CW01209418

THE DETERRENT

The Adam Drake series

SCOTT MATTHEWS

Published by Vinci Books

Published by Vinci Books 2024

Chapter One

THE KIDNAPPER WAITED PATIENTLY in the black Cadillac Escalade for the target and her boyfriend to drive from the brew pub in Bend, Oregon, to the Seventh Mountain Resort. His lookout had called to say they were on their way.

There were scattered patches of snow on the grass along the path that led to the door of the condo where Ashley Berkshire, a University of Oregon biology major, was staying. She had been there for a week of spring skiing with two of her sorority sisters. Her friends had left that afternoon so she could have a night alone with her boyfriend.

Ashley Berkshire was the daughter of a research biologist who was working on a new vaccine for the H7N9 avian influenza virus at a lab in Portland, Oregon. The H7N9 virus that had killed fifteen hundred Chinese in five reported influenza epidemics in recent years was at the top of the list of the Centers for Disease Control and Prevention (CDC) for known viruses most likely to start a world-wide pandemic.

Berkshire's vaccine and a sample of the live virus was the ransom they were demanding in exchange for the life of his daughter and only child.

He heard the throaty rumble of the boyfriend's dark green Ford Mustang Bullitt approaching in the distance. Ford built the special edition car to salute Steve McQueen's iconic 1968 Mustang in the movie BULLITT and he wasn't surprised the kid was driving it. Alejandro Pella, the girl's boyfriend, was Paolo Pella's spoiled younger brother.

Paolo Pella was known in the trade as 'El Blanco'. He turned dirty money white in a vast money laundering enterprise he ran for the drug cartels and Hezbollah in South America. To clean the dirty money, Pella purchased luxury homes, condos and exotic cars and then sold them to get the ill-gotten gains from the sales of his investments into legal financial systems around the world. The limited-edition Mustang he'd given his younger brother to drive while he was in college was one of Paolo's "investments".

He waited until the younger Pella parked the Mustang in front of the three-story building and walked Ashley Berkshire to her condo before he got out of his SUV and followed them.

The temperature had plunged below freezing when the sun went down and the warm moisture in his breath condensed into a cloud of vapor when he exhaled. He didn't mind the cold, but he was looking forward to returning to the warmer climate he preferred.

He walked confidently across the parking lot, keeping his head down and looking at the cell phone in his hand to keep anyone from getting a good look at his face. He was wearing a ski parka, jeans and a pair of hiking shoes to look like the other men at the resort, but he wasn't too worried about anyone remembering him. He would be at the resort just long enough to get what he'd come for.

When he was standing in front of the door of Unit 47, he knocked three times and waited for Alejandro to come open it. When the kid did, he motioned for him to lead on.

Ashley Berkshire was standing in front of the gas fireplace with her back turned to him as he approached.

"Who was it, Alejandro?" she asked without turning around.

He closed the distance to her in three quick steps and plunged a syringe loaded with ketamine into her neck with his right hand. With his left hand, he reached around and covered her mouth.

"Relax, Ashley. I'm not going to hurt you," the kidnapper said softly. He reached back and held out the syringe to Alejandro as he lowered her to the floor.

"Get her parka and help me put it on her. Make sure you're not leaving any of her things behind when you leave. We want it to look like she dropped out of school and ran off with you. Where will you be?"

"I'm driving to San Francisco tonight. My things are in my car and I've paid a year's lease in advance on my apartment. No one will miss me for a while."

"Make sure you stay out of sight, kid. We don't know how long it will take her dad to get the vaccine to us."

"Don't worry, Paolo wants me to take a yacht to a buyer in Costa Rica. They have great beaches there. I'll stay and surf for a while."

When Ashley's clothes, ski equipment and things were loaded into the black Escalade idling in the handicapped parking space outside, Alejandro and the kidnapper walked Ashley out between them.

To anyone paying attention to them, it would look just another college kid on spring break was being rushed to an emergency room because she'd too much to drink.

But no one at the resort paid any attention when he drove away from the Seventh Mountain Resort in the black SUV and her boyfriend left in his dark green Mustang.

Chapter Two

ADAM DRAKE FOLLOWED the lithesome woman gracefully skiing ahead of him down the Northwest Crossover run from the summit of Mount Bachelor.

It was a cloudless sunny morning and blue sky surrounded the snow-capped volcanic peaks of the Three Sisters mountains in the distance. Adam Drake had promised Liz Strobel, the skier ahead of him, that he would take her spring skiing in Oregon. He couldn't have picked a better day. It was thirty degrees and two inches of fresh powder snow promised to make the skiing as good as he told her it would be.

Liz was wearing a chic heel-to-toe all-white ski ensemble with red accents and a sleek visored red ski helmet she bought the week before. He, however, was wearing a black ski parka and black pants he'd had for years. A new white vented ski helmet was the only concession he'd been willing to make to update his ski apparel.

Drake skied beside Liz and pointed ahead with his ski pole to three other skiers who had stopped ahead of them and said, "That's the start of the Zoom Run I told you about. Ready to have some fun?"

She skied ahead to the other skiers, did a hockey stop and raised the visor of her helmet. "Are we racing?"

"Not unless you want to," Drake said. "It's a four-minute run down to the Northwest Express chair lift. Go as fast as you want, I'll be right behind you."

"Good luck with that," she taunted and did a jump turn to start her descent.

Drake laughed, dug his ski poles in and shoved off to follow her.

The Atkinson Zoom Run started at the top of a wide bowl and narrowed to a wide trail at the lower elevations, running between snow-draped fir trees on both sides. There was nothing to impede your progress and you could go as fast as you dared.

Liz wanted to go as fast as she could, judging by the ski-racing stance she was tucked into.

Drake copied her stance and sped after her. The wind whistled through the vents in his helmet and his eyes began to water behind his sunglasses as he picked up speed. He raised his hands in front of his face and lowered his hips until his butt was level with his shoulders to complete his racing tuck.

But he wasn't closing the gap between them. He saw Liz's skis were pointed straight down the fall line. She maintained her speed approaching a rise ahead in the snow and then soared over it.

For a moment she was out of sight and he said a quick prayer that she was all right. When he reached the jump, he sprang up and bent his knees to absorb the shock as he landed and looked ahead for Liz.

When he saw that she was already around the next bend, he shook his head and felt silly for worrying about her. She was a far better skier than she'd led him to believe. It was something he shouldn't have bought into when she'd asked about the difficulty of the runs on the mountain, as if they might be too difficult for her.

Drake let his skis run flat and raced after her and saw that he'd closed the gap slightly. They were halfway down the Zoom Run with enough time to catch her. Liz was skiing in the middle of the run instead of taking a proper racing line.

A proper racing line consisted of starting a turn in at the right point, hitting the apex at the inside of the corner and maintaining your speed through the corner, before lining up for the racing line through the next corner.

Drake swung to the outside of the run on the left for the next right-hand bend, turned in to clip the apex and then carried his momentum through the bend to swing wide to the left side of the run again. Liz was now thirty yards ahead of him.

The run had three sweeping bends ahead, where he could make up some ground. The first sweeping bend had closed the gap to her by a few yards. Then they were both on a straight stretch in the shade of the tall fir trees with his skis chattering on the crusty snow. She was closer now, maybe fifteen yards ahead, and had raised up out of her tuck a little as she encountered the icy conditions.

The next bend curved to the left and Drake swung wide and turned in to hit the apex, nailed it. He was only ten yards behind, with one bend ahead, before the run flattened out and they reached the loading area for the Northwest Express chair lift.

Drake grinned, anticipating the look on Liz's face when he shot passed her to take the lead. One more bend ahead to the right and he would have her. He ran wide to the left and turned in to sweep across the apex.

As he clipped the apex, he was forced to carve a tight turn back to the left to avoid ploughing through a group of skiers. They were standing right in his racing line, gathering around a trail map before their next run.

When he recovered from the near collision, Liz was ahead and already halfway across the loading area, with her arms raised above her shoulders celebrating.

Drake skied to her side where she was standing and touched his ski glove to the side of his ski helmet to salute her victory.

"You did a nice job convincing me that you're not a good a skier," he said. "Where did you learn to ski like that?"

Liz raised the visor on her helmet, grinning from ear to ear. "Didn't I tell you that I spent my junior year studying in France? My ski instructor won medals in two Winter Olympics."

Drake laughed. "You forgot to mention that. Would you like to make another run before we take a break?"

"I would, that was fun. What's your favorite run?"

He was thinking about which run she would enjoy skiing when his phone vibrated in the chest pocket of his parka. He took his right ski glove off, took his phone out and saw that it was Paul Benning calling.

"It's Paul, I'd better take this."

Chapter Three

DRAKE FLATTENED his skis on the snow and side slipped far enough away to avoid being overheard.

"Good morning Paul."

"I hope I'm not interrupting anything. I know you and Liz are away for a ski weekend."

"We just finished a run and waiting to get on the chair lift. You're not interrupting anything. What's on your mind?"

"Are you driving back to Portland or driving Liz back to Seattle?"

"We're driving back to Portland and staying a night on the farm before we return to Seattle. Why?"

"I've been retained to find a friend's niece. She was supposed to be staying at the Seventh Mountain Resort to ski Bachelor with a couple of her sorority sisters. They returned to campus without her and think she may have stayed after they left to spend time with her boyfriend. If you could stop and see if she's there, it would save me a trip to Bend."

"Why's your friend concerned? It's spring break. College kids run off to do all sorts of things. I know I did and I'm guessing you probably did too."

"I know, but her uncle says she's never missed calling him on his birthday. They're close and he's worried. She's a straight A biology major at Oregon. He says she's not the type to run off like this."

"Why is her uncle retaining you instead of her parents? Aren't they concerned as well?"

"That's what's a little hinky about this. Her father isn't concerned at all. He told my client to leave it alone, that it's none of his business."

"All right, we can stop at the resort this afternoon when we finish skiing. What is the niece's name?"

Her name is Ashley Berkshire. Her uncle is Alex Berkshire, the father's brother. He's the professor at Portland State who asked me to talk to his criminal justice class last year."

"I'll call you after we stop at the resort. Anything else I need to know?"

"You know as much as I do at this point. Thanks for helping me out with this. I owe you one."

Drake put his phone away and thought about his friend's new line of work. Paul Benning retired detective in the Multnomah County Sheriff's Office in Portland, Oregon, and married to his former secretary in the District Attorney's office where he'd been a prosecutor.

When he left the D.A.'s office to start his own private law practice, Paul's wife, Margo, had left with him to become his legal secretary and office manager. Following his setback when life threw him a curveball and he'd been diagnosed with prostate cancer, Paul decided to start a new career and became a private detective.

Paul and Margo Benning were family, as far as he was concerned. His father was a Green Beret who was killed when he was very young. His mother had been killed the summer before he left for college by a drunk driver. She was on her way home from the hospital one night when she'd worked a double shift to cover for another nurse. Drake was an only child and aside from friends he made playing football for the University of Oregon and later serving in the Special Forces in the United States Army, the Benning's had become his closest friends. Margo Benning, in fact, treated him as a son every bit as much as his mother did before she died.

If Paul Benning needed him to go a little out of his way and look for a young woman, who was probably with her boyfriend and didn't want to be disturbed, he was happy to do it.

Drake side stepped his way back to Liz. "Let's take the lift up and take a break mid-mountain at Pine Martin Lodge. You'll love the view from there."

As they got back in the lift line, Liz asked, "What did Paul want?"

"A client wants him to locate his niece. She was skiing with her sorority sisters and her uncle hasn't been able to get ahold of her. Paul asked if we would stop at the resort where she was staying and see if she's still there."

"Is she missing?"

"Her sorority sisters returned to campus without her. They think she's probably with her boyfriend."

"It sounds like her uncle is being a little overprotective. Does he have any reason to worry about her?"

"I don't know and to be honest, I don't really care. I'm here with 'my' girlfriend for a romantic ski weekend, just like she probably is with her boyfriend. She deserves her privacy, but we'll stop and ask about her because Paul asked us to."

"Is that why we're here, for a romantic weekend?" Liz grinned. "I thought you brought me here to show me how great a skier you are."

"How did I do? Don't answer that. Maybe I can romance better than I ski."

"I don't know, you've already set the bar pretty high. I'm not sure you can do any better."

Drake put his arm around her and pulled her close. "All I can ask for is a chance to show you."

"Let's finish skiing and maybe you'll get a chance."

Chapter Four

AFTER THEIR LAST RUN, they stopped for an Irish Coffee at the Clearing Rock Bar in the West Village before they left the ski area to drive east on the Cascade Lakes National Scenic Highway to the Seventh Mountain Resort.

Drake was enjoying driving the Porsche 718 Cayman GTS Puget Sound Security leased for him as its new special counsel, but they were stuck in a long line of traffic leaving the mountain and it was irritating him. It was like reining in a thoroughbred after the gate opened at the start of a race.

"Relax, Adam. Enjoy the scenery."

"I know, I know. Sorry, but they should make it illegal to drive motorhomes to and from the mountain and hold up traffic, like the one in front of the line is doing."

To get Drake's mind off the slow pace of the traffic, Liz asked, "Did Paul say which sorority this girl belonged to?"

"He didn't, why?"

"Just wondering. I was in a sorority in college, Kappa Kappa Gamma."

"Would you have left a sorority sister behind to spend time with a boyfriend?"

"It would depend on how well I knew the boyfriend, I guess."

They passed the Highway 45 turnoff to Crosswater, where they were staying in the summer home of Drake's father-in-law, Senator Robert Hazelton, Oregon's senior United States Senator, and drove on to the Seventh Mountain Resort.

Drake stopped at the resort's office and walked to the front desk with Liz.

"Hi, may I help you?" asked the bubbly young woman behind the counter.

"I hope so," Drake said. "The uncle of one of your guests asked us to take her to dinner tonight in his place. He's stuck in Portland for another day."

"Sure, what's her name?"

"Ashley Berkshire," Drake told her. "She was here with some of her sorority sisters to go skiing. Her uncle didn't know which unit they were in."

The clerk frowned. "I remember them, four Oregon students wearing bright yellow Oregon sweatshirts. But they checked out."

"Did all of them checkout? Could one of them have extended her stay?"

"That wouldn't have been possible. During spring skiing at Mt. Bachelor, we're booked a year in advance. Someone would have raised a fuss if the unit they paid for wasn't available."

"Have you seen her here at the resort since last weekend, by any chance?" Liz leaned closer and said softly with a wink. "She may have stayed over with a boyfriend."

The young woman grinned and nodded knowingly. "She may have, but I haven't seen any of those girls since they checked out."

Drake took out one of his business cards and handed it to the clerk. "If you do see her, I'd appreciate it if you'd call me and let me know."

"No problem, glad to."

They walked back to the Cayman and Drake held the door open for Liz. "Looks like Paul has his work cut out for him, if Ms. Ashley's run off with her boyfriend."

"Does Paul know anything about the boyfriend?"

Drake started the engine and backed out of the guest parking space. "Call Paul Benning," he instructed Bluetooth. "Let's find out."

"Still on the mountain?" Benning said when he answered.

"We're just leaving Seventh Mountain Resort. Liz is with me, you're on speaker."

"Did you find Ashley?"

"Her sorority sisters checked out of their unit last weekend. The clerk at the front desk remembered them but said she hasn't seen any of them since they checked out. Do you know the boyfriend's name? We could check and see if he's here."

"I don't know his name, just that he's a tennis player at Oregon. That's all my client mentioned."

"Why don't you give your client a call. We're going into Bend for a late lunch. We can stop at the resort on our way back to Crosswater."

"I'll call you when I have a name."

Before they drove the seven miles from the resort to Drake's favorite restaurant, The Drake, in downtown Bend, Benning called back.

"His name is Alejandro Pella. My client said all he knows is that he's Oregon's number one tennis player. I checked Oregon's roster to get his name and learned that he's from Argentina."

"Do we know anything else about him?" Drake asked.

"I haven't had time to do a background check."

"See what you can find out. And find out which sorority Ashley is in. We can return to Portland via Eugene and stop at her sorority to talk with her skiing friends, if you want."

"Paul," she said, "Find out if Alejandro's brother is Paolo Pella."

"Who is Paolo Pella?" Drake asked.

"If he's the same Paolo Pella I heard talk about when I was with the FBI, he's the son of Papa Pella, an Argentine who ran an international money laundering network. There was a rumor that Paolo Pella might have taken over the network when his father was killed, but there was no evidence we could find that he had."

"What happened to his father?" Benning asked.

"We were investigating individuals and networks providing support to Hezbollah. In 2013, Argentina was considering opening its banks to money launderers to prop up its economy. Papa Pella ran the international network known as 'Los Blancos' because they cleaned or made dirty money white. We put pressure on the government in Argentina to arrest him and were told he was dead. We never found out if the government had him killed or if he took his own life before they could arrest him."

"So, Ashley's boyfriend, Alejandro, might be related to the Pellas of Argentina?" Benning asked.

"The Pella name triggered a memory, that's all. The only thing we know is that Alejandro is from Argentina," Liz said.

"It sounds like my background check needs to dig deeper than I was planning," Benning said.

Chapter Five

JUAN PAOLO PELLA paced back and forth in front of the floor-to-ceiling windows in his luxury condo on the 52nd floor of One Rincon Hill in San Francisco. The yacht delivery service he hired to bring the Hatteras M75 Panacera motor yacht he purchased in Vancouver, B.C., Canada, to San Francisco was behind schedule.

The boatyard that was waiting to inspect the yacht, before it was delivered to his buyer in Costa Rica, had called to tell him he was going to have to reschedule the inspection. They needed the yacht in the next twenty-four hours, or he would have to find someone else to do the inspection and any work that it required.

If he could keep his buyer in Costa Rica committed to the purchase, despite the delay, he would clear two million dollars on the sale. With that profit, he'd be able to cover the debt owed to his friends in the Tri Border Area of South America and still have a million and half available for his current project.

He'd purchased the Hatteras Panacera at a bargain price from the estate of a recently deceased billionaire. The man had refused to sell the yacht for the price Pella offered him the month before and, tragically, had died in a drive-by shooting in Vancouver.

The money used to buy the yacht had been laundered once

through a bank in Florida. It would be cleaned once more when the yacht was delivered in Costa Rica and he was paid.

It was imperative that the delivery of the yacht remain on schedule for two reasons. First, a half million dollars was needed to fund his current project, and second, he needed to get his younger brother out of the country.

He knew the father of the young woman Alejandro had helped him kidnap hadn't gone to the police yet. His home, car and office were bugged and his man in Portland was watching him day and night. But he couldn't take the risk that the father would weaken and go running to the police. If that happened, and Alejandro wasn't out of the country yet, the police would soon discover Alejandro was his brother and come knocking on his door.

Paolo bought and sold luxury condos, like the one he was living in and the luxury home he owned in Las Vegas. He bought expensive cars, like the Ferrari LaFerrari coupe he had his eye on in Las Vegas. Then he sold them to clean the drug cartel's profits. In the last decade, his money laundering had provided him a very comfortable lifestyle.

Others in his network ran the casinos he had an interest in and operated the banks he owned on a day-to-day basis. But the image he'd perfected, as a wealthy international playboy, unfortunately, made it necessary to have the expensive things required to maintain that image.

But now, he needed more money than his cut from buying and selling expensive things earned him to fund his plan to take his business to the next level. The sample of the H7N9 influenza virus he was demanding as ransom in his kidnapping plan would provide him all the money he needed.

When he'd learned from his little brother that his girlfriend's father was developing a vaccine to prevent a world-wide influenza pandemic, he immediately saw the opportunity to make a huge profit. He'd remembered reading that a biologist in Pakistan or North Korea had bioengineered a microbe that mimicked the transmissibility and lethality of smallpox, with technology that could be ordered online for less than two hundred dollars.

It was the age of do-it-yourself synthetic biology. Inevitably, some terrorist group or nation state would develop a synthetically engineered bioweapon capable of decimating an enemy's population. And someone like that would need a sample of, say, the H7N9 influenza virus, the virus that was thought to be the most likely to cause a worldwide pandemic.

Someone, who wanted to do that intentionally, would pay a fortune to get their hands on a live sample of the virus, like the sample he was going to get from the girlfriend's father.

Even more valuable than the virus itself, however, was the vaccine that Alan Berkshire was working on. With that, you'd be able to survive the pandemic, if the bioweapon was ever deployed. He knew enough to know that if an influenza pandemic ever went viral, a vaccine that protected from living or dying was worth, what? How could you put a price on a vaccine like that?

The ringtone playing on his cell phone ended his thinking about his filthy rich future. When he picked it up, he saw that it was the one man he didn't want to be speaking to right now. Armin Khoury and his men were the ones who helped him kidnap the biologist's daughter.

"Will you be coming to see me as we arranged?"

"There may be a slight delay."

"That would be unfortunate."

"I always deliver, you know that."

"There is always a first time for everything. What's the problem?"

"Bad weather is making it difficult to get the yacht here on schedule."

"Do we need to renegotiate the terms of our arrangement?"

"You'll get your money on time."

"Make sure that I do. Our friends have payrolls that need to be made."

"How is our guest doing?"

"She's sedated. We couldn't keep her quiet. She was yelling obscenities so loudly at your brother that golfers playing outside could hear her. She's fine otherwise."

"We need her awake to provide 'proof of life' when her father demands it. Find a way to keep her quiet without sedating her."

"Don't worry, I've done this before. Why did you need this one? She says her father doesn't have a lot of money."

"He doesn't. He has something else I want."

"I know what he does. Is this something I might be interested in?"

"You might."

"If it is, make sure that I'm the first one to know about it."

"Of course."

Paolo waited to hear if there was anything else Khoury wanted to talk about and realized the call had ended.

His caller was someone you allowed to end a conversation on his terms. In addition to him being the most intimidating man he'd ever met, Khoury was also the commander of Hezbollah in North America.

Chapter Six

ARMIN KHOURY SELECTED a Montecristo No. 2 from the olive wood humidor that traveled with him, wherever he went, and walked out onto the back patio. The opulent home on the championship golf course that meandered through the gated community was one of the current assets in the western states that was available to him, whenever he required it, until Paolo Pella sold it.

The title to the property wasn't in his name, but that didn't matter; it was their money. Pella was just processing it for them.

Khoury, also known as '47' for the custom AK-47 he liked to use when he executed a rival or a traitor, was the commander of Hezbollah's criminal and terrorist network in America. The network had been in place for a decade, money laundering and fundraising for Hezbollah in North America.

His secret mission, however, as commander of the external military operations wing of the party, was much more than that. He'd been tasked with training and maintaining sleeper cells in major U.S. cities, cells capable of delivering a devastating blow to Israel's benefactor if Iran was ever attacked by Israel or America.

His teams were in place, living and working with false identities, as loyal Americans. They owned homes, paid taxes and made friends with the people in their neighborhoods. They were all highly trained fighters, each with a unique skill in the cell they were assigned, and they were very careful in the way they lived in America. When the time came for them to act, their neighbors would be shocked when they found out who they really were.

Khoury lit his cigar and looked across the golf course at the homes on the other side. They were politely called luxury homes, but they were mansions in his mind, examples of the lust Americans had for status in a society where you could never have enough of anything.

The house he was in had seven thousand square feet. There were six ensuite bedrooms, four and a half bathrooms, master suites upstairs and downstairs, two family rooms, a great room, a formal living and two dining rooms.

He thought about how this contrasted with the lifestyle in the Palestinian refugee camp in Lebanon where he'd grown up. The slum city of Shatila, a refugee camp built in 1949 to house three thousand people that was now home to over twenty thousand. Electricity there was unreliable and the salty water that ran through the pipes was undrinkable.

He remembered the night in 1982 when the Lebanese right-wing militia attacked the slum city. The militia's killing spree was aided by the Israelis, who fired flares overhead to light the way for the Christian savages. Three thousand or more of the slum city residents were killed in two nights of carnage.

He'd been eight years old.

He imagined how the people in this gated community in Red Rock Canyon on the outskirts of Las Vegas would deal with the horrors he'd grown up with. He thought not many of them would survive.

As soon as he had the means to give them the opportunity to find out, he would see if he was right.

Khoury heard the French doors behind him open and waited for the man to announce himself before he turned around.

"Jefe, what would you like for dinner?"

He turned and saw that Raul, the Portuguese fighter he brought back with him on his last trip to the Tri Border Area, was standing stiffly at ease with his hands behind his back.

"Why don't you decide for me, Raul."

"Would you like a steak or, perhaps, lamb?"

Khoury stepped into the man's personal space and locked eyes with him. "Did I tell you to decide for me?"

"Yes, Jefe."

"Then why didn't you?"

Raul swallowed and said, "I didn't want to disappoint you."

"You've disappointed me by not doing what I told you to do. Don't let it happen again or I will think you're not enough of a man to serve here with me."

"Yes, Jefe."

"Then go, Raul."

The man turned and left.

Khoury turned back around and considered the deference Raul had just shown him, in contrast with the double talk he was getting from Paolo Pella

He knew about the ransom Pella was demanding from the kidnapped girl's father. He knew what Pella intended to do with it. He also knew that he was not about to pay a penny for the virus, when it was there for the taking when he handled the ransom exchange for Pella .The man didn't have the cojones or the men to stand up to him if he kept the virus for himself.

Pella knew the consequences of not living up to his end of the agreement with Hezbollah. When Pella's father had been jailed in Argentina for laundering money through the bank he owned, Hezbollah had offered to support the family and protect his father in jail, if Paolo agreed to continue the arrangement they had with his father.

Paolo Pella had agreed and understood that if he didn't keep his promise to continue laundering their money, his family would die one at a time until he changed his mind.

He would regret having to kill the Pellas, of course, they had served the party well. But discipline had to be maintained.

Khoury took out the day's burner phone and called the man who was watching the girl's father for him.

"How close are we to getting what we need?" he asked.

"From what I'm hearing in his lab, the vaccine is in the final stages of its field trial. The volunteers they're using have been vaccinated twice and are being monitored. Their blood samples will then be tested for the H7N9 antibodies. As soon as he has the test results, we'll know if his vaccine works."

"When will that be?"

"Soon, maybe next week."

"When he knows if the vaccine works, we'll arrange the transfer. Make sure he doesn't involve anyone to help him with that. I don't want anyone getting in our way."

"He's doing what you told him so far."

"Make sure he continues to do so."

Chapter Seven

ALEX BERKSHIRE, the biologist's twin brother Alan, parked on the street in front of his brother's two-story home in the Rock Creek suburb of Portland, Oregon. Alan Berkshire lived alone, following the death of his wife four years ago, and the departure of his daughter for college a year later.

His brother's routine made it easy to know when he would be available to explain what he was doing to find his daughter. Alan Berkshire, Ph.D., left for work every morning at seven to drive to the Vaccine & Gene Therapy Institute on the west campus of the Oregon Health Sciences University in Hillsboro.

After his normal twelve-hour day at the Institute where he worked as a research scientist, he routinely stopped at the Rock Creek Country Club near his house for a single Bourbon Old Fashioned and a Chicken Caesar Salad before he returned home to read research articles until he went to bed.

Alex Berkshire also had a Ph.D., as a professor at Portland State University, who also lived life with a routine that involved, among other things, hearing from his niece on his birthday.

They had a special and close relationship and she hadn't called him last week on his birthday, the first time that had happened since she left for college. When he asked his brother if she was okay because he hadn't heard from her, he'd been told that she was fine and not to worry about it.

That hadn't set right with him and he'd called the sorority and learned that she hadn't been seen since she left to go skiing. Hearing that, he asked his brother if he'd been in touch with Ashley and been shocked at his brother's response.

Alan had bluntly told him to leave it alone.

Leaving it alone wasn't in his nature. His Ph.D. was in forensic psychology and he lectured on the criminal mind at the university. There were too many men in the world who would be tempted by the beauty of a young woman like Ashley and want to do her harm.

Alex watched in the rearview mirror of his new red Mazda MX-5 Miata roadster as his brother turned into the cul-de-sac in his nine-year-old Volvo XC70 wagon. He waved at his brother and watched him open his garage door and drive into the garage.

Alan considered leaving and decided to try again to talk to his brother about Ashley. He walked up to the front door and rang the doorbell.

He waited for a long minute before he finally knocked. "Come on, Alan. I'm not going to leave until you let me in and we talk."

"Go away, Alex. I know why you're here and I'm not going to argue with you again about Ashley," Alan said without opening the door.

"I had someone try to find her in Bend. She wasn't at the resort with her friends. No one knows where she is. If you're not willing to report her as a missing person, I will."

The door flew open and Alan pulled his brother inside.

"I told you to leave it alone," he hissed. "No one's going to the police. She's okay and she doesn't need you or anyone else searching for her."

Alex brushed his brother away and stepped back. "Then tell me where she is, if you know she's okay. That's all I'm asking. I love her too, Alan. I need to know that she's okay."

"For God's sake, why can't you trust me with this? I'm telling you she's okay."

"I don't believe you," Alex said loudly. "What's going on, Alan?"

Alan Berkshire turned abruptly and marched down the hall to the kitchen with his brother right behind him. He grabbed a bottle of bourbon out of the liquor cabinet, along with two glasses, and poured two fingers of the bourbon for each of them.

"Tell me what you've done, after I told you to leave this alone."

"I did what you should have been doing. I tried to find her."

Alan took a deep breath. "How did you try to find her," he said patiently.

"I had someone look for her at the ski resort where you told me she was going to be for spring break."

Alan stared at his brother and took a big drink of his bourbon. "What else did you do?"

"I had someone stop by her sorority in Eugene. No one there knew where she was either."

"Who was the person you asked to find her?"

"A friend of mine. He's a private detective I know."

"What's his name?"

"Why?"

"Because I need to tell him, in person, to stop looking for my daughter. I can't trust you to tell him."

"I'll ask again, what's going on? Don't you want to know where she is?

"Tell me his name, Alex."

"His name is Paul Benning. He's a retired detective from the Sheriff's Office."

Alan Berkshire set his glass down and leaned forward with both hands on the granite top of the kitchen island between them. "All I can tell you, Alex, is that what you're doing isn't helping Ashley. In fact, it's just the opposite. Please let me handle this."

"Handle what?"

"I can't tell you."

"Is Ashley in trouble?"

"I can't tell you that either. You have to trust me on this, Alex, please."

The look of helplessness and despair on his brother's face told him that something was very wrong. Until he knew what it was, there was no way he was going to let his brother handle it was by himself.

"All right, I'll trust you. But know this, if there's anything you need help with, I expect you to call me. Will you do that?"

"I will, I promise."

Alex stayed to finish his drink and left convinced that his brother needed his help, even if he wasn't going to ask for it.

Chapter Eight

PAUL BENNING ORDERED a cup of coffee at the Little River Café near his office and took it outside to a table on the waterfront River-Place Esplanade to wait for Alex Berkshire to arrive. Berkshire had called the night before and asked to meet with him before his morning class at the university.

He knew Berkshire was still worried about his niece. But tracking down a young woman who might not want to be found, if that was what this meeting was about, would be time-consuming and expensive. Unless Berkshire had new information that would narrow his search, he wasn't sure he wanted to take on a missing person case right now, especially if the person really wasn't missing.

Benning saw his client walking briskly toward him. His shoulders were hunched, his head down, as if he was looking for a penny someone dropped. Alex Berkshire was a tall man with a full head of graying hair and a classic Van Dyke beard. The combination gave him the distinguished look of a professor or artist, confident and learned, but his posture betrayed his personae.

Benning waved to him as he approached and held up his cup of coffee. "The coffee is good, if you haven't had your quota for the morning."

Berkshire shook his head pulled out a chair to sit down. "I'm good. Thanks for meeting me this morning, Paul. I saw my brother last night and I think he's in trouble. He won't tell me what it is, but I know that whatever it is, he's scared."

"I assume this involves his daughter in some way?"

"I'm sure it does. He said it's something he needs to handle, that what I'm doing isn't helping Ashley, just the opposite. He said he couldn't tell me what it was he needed to handle, and he couldn't tell me if Ashley was in trouble or not. He said I just need to trust him. I think Ashley's been kidnapped."

"Why?"

"Because of the way he acted when I said I was going to make a missing person report if he didn't tell me where she was. Until I said that, I couldn't get him to open the door. He pulled me inside and wanted to know everything I had done. He demanded to know your name, so he could tell you in person to stop looking for Ashley because he couldn't trust me to tell you."

"Is he doing anything to find Ashley?"

"He hasn't mentioned it, if he is."

"You know your twin brother better than anyone else, Alex. Do you think whoever took Ashley, assuming someone did, is demanding a ransom and told him not to go to the police or get anyone else involved?"

Berkshire nodded his head. "That's exactly what I think."

Benning stood and said, "I'm going to get another cup of coffee. You sure you don't want anything?"

"Do they have bagels? The acid in my stomach is crying out for something to work on."

"Sure, I'll get you one. Stay put, I'll be right back."

He didn't need another cup of coffee, he needed time to think. He'd been involved in kidnapping investigations but had never been the lead detective on one. The investigations were always complicated with the competing interests involved.

The family or company the victim worked for had one focus, returning the kidnapped person alive. Law enforcement wanted that too, but it also wanted to capture and prosecute the kidnapper.

Private kidnap and ransom consultants and negotiators the family hired or its insurance company, if they were lucky enough to have kidnap and ramson (K&R) insurance, were tolerated but resented by the law enforcement personnel conducting the investigation.

He still had a good relationship with the Sheriff's Department he had just retired from and he wasn't willing to jeopardize it by taking on a kidnap and ransom case. He wasn't going to put him in the middle of the competing interests he knew would develop. If he was going to help his friend, it would have to be on the basis that he was being retained to find a missing person and nothing more, at this point.

Benning returned with a bagel, cream cheese and his second cup of coffee.

"Alex, I'll do what I can to help you if you will agree to two things. First, that you are retaining me to locate Ashley as a missing person. I'll have Margo prepare a retainer agreement that makes that clear. Second, if we find out that Ashley has been kidnapped, you will agree to bring in the security services firm I do work for. They have the expertise to handle Ashley's return and negotiate any ransom that's demanded. Puget Sound Security is in Seattle and it has a kidnap and ransom unit with years of experience that we'll need."

"Agreed. What do you need from me to get started?"

"Any personal information about Ashley that you can get to me without letting your brother know what you're doing. Date of birth, a recent photograph, her driver's license, anything that will help identify her when I ask people if they know her or have seen her. And anything you can tell me about her boyfriend, the tennis player."

"I'll bring you everything I can after my last class this afternoon. I appreciate this, Paul."

"It's what friends are for," shaking Alex's outstretched hand. "I'll do everything I can to help you find her."

Benning watched Berkshire walk away with his head up and his shoulders squared.

He didn't pay any attention to the man sitting on a bench reading down the esplanade. He was thinking about the first thing he needed to do to find Ashley and didn't notice when the man got up and followed his client.

Chapter Nine

THE HEZBOLLAH ASSASSIN stalked his target to the turnaround at the south end of the RiverPlace Esplanade and watched him get into his red Mazda Miata convertible. He waited until the professor drove around the circle and started up SW Market Street before he sprinted to his motorcycle parked four parking meters behind the red sports car.

He saw the professor turn left onto SW Harbor Drive at the intersection and disappear around the corner. The assassin raced after him. By the time he caught up with the Miata on the SW Harbor viaduct, there were three cars between his black and blue Suzuki GSX-S1000F and the red sports car.

He knew where the professor was going. He'd followed him to the university after hearing him ask his brother if his niece was okay, on a bug he'd planted in his brother's house. When it semeded that Alex Berkshire was letting his brother handle things, he'd left him alone.

That was until last night, when he heard him arguing with his brother and threatening to go to the police to file a missing person's report if his brother didn't tell him that his niece was okay.

Now that the brother had met with a private investigator, he had to make a call before he had a green light to silence the professor.

As he expected, the professor drove straight to the parking structure across the street from Cramer Hall at the university where the Psychology Department was located. He pulled to the curb at the first empty metered parking spot and patted his pockets for change as if he intended to park his motorcycle. When he saw the professor cross the street from the parking structure and enter Cramer Hall, he started the 999cc engine of the Suzuki and pulled out from the curb to find a place off campus to call Las Vegas.

Retracing his route back to RiverPlace and the South Waterfront Park, he parked his motorcycle and walked through the park to an empty bench beside a reflecting pool.

"Yes?" Armin Khoury answered on the first ring.

"The brother met with that P.I. again. I think he's going ahead on his own to find the girl."

"Has he gone to the police as he threatened?"

"I followed him this morning from his house. He hasn't gone there yet."

After a long pause, Khoury said, "Make sure he never does. A drive-by shooting isn't unusual there. Make it look like a random gang thing. We'll worry about the P.I. later, if he continues looking for the girl without a client."

The assassin sat on the bench with his right hand resting on the top of his helmet, staring into the reflecting pool at the scattered rocks on the bottom. He wasn't thinking about what he had been told to do, he'd done it many times before. Instead, he was thinking about how the rocks made him think of the people walking the paths of the park, without a thought about the violence that might confront them someday.

In the world he grew up in, it was a part of everyday life that you didn't think about. It couldn't be prevented, you just learned to accept it as a part of the cycle of life, like a lion bringing down a gazelle for dinner. There were predators and those who were preyed upon. You had to choose which one you wanted to be, but the end was the same for everyone.

He looked at the black military-style watch on his wrist and calculated the time he had before he needed to get back on campus to follow the professor. When he finished teaching his last class at four in the afternoon, the professor played raquetball at the Multnomah Athletic Club. He played four days a week, starting on Monday and skipping Wednesday. Today was Tuesday and he would leave the club sometime around six o'clock and walk across the street to the parking structure.

The assassin had plenty of time to get ready to be there when he crossed the street.

Before returning to his apartment near the campus of Portland State University, where he was registered as a student, he stopped for a lamb gyro at a food cart and ate it while sitting on his motorcycle.

His routine on the days he was ordered to use his deadly skills was always the same. A light halal meal early in the day, followed by an hour of sweating through the basic drills of the ancient Persian martial art of Razmafzar with a sword and a hand shield.

After a break for water, he did another hour of the Muslim martial art of Pencat Silat drills, an Indonesian martial art form, to prepare his mind for the unexpected that always seemed to occur when he was sent out on a kill.

At ten minutes to six o'clock that evening, he was in position. He sat on his motorcycle in a parking space between two cars on SW Salmon Street, across the street from the Multnomah Athletic Club. He had a black messenger bag hanging from his right shoulder and a map that he was studying open and laying on the gas tank. The visor of his black helmet was up, but with his head down looking at the map, anyone walking by wouldn't get a good look at his face.

At two minutes to six o'clock, he saw three men in his peripheral vision walk out and wait on the curb for a car to pass before crossing the street. Alex Berkshire was the one in the middle.

The assassin pulled his visor down with his left hand, slipped the map into the messenger bag with his right hand and pulled out a Heckler & Koch MP5-SD 9 submachine gun. Revving the idling engine, he shot out from the curb and raced toward the men who had stepped back to the curb to keep from being hit.

As he swept by them, he fired a stream of 9mm rounds from the submachine gun, cutting down all three men in a flailing tangle of bloody bodies.

In his rearview mirror, he saw that no one rushed out to give aid to the three men as he sped away.

Chapter Ten

ADAM DRAKE and Liz Strobel stood on the aft viewing deck of the M/V Walla Walla ferry, looking back at the night lights of Seattle, when Paul Benning called. It was ten minutes to eight on Tuesday evening and they were halfway to Bainbridge Island.

"Are you in Seattle?" Benning asked Drake.

"I'm on the ferry to Bainbridge with Liz, why?"

"The client who was worried about his niece was gunned down tonight in a drive-by shooting. I may need your help."

"In what way? The police will investigate the shooting."

"That's not what I think I'll need help with. Alex Berkshire asked to meet me this morning. He thinks his niece has been kidnapped. I told him that I was willing to look for her as a missing person, but if we found out that she was kidnapped I would bring you and the PSS kidnap and ransom team in to handle it."

"Did you find out that she was kidnapped?"

"Not exactly. Alex talked with his brother last night, who told him it was something he could handle himself and didn't want anyone else to be involved. He made Alex promise again that he wouldn't go to the police. I think he's trying to deal with the kidnappers by himself."

"Has there been a ransom demand?"

"Not that Alex knew about."

"Then we don't know if it is a kidnapping."

"I think Alex being killed says there is. I talked with the detective handling the drive-by. Three men were killed, Alex and two others. Alex was the only one who had a regular routine playing racquetball at the MAC every Tuesday. The killer was waiting in ambush across the street for him to come out at the time he always did. It wasn't a random drive-by."

"If you're right about this being a kidnapping, what do you want me to do?"

"Help me find her boyfriend. He was the last person to see her, as far as we know. He's dropped out of school and no one at the university knows where he is. His next of kin is a brother in San Francisco, I thought I'd start there."

"Get me everything you know about Ashley, her boyfriend and his brother. I'll see what I can find out before you make a trip to San Francisco."

"Thanks Adam. I'll get you what I can put together."

Drake put his phone away, turned and put his arm around Liz and pulled her close.

"What did Paul want?"

"I thought we agreed to leave work in Seattle for a night."

"You answered your phone, not me."

Drake turned to face her. "What's wrong? I thought you were looking forward to a night in the cabin?"

"Bainbridge didn't seem so far away when you're looking at a map. A thirty-five-minute commute each way means seventy fewer minutes a day I have you," she said, pouting.

"Liz, you know I'm not sure I want to live here. I don't think I can live in the city. Lancer would be cooped up in a condo or a back yard somewhere. We can look at other places if we decide this isn't for us. It's only a six-month lease."

Liz turned and looked down at the dark waters of Puget Sound trailing behind the ferry. "Adam, you need to find a place you like. It doesn't have to be a 'we' thing. I didn't give you a vote when I bought the condo."

"That was before I decided to move to Seattle. I'd like it to be a 'we' thing now that I'm here."

Drake turned her around and kissed her. "If it doesn't work for 'us', it doesn't work. Tomorrow we'll go for a run to get to know the place better and then I'll take you out for breakfast."

"Isn't Paul sending you something tomorrow?"

"Paul thinks the girl we looked for in Bend has been kidnapped. He's sending me the information he has and wants me to look at it, that's all."

"If he thinks it's a kidnapping, why not get the PSS K&R unit involved?"

"He's handling it as a missing person case, for now. He will if he finds something that proves it's a kidnapping. Let's go up front, we're getting close to Bainbridge."

The M/V Walla Walla arrived at the Bainbridge Island ferry terminal at five minutes after eight o'clock, exactly on time. A short walk to the terminal parking lot and a quick search brought them to a blue Range Rover Drake's realtor left for him to drive for the two days he was on the island.

"How far is this cabin you want me to see?" Liz asked.

"It's at the north end of the island. Sit back, relax and enjoy the ride. It's a beautiful new log cabin, on two acres with one hundred and eighty feet of waterfront. You'll love it."

Chapter Eleven

PAUL BENNING CARRIED his laptop and a legal pad into the conference room and turned on the lights in Adam Drake's former law office. His wife, Margo, was upstairs watching a movie in the condo they leased from Drake.

He'd promised Drake he would send him everything he could find on Ashley's boyfriend, Alejandro Pella, and his brother, Paolo Pella. He hadn't finished his research and it was getting late.

There wasn't much about the younger brother he could find. Alejandro was a foreign student from Argentina, twenty years old, playing tennis for the University of Oregon. He'd lived in Buenos Aires, Argentina, with his mother and a younger sister before leaving to play tennis in North America. He listed his brother, who lived in San Francisco, as his next of kin, not his mother or father in Argentina.

He was the Number One player on the Oregon tennis team and had been selected for the Pac-12 first team in his sophomore year. He lived in the Skybox Apartments across the street from the Matthew Knight Arena, drove a new Ford Mustang and from the photos he'd been able to find, was a good-looking kid. He'd even found a photo of Alejandro and Ashley together in the Daily Emerald, the campus paper, after one of Alejandro's matches.

He also learned, when he called the Registrar's office at the university, that Alejandro had suddenly dropped out of school during Spring Term and did not play in the NCAA national tennis championship in Orlando, Florida, even though he'd qualified. The tennis coach hadn't returned his call, but his secretary told him that they were all shocked that Alejandro missed the championship. Tennis and pretty girls were his main interests and Benning was given the impression that his interest in his academic studies paled in comparison.

Alejandro's brother was a different matter, altogether. Paolo Pella, age thirty-four, had an MBA in finance from the University of Southern California and lived in San Francisco in a luxury condo. He was a member of the San Francisco Yacht Club and appeared to be successful and well-liked. Benning could find no mention of what he did for a living.

Given the criminal history of his father in Argentina, he could understand why Paolo stayed out of the spotlight. Hernando Pella was in prison for laundering money for the cartels in the Tri Border Area of South America. He had made his fortune exporting soybean meal in Argentina, the biggest soybean meal exporter in the world. His financial empire included ownership of banks, casinos and ranches in Argentina, but it was one of his casinos that led to his downfall.

In 2009, Argentina had granted amnesty to anyone who wanted to pull undeclared cash out of tax havens and deposit it in Argentinian banks to replenish its coffers and prop up its failing economy. It was widely accepted that some of the four billion dollars that has been deposited was illicit, but the move was necessary that no one complained.

After the amnesty, Hernando Pella, allowed a casino he owned in Puento Iguazu, in western Argentina and the infamous Tri Border Area, to be used to launder money. Cartel men would bring cash to the casino to buy chips for their gambling. After a short amount of time, and very little gambling, they would cash in their chips and walk away with clean, or laundered, money. Pella became known as "El Blanco", because he made dirty things clean again.

Pressure from the United States on Argentina to crack down on the cartels and the laundering of the cartel's money, as well as that of the terrorist organization Hezbollah, subsequently led to the arrest and conviction of Hernando Pella and the seizure of his assets.

Benning according to a friend in the FBI he called, Paolo Pella was suspected of being the new "El Blanco", but nothing had been found to substantiate the suspicion. Paolo Pella's record was supposedly clean, not even a parking or speeding ticket.

After twenty-five years in law enforcement, with the last twenty years as a detective in the Multnomah County Sheriff's Office, Benning knew, without digging deeper, that Alejandro Pella was involved in the disappearance of Ashley Berkshire in some way. With his family's history of involvement with drug cartels, well known for their kidnapping and ransom demands, Ashley's boyfriend had to be involved in her disappearance. It was possible the two young lovers ran off somewhere, but he doubted it. Why would a tennis player, who moved to North America to play collegiate tennis and pursue a career as a professional tennis player, miss such a big tournament?

Whatever the reason, Ashley and her boyfriend were missing. San Francisco was the only place he could think of to find information to help him find Ashley. He knew how to get answers from people.

If Paolo Pella was involved in a kidnapping, he'd know it. If he knew something about his brother running off with Ashley, he'd know it. If he didn't know anything at all and was genuinely worried about his brother, Benning would know that as well. His experience of over twenty years as a detective had taught him to recognize deception and he was very good at doing just that.

Chapter Twelve

DRAKE'S "NEW LOG CABIN" was an architecturally designed two-story log home with soaring roof lines and deck off the upstairs master bedroom that had a view of Puget Sound to the east. The yard surrounding the cabin had wide, graveled paths weaving around landscaped flower beds with blooming rhododendrons. One of the paths led to a sunken fire pit down on the waterfront.

With every modern convenience and a kitchen that a master chef would be proud to call his own, the two thousand square-foot home was a compromise he'd been willing to consider from the big city across the waters of Puget Sound.

They left the cabin at seven in the morning and ran side-by-side north on Sunrise Drive NE to the end of Hedley Spit and back before showering and setting off for breakfast.

"Wherever you're taking me for breakfast, it had better have more than just coffee and croissants on the menu," Liz said. "I'm hungry."

"My realtor suggested the 'Good Egg' in Winslow. It's at the other end of the island, but the drive will let us see the place in the daylight."

"The same one who's letting you drive her Range Rover? What's she like?"

"What makes you think it's a woman?"

"Gee, I don't know, maybe it's the perfume I'm getting a whiff of."

"Relax, Suzette is a very attractive and accommodating lady, with the emphasis on 'Lady'. When I told her what I was looking for, she said she had the perfect place in mind. It was built for a doctor who wanted to live on the island, but a divorce changed his mind. Suzette bought it as an investment and was willing to lease it for six months, with a refundable earnest money if I decide not to buy it. What do you think about it, so far?"

"It's growing on me. Do you think you could adjust to using the ferry all the time to get to and from Seattle?"

Drake smiled and said, "I was thinking I might have Mike teach me how to fly and getting him to loan me his helicopter."

Liz laughed. "Good luck with that. Mike loves his helicopter like you love your old Porsche."

A sexy sounding male voice with an Australian accent advised them that they were nearing their destination.

The Good Egg was on the corner of the Winslow Green. It was exactly what Drake had hoped it would be. They were sitting inside at a window table, after ordering poached eggs with buttered sourdough toast, when Liz looked over the top of her coffee cup she was holding up in both hands and nodded. "Good choice, Mr. Drake".

"Glad you like it, Ms. Strobel."

"What are we doing after breakfast?"

Drake started to suggest visiting some of the nearby shops when his phone vibrated in his pocket. When he saw that it was Paul Benning, he stood and motioned that he was going to step outside.

"Morning Paul."

"There's an email on your computer with everything I could find about Ashley's boyfriend and his brother. Turns out the Pella's are an interesting family."

"Liz thought the Pella name sounded familiar. The father was a money launderer for the cartels in Argentina or something?"

"He was, indeed, maybe he still is. He's in prison but that doesn't mean much these days. I'm going to San Francisco to see the older Pella brother. Want to join me?"

"When are you going?"

"Tomorrow."

"I won't be back in Seattle for another day. Are you thinking that you might need some backup? I could get someone from the Los Angeles office to go with you."

"No, I just thought you might like to go along since I got you involved in looking for Ashley. I haven't found anything that makes me think Paolo Pella is anyone to worry about. The guy's as clean as a they come, a real model citizen."

"That alone is enough to make me suspicious."

"I'll be fine. Say hello to Liz for me."

"I will. Tell Margo I'll be back in Portland later in the week."

Drake went back inside and sat down across from Liz. "Paul says the two Pella brothers are sons of the Pella you remembered as a money launderer in Argentina. He's going to San Francisco tomorrow to ask the older brother if he knows where Alejandro is."

"Do you think you should go with him?" Liz asked.

"Paul has plenty of experience questioning dangerous people, he'll be fine. He doesn't think the older brother is anyone to worry about."

"He was a detective when he got that experience. He's not wearing a badge now."

"True enough, but I think that he'll be fine."

Drake watched Liz smile when she looked in the direction of the kitchen and smiled. He turned and saw that their food was arriving.

When the waiter set his plate in front of him, Liz leaned forward, "You're doing okay, so far. What's next on the agenda?" she asked and picked up a slice of sourdough toast.

"Do you like to shop?"

"Sure."

"Then that's what we'll do, until you tire me out and I'll need to go back to the cabin for a siesta. Then we'll explore the island a little more before dinner."

"If I'm going to wear you out with a little shopping, maybe we should leave it for another time. I don't want to be responsible for you needing a nap in the middle of the day."

Drake smiled at her and said, "You're already responsible for the nap I'm thinking about. Of course, we could skip the shopping?"

Chapter Thirteen

PAUL BENNING LANDED in San Francisco Thursday morning on Alaska Airlines 2370 at 10:45 AM and took a cab to 425 1st Street on Rincon Hill, one of the city's original 'Seven Hills'. Paolo Pella lived in a three and half million-dollar condo that he purchased the year before.

His wife, Margo, had called the day before to make an appointment to meet with Paolo Pella to discuss his brother's disappearance from the University of Oregon and the tennis scholarship that was at risk. Paolo Pella had already been told that it was, because he was listed as Alejandro's next of kin. The university athletic department, however, had asked him to follow up and find out if Alejandro would be returning or if his tennis scholarship was available to be awarded to someone else.

When the security guard checked the list of Pella's expected guests for that day, Benning's name was on it and he was directed to the elevator and given Pella's unit number.

The elevator stopped at the fifty second floor and he found Pella's condo, rang the doorbell and waited.

Paolo Pella had on a gray cashmere sports coat and black slacks, a white shirt open at the neck and brown Italian loafers. He was five eleven, trim and relaxed.

Benning held out his hand and said, "Thank you for seeing me. I won't need much of your time, Mr. Pella."

Pella stepped back and motioned for him to enter. The floor-to-ceiling windows on the other side of the living area provided an awesome view of the San Francisco skyline and the bay. The condo was furnished appropriately, if sparsely, with chrome and glass and black leather chairs and sofas.

"What's this about Alejandro's scholarship? My personal assistant didn't fully explain to me why you needed to see me?"

"Do you know where your brother is, Mr. Pella?"

Pella blinked quickly before answering. "He's at school. Why do you ask me that?"

"He hasn't been at the university for several weeks. Have you spoken to him recently?"

Pella turned around and walked to a wet bar and picked up a coffee cup. "Would you like coffee, Mr. Benning?"

"No thank you. I had some on the flight here."

"Do you remember your college days, Mr. Benning?"

"Yes."

"Then you know that young men aren't so good at staying in touch with their families. Alejandro is no exception."

"But you speak to him occasionally, correct?'

"I do, yes."

"Has he said anything about dropping out of school?"

"Not to me."

"Has he mentioned his girlfriend, Ashley Berkshire?"

Pella's head tipped slightly to the right and furrowed his brow. "He's mentioned girlfriends, I don't recall that she was one of them. Why do you ask?"

"She went missing around the time that Alejandro left school."

"And you think they might be together?"

Benning shrugged his shoulders. "I guess that's a possibility. If they did run off together, do you think Alejandro will return to play tennis again for the university?"

Pella smiled and said, "Who knows what a young man will do these days. I have no idea where Alejandro is or what he intends to do, Mr. Benning. I suggest you ask him."

"I will when I find him, Mr. Pella," Benning said and handed him his business card. "When you hear from him, have him call me. We can't hold his scholarship for next year much longer if he isn't coming back."

"If I hear from him, I certainly will. Is there anything else?"

"I have everything I need for now. Thank you for seeing me," Benning said and turned to leave.

"Vaya con Dios, Mr. Benning," he heard Pella say behind him as he opened the door.

In the elevator on the way down to the lobby, Benning knew Pella was lying. The decision he had to make was what he was going to do about it. Without a way to make Pella tell him where his brother was, there wasn't much more he could do in San Francisco except kill some time. His flight home to Portland didn't leave for another six hours.

Alejandro could be anywhere. Even if Pella knew where his younger brother was, and Benning was sure that he did, he didn't seem to be eager to volunteer the information.

He decided to call a cab and go to Fisherman's Wharf for lunch at his favorite restaurant, the Fog Harbor Fish House on Pier 39. He was waiting in front of the One Rincon Hill condo tower when he saw Paolo Pella drive by in a gold and black Bugatti Chiron.

Before the Bugatti was out of sight, Benning's Yellow Cab pulled up and he jumped in.

"Did you see that gold and black Bugatti, I need you to follow it," he told the driver.

"You always wanted to say that, right?" the old black cabbie chuckled. "This ain't the movies, man."

Benning held up his worn leather ID holder with twin windows for the man to see in his rearview mirror. One side had his private investigators license and the other his old detective's ID. He held up the ID holder so in a way that made it easier to read his detective ID.

"No, it isn't, but I still need you to follow the Bugatti."

The cabbie's eyes darted back and forth from the ID holder and Benning's eyes before he nodded and turned the cab around to do what he was asked.

"Is this where you hold up a 'Benjamin' if I don't lose him?"

Benning shook his head. "Maybe a 'Grant' if you're lucky."

Chapter Fourteen

PAOLO PELLA DROVE CAUTIOUSLY on the way to the San Francisco Yacht Club where the yacht was moored. The Bugatti was worth two and half million dollars, easy, and he couldn't risk getting a scratch on it before he found a buyer.

The car's exotic looks turned heads and he needed to be prepared for anything. Drivers wanted to pull beside it to get a better look and cars in front of it often slowed down for the same reason. If he wasn't careful, some fool could cost him a small fortune if the car had to be repaired after an accident.

In fact, he couldn't afford to lose any part of a fortune, even if it was small. His "investors", as he preferred to call them, were acting like they no longer trusted him. He assumed it was because he'd stepped out on his own and initiated the kidnapping of the biologist's daughter without involving them first. But he had to seize the opportunity when it presented itself.

When Alejandro told him about his new girlfriend, he did what he always did when someone got close to his young and reckless brother; he had her investigated. He worked hard to keep his enterprise off law enforcement's radar, and he wasn't about to let some attractive young undercover cop bring him down.

While he'd been pleased to learn that Ashley wasn't a threat, he'd also recognized immediately that her father had access to a commodity that could make him a lot of money. Bioweapons were the hottest item on the dark web black market and having a live sample of the deadly virus could be worth millions. With a vaccine to go along with it, he could quadruple the asking price.

By the time he got to the yacht club, he was daydreaming about the day when he could afford to stop working for Hezbollah and the cartels. Armin Khoury had called that morning and said he was flying in from Las Vegas. Khoury wanted to meet him at the yacht to discuss business and the young woman he was keeping an eye on.

Khoury was leaning against the side of a black Mercedes sedan, with his arms folded across his chest, when Pella drove up and parked the Bugatti next to it.

"Beautiful boat," Khoury said. "Do you know why they call this Hatteras the 'Panacera'?"

"Panacea, from the Greek word for 'all-healing', or the solution for all difficulties," Pella answered. "Being on this yacht will make you forget what's troubling you."

"That's correct. What's troubling me, Paolo, is that it's still here in San Francisco. It's supposed to be halfway to Costa Rica by now. Do you still have a buyer for it?"

"He says he still wants it and he'll wait. Don't worry, you'll get your money."

"Yes, but I won't be getting it when you promised me I would. Because of that, I've had to use my own money for something that had to be done. Now I'm going to need the whole two million from the sale, I'm afraid Paolo, for it to be a solution for me."

"That's not what we agreed to, Armin."

"Consider this our new agreement. To guarantee that you abide by its terms, I'm putting one of my men on board the yacht for the trip to Costa Rica. Don't let the boat leave without him."

"There isn't room for another man, Armin. With the captain and his two men and my brother, Alejandro, there's no place for him to sleep."

Khoury shoved off from the side of the Mercedes and took a

black folding knife from his pocket and opened it. It had a hawkbill blade that he used to trim his cigars with and he took a Montecristo No.2 from his shirt pocket and began trimming it.

"Alejandro can sleep on the floor, he's young. When will your captain and crew get here?"

"In two hours, he wants to leave before dark."

Khoury finished trimming the cigar and took a gold lighter from his pants pocket to light it. "When will Alejandro get here?"

Pella turned his head and saw his brother standing in the aft deck watching them. "He's already on board."

"Does he have the keys for the boat?"

"He does, why?"

"If he does, there's no need for you to be here. Say goodbye to him. I'll stay until the boat leaves to make sure my man is on board and then I'll head back to Las Vegas. You're taking up a lot of my time, Paolo, I hope this is worth it, for your sake."

"What's that supposed to mean?"

"You know what it means. Say goodbye to Alejandro and go find a way to pay me what you owe me."

PAUL BENNING SAT in the back seat of the Yellow Cab and watched Pella and the other man through an open window. He didn't recognize the other man, but with the photos of him on his Samsung S10, he was sure he could find out.

Whomever he was, Pella didn't seem to enjoy meeting with him, judging by the way he was marching to his Bugatti after talking with someone on the yacht.

"How much longer do you want to stay here," the cabbie asked. "You used up that 'Grant' a while ago."

"Let's follow the Bugatti when it leaves, and I'll consider giving you that 'Benjamin' you wanted."

"Why are you following this guy? He some crook or something? Whatever he's doing, it looks like he's making good money at it."

"Looks like it, doesn't it? If that's his yacht and Bugatti, I'd say he's making more money than either of us will make in a lifetime."

"Don't you be so sure about that," the cabbie said and held up a lottery ticket. "This is the winning ticket that will prove you wrong, mister."

Chapter Fifteen

ARMIN KHOURY RETURNED to Las Vegas more determined than ever to finish the kidnapping business as quickly as possible and get on with his assignment in North America.

The money launderer thought he was going to pay for kidnapping the girl with the money he made from selling the sample of the virus and the vaccine. The fool, Pella was never going to get his hands on the ransom.

He had a biologist waiting in a makeshift lab, with equipment purchased online for less than a thousand dollars, that could synthetically engineer the sample of the virus into the perfect bioweapon. Modified to have a lethality rate close to fifty percent and the airborne ability to pass from one human to the next, the bioweapon would provide his sleeper cells in all the major cities with the capability to unleash a bioengineered viral pandemic.

Western civilization was urbanized and received its food and water from distant locations through a supply chain that would simply shut down if there was a lethal virus spreading across the land. People would be afraid to report to work. Those who did keep working, like emergency medical personnel and the police, would catch the virus from the infected. Economic activity, public services and transportation would cease along with the flow of essential goods. Panic buying and hoarding would begin and when the food and water supply was threatened, widespread marauding and looting would start and the police would be so shorthanded they couldn't stop it.

That was the power he would soon have in his hands: a weapon so destructive no nation could stand against it: a deterrent that would create a mutual destruction stalemate with a nation even as powerful as the U.S., if it became necessary. That was the mission he'd been given: to find a way to protect Iran and prevent it from being attacked by Israel or its puppet sponsor.

Sitting in the back of his Mercedes on his way from the airport to Pella's house in Red Rock Canyon where he was staying, he called his man in Oregon for an update on the situation there.

"Talk to me."

"He's out of his lab arranging a funeral for his brother. Before he left, it sounded like he was getting close to having the vaccine."

"We need him to complete his work. Pella worries me. It's all about the money for him. I think he's trying to line up a buyer for the virus on the dark web. If an intelligence agency figures out what he's offering, they'll make sure all samples of the virus are secured and protected. We may not have much time."

"What do you want me to do?"

Khoury considered his options. "Why don't I give him some face time with his daughter tonight. I want the vaccine as well as the virus, but I'll take just the virus now to make sure we get it."

"Will he hand over the virus if he doesn't get his daughter?"

"He'll be making a down payment to keep her alive until he gives us the vaccine. Call me tonight when you know that he's home and alone."

As soon as the garage door closed behind the Mercedes, Khoury got out and entered the seven thousand square foot estate home, and went directly to Ashley Berkshire's bedroom on the second floor.

The guard sitting on the chair outside her door jumped to his feet and stood at attention as he approached.

"At ease, Haasim. How is our guest?"

"She's not crying as before, but she refuses to eat."

Khoury nodded toward the door and Haasim opened it for him.

Ashley was standing at a window, looking down at the golf course outside, and spun around when she heard the door open.

"I hear that you are not eating. Your father would not be pleased," Khoury said.

"Does my father know I'm here?"

"Yes, he's seen you and knows that you're alive. He'll get to see you again tonight, if you will agree to cooperate."

"Why are you doing this? Where is Alejandro? Is he here?"

"Your boyfriend did not travel here with you."

Ashley's lips quivered and she looked like she was going to cry. "Is he okay?"

"I have no way of knowing but I'm sure that he is."

She shook her head. "I don't believe you," she said quietly.

"We didn't hurt him, Ashley, and we're not going to hurt you. Your father has something we want. When we get it, he gets you back in the exchange. Hurting you or your boyfriend would only complicate things."

"Are we in Las Vegas?" she asked. "I saw one of the golfers with Red Rock Country Club on his golf bag. One of my sorority sisters lives around here."

Khoury smiled but didn't answer her. "Is there anything you need?"

"A phone would be nice."

"Get some rest, Ashley. You want to look your best when we call your father tonight," Khoury said and left the room.

He went downstairs to one of the two master suites to change for a swim in the solar-heated pool. One of the perks for being the Hezbollah commander in North America was the opportunity to do things without worrying about his safety. He had twelve men guarding Pella's home, four men for each eight-hour shift and another twenty men in and around Las Vegas if he needed them.

Alan Berkshire would be on his guard now, with the murder of his twin brother and the kidnapping of his daughter. He would have to be carefully managed from here on out.

Persuading him to hand over a sample of the virus, without the release of his daughter, wouldn't be easy. He needed to sincerely believe he would see his daughter alive and well soon and, at the same time, understand that she was a moment away from having her throat cut if he didn't do as he was told.

Khoury knew from experience how to convince Alan Berkshire of that.

He summoned two of his men who were playing pool in the game room.

"Go to town and bring me a young prostitute who looks like the girl upstairs. I want him to see how someone dies when their throat is cut."

Chapter Sixteen

KHOURY WAS WATCHING BBC World News in the media room when his men returned with a young prostitute. She had duct tape over her mouth, a zip tie around her wrists and a wild look in her eyes. She had been crying and her mascara had run and darkened her cheeks.

He circled her and nodded his approval. "Take her to the garage and get things ready. Hang a sheet behind the chair she's in. I don't want anything in the background that will provide information about our location."

The prostitute was led away and Khoury headed upstairs to get Alan Berkshire's daughter ready for her father to see her. Outside the door of her room, he told the man guarding her what he wanted.

"Get someone to help you," he said. "I'll stay here until you get back. When you return, bring one of the dining room armchairs. Sit her in it and use duct tape to secure her arms and feet. Put tape across her mouth. Stand behind her wearing your balaclava. When I tell you, rip off the tape and we'll let her talk. If I signal you, put the tape back on quickly. I don't want her saying much."

Khoury opened the door and saw that Ashley was lying on the bed staring at the ceiling.

"I'll be back in ten minutes and we'll call your father. Think about something you can tell him that will make him do what he's told, if you want to go home."

Ashley sat up and swung her legs over the side of the bed. "What is it you want from him? He's a research scientist. He doesn't have a lot of money, if that's what you're after."

"He knows what I want. Just make sure you remind him that what you want is to go home."

Khoury closed the door and saw his men coming up the stairs. "Don't hurt her when you put her in the chair. I want her father to see that we're taking good care of her and that we will continue to do so as long as he does what he's told."

He went downstairs to the garage to see if his men had done what he'd asked. The prostitute was sitting in a folding chair in the middle of a sheet of clear plastic with a black bag over her head. Her arms and feet were zip-tied to the back and legs of the chair and there was a white sheet hung behind her.

Khoury nodded his approval. He took the cellphone he bought to communicate with Berkshire and send him a text.

I will call and allow you to see your daughter in five minutes. Accept facetime request when I do.

While he waited, he walked out to the patio and lit a cigar to pass the time. When five minutes passed, he continued smoking for another five minutes to allow Berkshire's anticipation to build.

When he entered and opened the door to the garage, he handed his cigar to the man by the door and took the black balaclava held out for him. He pulled it on and called Berkshire.

When he saw that Berkshire was staring back at him, he said, "Before I let you see your daughter, I want to show you what will happen to her if you disobey me in any way."

With that, he turned the phone around to show him the prostitute sitting in the chair with the black bag over her head. When he nodded to his man standing behind her, the bag was pulled off and the duct tape was ripped from across her mouth.

"Watch carefully, Mr. Berkshire."

When he nodded a second time, the man behind the chair pulled a knife from the sheaf on the center of his belt and held it high, before he slashed it down and pulled the curved blade of the Jambiya quickly across the prostitute's throat.

A gush of blood shot out from the gaping slash across her throat and her eyes opened wide.

Alan Berkshire cried out in shock. "You bastard! You didn't have to kill her. I'm doing what you ask," he shouted.

Khoury kept the phone focused on the prostitute. "You need to know that I'm dead serious when I tell you that I'll do the same to your lovely daughter. I'll call you back in a minute or two."

He made a circling motion with his index finger to tell his men to clean things up in the garage, took his cigar back from his man at the door and headed inside to let Berkshire see his daughter.

Ashley Berkshire was sitting in the armchair with duct tape across her mouth with his man wearing a black balaclava standing behind her, like his other man had done in the garage.

Khoury called Berkshire and focused the phone on her as soon as he saw Berkshire's face.

"You see, Ashley is fine and will remain so as long as you do as you're told. You may say something to her, if you want."

He motioned for the tape to be taken off her mouth.

"Ashley, honey, are you okay?" Berkshire said.

"I'm okay, Dad, but please do as they say. I want to come home," she said and started to cry.

"I will, honey. We'll have you home soon."

"Say goodbye to your daughter and hope that it's not for the last time. I'm going to text instructions. Follow them exactly," Khoury said and ended the call.

He went downstairs to the patio and sat in one of the cushioned chairs under the maroon umbrella of a poolside table.

Time to let Berkshire know there was a change of plans.

I want a sample of the virus tomorrow. I'll release your daughter when you give me the vaccine, but not before. My schedule has changed, but you have

my word, you will get your daughter back soon. When you receive a call, follow instructions.

Chapter Seventeen

PAUL BENNING WALKED down the back stairs from the condo he leased above Adam Drake's law office to call his friend in Seattle. He'd gotten back from San Francisco after midnight the night before, because his flight had been delayed due to unspecified "mechanical difficulties", whatever that meant.

When he finally got home, he hadn't been able to sleep and downloaded the photos on his smartphone to his laptop to study them. That was when he'd noticed the young man standing in the aft cabin of Paolo Pella's yacht and realized it was Alejandro Pella, Ashley Berkshire's boyfriend.

He used the number he had for Drake's mobile device. It was midmorning and Drake should be in his office at Puget Sound Security by now.

By the sound of the wind whistling in his ear when his call was answered, he knew he'd reached Drake somewhere out of his office.

"Late for work?" he asked.

"What gave me away?"

"The sound of the wind I'm hearing."

"I'm on a ferry headed back to Seattle."

"Good, then you have time to hear about my trip to San Francisco. I met Paolo Pella. He said he didn't know where his brother was and didn't know anything about a girlfriend named Ashley. He was lying about his brother and probably Ashley as well."

"Why?"

"Because I followed him to his yacht club and took a picture of him standing in front of a yacht. His brother was watching him from the yacht/"

"That doesn't mean he's lying about Ashley."

"Before I left the yacht club, three men arrived with duffel bags and got on the yacht. I think Paolo hired a crew to take the yacht and his brother somewhere."

"And get Alejandro out of town before anyone can talk to him. What can I do to help, Paul?"

"Two things. Can you get Kevin to find out where that yacht is going? There's a shot of the yacht I'm sending you. Kevin should be able to identify it. The photo also shows a man sitting on the hood of his Mercedes talking with Paolo. See if Kevin can identify him as well."

"If Pella is lying about his brother, it looks like you may be right about Ashley being kidnapped. Maybe it's time to hear what her father has to say."

"He was pretty adamant that he didn't want anyone getting involved, according what to his brother said, before he was killed."

"If Paolo Pella is involved, with his family background, Berkshire needs someone getting involved, whether he likes it or not," Drake argued. "It won't hurt to talk with him."

"I suppose. You mentioned that you were going to be back in Portland later in the week. It's Thursday, would you like to go with me tomorrow and see what Berkshire has to say?"

"I don't think you need me for that, but I will if you want me to."

"If Berkshire admits that his daughter has been kidnapped, I thought it might help if you were there to offer the assistance of the PSS kidnap and ransom unit."

"Good thinking, Paul. I'll see what Kevin can find out and drive down tomorrow."

"Let me know when you're headed my way."

DRAKE WENT BACK into the main passenger cabin on the ferry and found Liz sitting in a booth looking out the window toward a sailboat in the distance.

"That was Paul," he said, and sat down across from her. "He's convinced the girl was kidnapped."

"Are you?"

"Things are pointing that way. He wants me to go with him to talk with her father."

"Why?"

"To offer the services of our K&R unit, if he admits she's been kidnapped and would like someone to handle the negotiations."

"If he says that he would like PSS involved, what role will you play?"

Drake shrugged his shoulders, "It depends, I guess. If it's a straight-forward ransom exchange, the K&R unit can handle it. If it turns out there's more involved, I'll do whatever I can to help out."

"When I was in the FBI, I was involved in several kidnap investigations. I don't remember one of them being straight-forward or routine."

"Were there private negotiators in those kidnappings?"

"A couple of them. The FBI tries to discourage it as much as they can. When there are private security services and K&R teams involved, there's a lot of friction that develops. The negotiators are focused on getting the victim back alive and the FBI focuses on prosecuting the criminal, as well as getting the kidnapped person back. The two interests were often in conflict."

"If it's our call, and it might be, do we get the FBI involved or handle it ourselves since it's a federal crime to deliver the ransom in a kidnapping,"

Liz laughed, "I think you know the answer to that. I don't remember anyone being prosecuted for handling a ransom but why risk spending ten years in prison?"

"That's why I wanted PSS to hire you, because you get along with the FBI so well, in case we decided to handle this ourselves," Drake said with a smile.

Liz shook her head. "With the way you've crossed swords with the FBI lately, I wouldn't count on my relationship helping out very much."

"Good point. I'll try to keep from drawing my sword unless it's absolutely necessary."

"Why doesn't that reassure me?" she asked.

"Probably because you know me so well."

Chapter Eighteen

ALAN BERKSHIRE SHOUTED "NO!" to stop the hooded man from cutting the girl's throat and bolted upright in his bed in a cold sweat. The nightmare had been playing in his mind all night, a horrible snuff film running on a continuous-play loop.

He got out of bed, feeling old and helpless. He'd prayed for an end to the gnawing pain in the pit of his stomach that developed after he was told what he had to do that day to keep his daughter alive. God didn't seem to be listening.

He'd devoted his life to researching the deadly epidemics of the past and developing vaccines for the pandemic viruses of today. He knew they could kill millions if they returned to plague the modern interconnected society of today. One air traveler in a crowded airport could start a pandemic that would spread around the world in a matter of days, by infecting people with something like the avian H7N9 influenza from China.

He knew the Spanish flu pandemic of 1918 killed just two percent of its victims, but it still eventually killed fifty million people. The current flu virus that was constantly evolving in nature or could evolve, with the help of some insane amateur biologist making it more easily transmitted from human to human, could cause billions of deaths around the world. That was why he had been working so tirelessly to develop a vaccine that could prevent such a pandemic.

And now he was being forced to choose between saving the life of his only child or potentially being responsible for the death of millions of people. He knew full well the latter possibility was more likely, because he was sure that what the kidnappers wanted was a sample of the live virus to weaponize it. And he couldn't think of a way to prevent that and save Ashley.

Standing in the shower with water as hot as he could stand it hitting between his shoulder blades, he shook his head from side to side thinking about the irony of it all. Twenty years after graduating the University of Oregon, where Ashley was studying biology to follow in his footsteps, he was being forced to betray both her belief in him and his profession.

He was glad her mother wasn't alive to have to endure this nightmare with him. She had suffered enough in her struggle with leukemia, but, then again, maybe that would have given her the strength to handle this better than he was, if she had lived.

Berkshire toweled off and glanced at the time on his cellphone laying on the countertop. It was five o'clock in the morning. He had one hour before he was supposed to meet one of the kidnappers and hand over a frozen nasopharyngeal swab specimen of the H7N9 virus from his lab.

The specimen was frozen at minus 70 degrees Celsius and had to be transported in a sterile vial packed in dry ice to keep it from thawing. He'd asked the kidnappers if they knew how to transport a frozen specimen and was told it was something he didn't need to worry about. Bring the specimen frozen and at the appointed time and place and they would take it from there.

For a fleeting moment he'd considered letting the specimen thaw enough to make it unviable for anything outside his lab. But the kidnappers would just be back for another sample before they released Ashley.

That wasn't the only thing he had to worry about right now. He was close, but he didn't have a vaccine for the H7N9 virus yet. Once he handed over a specimen of the virus, though, he was committed.

They would have to trust him to keep working on a vaccine, just as he had to trust them to keep Ashley alive until his work was finished.

Berkshire dressed quickly in his workout clothes for the gym and jogged through the house to his old Volvo wagon in the garage. It was a three-mile drive to his lab at the Vaccine & Gene Therapy Institute and he wanted to get there before the staff routinely came to work. Smuggling the frozen specimen out wasn't going to be a problem. But he couldn't allow a gabby lab tech to delay him in getting the frozen specimen into the dry ice transport container in the back of his Volvo.

He'd stopped at his grocery store to buy dry ice the night before. It was now chilling in the small polystyrene insulated transport container he'd borrowed from the lab. Now all he had to do was get to his lab and then rendezvous with the kidnapper.

At the Vaccine and Gene Therapy Institute gate house, Berkshire was waved through by the night guard who barely glanced at the staff sticker on the windshield, and drove on to the parking lot of his building.

He placed his hand on the biometric scanner to enter his lab and walked on through it to the room where the frozen specimens were stored. He used his lab keys to enter the room and walked directly to the vault where the frozen samples of the deadliest virus on the planet were kept. He compared the number he'd written on a piece of paper against the numbers on the storage chambers in front of him and took out a key to open the frozen sample he'd chosen to give to the kidnapper.

Five minutes, from the time he entered the lab, he was back in his Volvo and driving past the gate house. His instructions were to meet the kidnapper in the parking lot of the Tualatin Hills Nature Park.

The two hundred and twenty-two-acre wildlife preserve had four and a half miles of trails that he'd run through dozens of times in the early morning. Today, the parking lot adjacent to the nature center was empty except for a rider sitting on a black and blue motorcycle at the north end of the parking lot.

Berkshire drove the length of the parking lot and slowed to a stop in front of the motorcycle, staying in the car with his hands on the top of the steering wheel, as he'd been ordered to do.

The man sitting on his bike wore black motorcycle leathers and had a pistol with a suppressor on its barrel in his hand as he dismounted. When the kidnapper walked forward, keeping his pistol aimed at Berkshire's head, he noticed the blue specimen transport container strapped to the rear of the motorcycle.

Berkshire turned his head to the left as he tracked the man's approach. When he was standing next to the driver's side door, he tapped on the window with his pistol.

The visor on the kidnapper's black helmet was down and Berkshire rolled down the window to hear what he had to say. Instead, the man motioned for him to get out of his car and pointed with his pistol to the insulated transport container sitting on the seat behind him.

When Berkshire got out, the kidnapper handed him a folded sheet of paper, with typed instructions:

PUT THE SPECIMEN IN THE TRANSPORT CONTAINER

ON THE BACK OF THE MOTORCYCLE LEAVE. FOLLOW

THE INSTRUCTIONS OR SAY HELLO TO YOUR BROTHER

Chapter 19

Adam Drake kissed Liz at the front door of her condo and left Seattle to drive to Portland and accompany Paul Benning when he talked with Alan Berkshire. Ashley's father might not want any help, but his twin-brother had retained Paul to find the girl and his death didn't close the case, as far as the private investigator was concerned.

Drake was looking forward to the next couple of days. He always enjoyed his time on the farm, but he really was also looking forward to seeing Lancer, his German Shepherd buddy. He'd left Lancer in the care of his neighbor and vineyard manager, Chris Conners, while he looked for a place to live in Seattle. Lancer didn't mind staying with Chris and his German Shepherd, Max, but Drake always felt guilty when he had to leave his dog behind.

Drake couldn't help wondering how Lancer would adjust to a new home on Bainbridge Island.

He'd left everything behind, except personal belongings, in the old stone farmhouse he'd restored with his wife, Kay, before she died. He returned there as often as he could, to maintain the place and meet with Conners, who was managing the vineyard that he had finally talked Drake into replanting and restoring.

Moving to Washington, however, was going to be a fresh start, but before the transition was complete, he had a few things to take care of.

PSS used Paul Benning on several occasions to act as a private investigator on its behalf. With their new offices the company had opened on the west coast and in Hawaii, there was plenty of work to keep an investigator on retainer or as an employee. Drake hoped to talk Paul into taking a full-time position with PSS and work out of his law office in Portland that the company would lease for him.

He also planned to offer his condo above the law office to the Bennings and let them set the terms for purchase. With the money Kay left him from her trust fund when she died and the money he'd saved over the years, plus the profit he expected from the vineyard, Paul and Margo could take as long as they wanted to pay him for the condo.

The only glitch he foresaw in his plan was getting Margo to agree to continue as her husband's secretary for his P.I. work. She was used to running the law office her way and Drake had let her. At the beginning, when Paul had retired to begin working as a private investigator, he'd seen that the two of them weren't always on the same page when it came to managing the office. He hoped that had changed.

Drake walked down the back stairs from the parking garage to his office at ten minutes to twelve and found Margo talking on the phone. He walked slowly around to the front of her desk to keep from startling her and gave her a two-finger salute.

"I need to call you back, Cathy. A strange man just walked in and looks like he's lost," Margo said and hung up the phone.

"Hello, Margo. It's only been a week. What's with the lost stranger thing?"

"Must be my eyesight, because you don't look like the man I used to work for, all relaxed and such. I figured you had to be a stranger."

"Used to work for? I didn't get the memo."

"I didn't quit, there isn't a lot of work for me anymore. All I get to do is work for my husband, the private investigator. I'm the best legal secretary in Portland and you put me out to pasture before I was ready."

"Ah, that."

"You haven't had any new clients, except for what you do for Mike Casey at PSS. What needs to be done for the others is about finished. Thought it might be your way of telling me it's time to move on."

Drake glanced over his shoulder toward the stairs to the loft. "Is Paul here?"

"No, why?"

"Because I want to take the two of you to lunch, that's why."

"He should be back anytime now."

"When he gets here, meet me at the Harborside."

Drake turned to walk away and heard her say, "I knew it."

He turned around with a big smile on his face. "I couldn't resist teeing it up that way, just to see the look on your face, Margo. There's nothing for you to worry about, trust me. Come have lunch with me and hear what I have to say."

He hoped she would forgive him for not explaining himself, but what he wanted to propose was for both of them. Liz and Margo were friends and talked at least once a week and he knew that Margo was worrying about their financial future. But she should know by now that he wasn't going to do anything that wouldn't work out for all of them.

Chapter Nineteen

DRAKE HAD CALLED AHEAD on the drive down from Seattle to reserve a table at the Harborside, on the main floor next to the windows. He was on his second cup of coffee when Paul and Margo Benning entered and saw him waving at them.

He stood and shook hands with Paul. Margo just nodded and sat down in the chair across from him.

"Paul, I can see that Margo is not going to enjoy her lunch until she knows what I wanted to talk about, so I'll get that out of the way first. It's a proposal in three parts. First, PSS wants to make it official and hire or retain you as its lead investigator to work from here in Portland. PSS will lease my office for you and hire Margo to manage your office and keep doing what she's doing now. You can work full time for PSS or work with a retainer and continue as a private investigator.

Margo started to ask a question and Drake held up his hand. "Let me finish and you can ask me anything you want. I also want to sell you my condo at market value, with a family discount, on whatever terms that work for you."

"You haven't said anything about your law practice, Adam. What are you going to do with it?" Margo asked.

"Close out pending matters and refer our clients to a law firm we'll recommend. I'll work full time for PSS as special counsel and head of 'Special Projects' or whatever we choose to call what I've been doing for the last couple of years."

A waiter came to their table and asked if they wanted to begin with something to drink.

Margo took a deep breath and said, "Yes, I need a drink. How about a Bloody Mary, heavy on the vodka?"

Her husband chuckled and said, "Easy girl, I'm sure Adam doesn't need an answer from us right now. If you have questions you want to ask, now's the time."

"Where will you live?" Margo asked. "Are you moving to Seattle to be with Liz?"

"That's the plan. I found a place on Bainbridge Island and I'll commute from there. My neighbor has agreed to manage the vineyard and I'll keep the farm."

Margo's Bloody Mary was brought to their table and she stirred it with the pickled green bean and a deeply furrowed brow. When the green bean was halfway to her mouth, she turned it around and pointed it at Drake.

"I'm not surprised about your moving to Seattle. I saw that happening as soon as Liz moved there from Washington, D.C. But are you sure you want to give up the freedom you've enjoyed without having a boss?"

That made Drake laugh. "Since when have I not had a boss?"

Margo wrinkled her nose and snorted. "Someone had to make sure the work got done."

Their waiter returned, and they ordered cheeseburgers for the men and a grilled salmon Caesar Salad for Margo. While they waited for their food to arrive, Drake asked Paul if there were any developments in the Ashley Berkshire matter.

"Just one. Alex Berkshire is being followed," Benning said. "I've watched him for the last two mornings. He leaves his house for a morning run before work. Then he drives to the Vaccine and Gene Therapy Institute. A guy on a motorcycle followed him both mornings."

"Then his daughter has been kidnapped," Drake said. "They're making sure he doesn't go to the police."

"What did the motorcycle look like?" Margo asked.

"A black and blue Suzuki," Paul said. "Why?"

"The police report you got when his brother was gunned down described the shooter's motorcycle as being black and blue," Margo said. "I read the report, but it didn't identify the make of the bike."

"Alan Berkshire told me he was trying to get him to go to the police. The kidnappers must have found out."

"How would they find out?" Drake asked. "Alex wouldn't have told the kidnappers what his brother was thinking of doing."

"There's only one way," Paul said. "Alex Berkshire told me his brother wouldn't return his calls, so he went to his house to confront him. They must have bugged his house."

"If they bugged his house," Drake said, "They've probably bugged his car, and anywhere else Berkshire spends a lot of time, like in his lab."

"How are you going to talk with him without the kidnappers finding out?" Margo asked. "He's not going to volunteer to meet with you, after what they did to his brother."

"I think I know how," Drake said. "Did he run the same course both mornings, Paul?"

"Four point two miles on the same route both times."

"Then he's likely to do the same thing tomorrow morning. If some neighbor joins him on his morning run, the guy on the motorcycle won't suspect anything. Especially if I take a running partner with me."

"Adam, Paul hasn't fully recovered from his surgery. He can't be your running partner," Margo said forcefully.

"He won't have to be. I'll take Lancer."

"Would you want me to follow the guy on the motorcycle, in case this goes south?" Paul asked.

"That won't be necessary. Lancer can handle things if the kidnapper tries anything. I'll carry concealed, just in case."

"Do we know why Berkshire doesn't pay the ransom and get his daughter home?"

"Maybe he can't raise the ransom, Margo. Alex told me his brother didn't have a lot of money Benning said, "It could be this isn't about money."

"If it isn't about money, what is it about?" Margo asked.

Drake sat back in his chair and folded his arms across his chest. "It could be something he's working on at the vaccine institute."

Chapter Twenty

DRAKE LEFT his farm at sunrise with Lancer sitting in the passenger seat beside him. After leaving Paul and Margo at the Harborside, he'd driven to his farm outside of Dundee, Oregon, and spent a glorious afternoon inspecting the vineyard and playing with Lancer.

Nothing in the old stone farmhouse had been changed since he was last there, but it didn't feel the same. In a way, he felt sad that it didn't. The best years of his life had been living there with Kay, working to restore the abandoned vineyard, then working to keep his promise to complete the project after she died. Even then, when he lived there alone, it felt like home.

Now that he was moving north, everything was changing; where he was going to live, who he was going to be working for and, possibly, who he might be living with. It was all a little disconcerting.

He could only imagine what Alan Berkshire must be feeling, losing his wife, his brother and his only child being held by kidnappers. He needed to be persuaded to let them help him get her back.

Drake reached over and patted Lancer on his back. "We will get her back, Lancer, with you and me working together again."

He pulled off the Sunset Highway and drove west on NW Rock

Creek Boulevard to Rock Creek Park, south of Berkshire's home, and parked. Paul Benning was already stationed a block away and would let him know when Berkshire left on his morning run. From their location at the park, he and Lancer could see when Berkshire ran onto the boulevard in time to run and catch up to him.

They didn't have to wait long before Benning called. "He's leaving now. He should reach you in five minutes. The last two mornings he's turned west and run the same route, but he could turn east this time. Either way, you'll see him. Let me know when he shows up."

"Let me know if he's being followed."

"I will. Good luck."

Drake got out of the Cayman GTS and started stretching. Lancer sat on his haunches next to him with his head canted sideways, eager to start their run.

"We'll have to sprint to catch up with him, but don't go running ahead when we do. Stay with me, okay?"

Lancer turned away and looked in the distance with his ears up.

Drake looked in the same direction and saw a runner come into sight on NW Malheur Avenue. He kept stretching until Berkshire was turned west and headed up Rock Creek Boulevard.

"Let's go, Lancer. Time to meet Mr. Berkshire."

Drake jogged across the parking lot and then sprinted after Berkshire on the boulevard. He caught up with him in half a minute and called out, "On your left!"

When he ran up beside Berkshire, he slowed and said, "Morning, Alan. I'm a friend. Keep running with me so we can talk. You're being followed, so let's make this look like two runners out for our morning run."

Berkshire turned and studied Drake. "Who are you?"

"Adam Drake. I'm a lawyer working with the man your brother hired to find Ashley."

Berkshire looked straight ahead and ran a little faster. "Leave me alone. I don't need your help."

"Ashley's not back, I think you do. What ransom are they demanding?"

Berkshire didn't answer.

"Does this have to do with your work?"

Berkshire's head jerked around. "How...?"

"How did I know? We checked. You're not trying to refinance your house. Your brother said you're not wealthy. It had to be something else."

"Please, I can't involve anyone, or they'll kill her."

"Alan, we can make sure they won't. Tell someone at work that you're going to the Research Development and Administration office this afternoon to check on next year's research funding. Go to OHSU South Waterfront and take the aerial tram at four o'clock. I'll be waiting at the top in the Café on the third floor. We'll make sure you're not followed."

"It's too late."

"Too late for what? Is Ashley dead?"

Before Berkshire could answer, Drake heard Benning say in the earbud from the iPhone in his runner's belt, "Black and blue motorcycle following you, two hundred yards back."

"Alan, one of the kidnapper's is following you on a motorcycle. Finish your run and meet me at the Café. I'm going to turn off at the soccer fields up ahead. You can trust me, Alan. Bring something Ashley has worn. My dog will help us find her, if she's alive."

Berkshire didn't say anything. Drake split off at the entrance to the soccer fields and kept running.

"The motorcycle is still following Berkshire," Benning reported. "He's past where you turned off. Want a ride back to your car?"

"We'll run back. Running with Lancer feels good. Let's find someplace to have breakfast and figure out where we go from here."

Drake and Lancer reversed their route and ran back to the park. When they were two hundred yards away, he slowed to a stop and threw down the challenge. "Lancer, stay."

He stopped when he was seventy-five yards away from the entrance to the park and turned to see his dog watching him with his tail wagging.

Drake turned around and took the position of a miler at the

start of his race. Over his shoulder, he shouted, "Lancer, come!" and sprinted ahead.

When Lancer streaked past him, Drake smiled. He was still ten yards away from the entrance to the park.

Paul Benning was leaning against the fender of his red Ford 150 shaking his head. "Next time, take a two hundred-yard head start and he'll still beat you."

"Only if I let him."

"Right. Since you lost, Lancer says you buy breakfast."

"I usually do. But since I'm helping you with your case, you can buy both our breakfasts. We both like steak and eggs."

"Fair enough. Did Berkshire agree to meet you?"

"We'll know if he shows up."

Chapter Twenty-One

THAT AFTERNOON, Drake and Benning took the elevator from the underground parking at the OHSU Family Medicine Clinic at the South Waterfront campus in Portland. They walked together to the lobby, where Benning was going to stay and watch to see if Alan Berkshire was being followed.

It was thirty minutes before Drake's scheduled meeting with Berkshire at the Café in the hospital up on Marquam Hill.

Benning spotted a small table next to the bank of windows with an unobstructed view of the aerial tram terminal outside. He laid a copy of the Oregonian newspaper, the oldest continuously published newspaper on the west coast, on the table and motioned for Drake to take a seat to hold the table.

"I'm going get a cup of coffee. I'll be right back."

Drake sat down and watched the people lining up outside to take the tram up to the hospital. Benning would be able to see anyone coming through the lobby to the tram and see anyone through the windows walking to the terminal outside as well.

Benning hadn't met Alan Berkshire, but Drake had described him. He hadn't met the kidnapper either, but the former detective knew he'd be able to spot someone trying to keep Berkshire in sight.

With the meeting ostensibly happening at the office of Research Development and Administration (RDA), with the confines of the hospital on the hill, there was a good chance the kidnapper wouldn't risk being seen anywhere near Berkshire.

If they were wrong and the kidnapper was following Berkshire closely, the meeting would be aborted, and they would find another way to meet him.

Benning returned with his coffee and sat down across from Drake. "If he's being followed, do we want to risk being seen if I try to get a picture of him?"

"That's up to you, Paul. You'll know if it's worth the risk."

"I'll see what I can do. I couldn't forgive myself if I was responsible for getting Ashley killed."

"She might be dead already. Berkshire did say that it was too late for us to help."

"I hope that's not the case."

"I need to catch this tram. Text me when you see Berkshire."

Drake walked outside and stood at the back of the line of people waiting for the three-minute ride up to the Kohler Pavilion and the OHSU hospital. When the tram arrived and emptied its passengers, it quickly filled again. He was the last one in and faced to the rear of the tram to have an expanding view of the riverfront and the city, as the tram quickly climbed thirty-three hundred vertical feet to the pavilion above.

When the tram's door opened, he stepped aside to let people pass him as they rushed to their appointments or to visit a friend or a relative being treated at the university hospital. He followed them and made his way to the café on the third floor to wait for Berkshire.

The café was crowded with a mix of hospital staff eating hurriedly and anxious-looking family members waiting to hear if surgeries had been successful or critical diagnoses made that would change their lives forever.

It was a strange mix of professional aloofness and worried concern that Drake remembered all too well. He'd spent hours drinking coffee waiting in the place while Kay received her chemotherapy treatments that had done little to slow the rapid advance of her cancer.

Drake hated the place and the memories that came flooding back as he stood in line for coffee. He hoped in the future he would remember this visit for the good that came of it.

He chose a table at the far end of the room and sat with his back to the windows and the view of the river and the city below. His focused on the constant stream of people coming into the café.

At ten minutes after four o'clock, he sent a text message to Benning asking if there was any sign of Berkshire. He didn't know enough about the man to know if he was one who never arrived on time or had been delayed in the late-afternoon traffic, but he was beginning to worry.

No sign of him.

Let's give him until four thirty.

He hadn't had enough time when he was running with Berkshire to give him a reason to trust him, but he'd had to try. Berkshire had ignored the pleading of his twin brother to go to the police, but that wasn't unusual. The threat of harm to a loved one was enough to paralyze most anyone. His only hope was that Alan Berkshire wasn't most people and was ready to let someone other than the police help him.

He just rushed through the lobby. He's on the tram.

Drake watched the entrance of the café and five minutes later Ashley's father walked in with a brown canvas messenger bag hanging from his shoulder. He stopped just beyond the cashier's stand and looked around for his morning's running mate.

When he saw Drake sitting at a table near the windows, he nodded and hurried over.

"You weren't followed," he assured Berkshire. "Please, sit and let me explain why I asked you to meet me. I know your daughter has been kidnapped, probably by her boyfriend or someone he's working with. I know that you've been told not to go to the police, or she'll be killed. That's the leverage that kidnappers always have, the threat of harm to their captive.

"I can't begin to imagine what you're feeling, Alan, but I do know I can help you. I'm special counsel for a security firm that has a very good kidnap and ransom unit that specializes in managing the crisis and negotiating with kidnappers. It has an outstanding record getting hostages released and helping deal with the stress of it all.

"If you'll let me, I'll help you any way that I can. And with your permission, I'll get our K and R unit involved to assess your situation. Can we start by you telling me what's going on and why you said that it's too late?"

Berkshire stared out the window and then looked Drake in the eye. "They killed my brother, didn't they?"

"We think so. Th motorcyclist the witnesses described matches the description of the man we've seen following you."

"Why do you think her boyfriend is involved?"

"Because he dropped out of school. Recently he was seen on a yacht his brother owns. Now it's on its way to Costa Rica."

"Why do you want something of Ashley's?"

"Because I'll be flying to Costa Rica to see if she's on the yacht. My dog you saw with me is a police-trained German Shepherd. He's going with me."

"Why are you doing this?"

"Paul Benning, the private investigator your brother hired, asked for my help. He's not going to quit until he finds Ashley."

"Even if his efforts to find Ashley get her killed?"

"The kidnappers will know someone is looking for her. They won't know we're looking for them as well."

Berkshire took a deep breath and hung his head.

"Do you mind if I ask you something?"

Berkshire shook his head.

"Why did you say it was too late?"

Without looking up, Berkshire said, "Because I gave them what they asked for. They haven't let her go."

"What did you give them?"

"Something I shouldn't have."

"Something you were working on in your lab?"

Berkshire's nodded.

"It was just a guess. What I think you're probably working on has value to some people."

"You mean terrorists."

"Most likely, or criminals who want something to sell to terrorists. What was it?"

"A live specimen sample of the H7N9 avian flu virus. There are other places they could get a sample. I thought if it would get Ashley back, it was a risk I had to take. They'd just get it somewhere else if they didn't get it from me."

"When did you give them the specimen sample?"

"Yesterday."

"Did they say why they didn't release Ashley?"

"They want something more. They want the vaccine for the virus I'm working on."

"Why would they want that?"

Berkshire sighed. "I don't know."

"If you had to guess…?"

"If they weaponize the Asian flu virus, the vaccine would allow them to protect themselves if they ever use it."

Chapter Twenty-Two

DRAKE REMAINED SEATED with Ashley's blue scarf in his hand and watched Berkshire walk out of the café. The job of finding his daughter had just gotten a lot more complicated.

The kidnappers were terrorists and brutal ones at that. Berkshire had described how he had screamed, watching a young girl have her throat cut, to warn him the same thing would happen to his daughter if he didn't do as he was told.

Berkshire had also explained that in the current age of bioengineering, it was easy to modify an existing pathogen to make it more lethal and transmissible. With new technology, the genetic material of an organism could be manipulated in a simple and cheap lab in a neighbor's garage for less than two hundred dollars.

Intentionally and strategically released in a densely populated city or crowded airport, the rapidly spreading virus could quickly cause a worldwide pandemic. Berkshire also said that if a virus was genetically modified, there would be few, if any, vaccines available that would be effective. That was why he was working to create a vaccine for the H7N9 avian flu that could be effective, even with genetic manipulation.

Berkshire remained adamant that the police or FBI must not be brought in. He needed to complete his work on the H7N9 vaccine to get his daughter released. The first thing the FBI would do is make sure his lab was closed to prevent him from providing anything else to the kidnappers. He didn't see that there was anything the FBI could do that Drake's company couldn't do. With the head start that Drake and the private investigator had, Berkshire thought they could find Ashley faster than anyone else.

Drake hoped that was true. He knew the FBI had more assets at their disposal than Puget Sound Security would ever have. The only edge they had was knowing that Ashley's boyfriend was last seen on a yacht that was now in Costa Rica and that he could get there faster than anyone else by using the PSS Gulfstream G650.

Drake called Paul Benning in the lobby watching the aerial tram come and go. "Has Berkshire passed your way?"

"He's just getting out the tram."

"I'm coming down."

"Is Berkshire willing to work with us?"

"I'll fill you in when I get there."

Drake walked to the tram loading dock and took the next tram. He stood with the other passengers, thinking about what Berkshire had told him and the possible consequences of not involving the FBI. Given the nature of the work Berkshire was doing, the FBI would quickly takeover any investigation of Ashley Berkshire's kidnapping and focus on capturing the terrorists and recovering the specimen sample.

He understood the FBI's priorities and didn't disagree with them. But he also agreed with Berkshire that involving the FBI would probably get his daughter killed. The terrorists already had the sample specimen of the avian flu virus They were more likely to risk using the modified virus without the vaccine than risk being caught, if they learned the FBI was involved. Ashley was the only one who could identify them, and they would certainly kill her if they decided to cut and run.

Benning was standing outside on the terminal platform when Drake stepped out of the tram and kept walking into the lobby of the South Waterfront. He turned and followed Drake inside.

When he caught up with him, Benning asked, "What did he say?"

"He said we have a bigger problem than we thought. Let's get back to the office and figure out what we're going to do about it."

"How big?"

Drake stopped and stepped closer so that no one could hear what he was about to say. "The kidnappers are terrorists and he's already given them half of the ransom, a specimen sample of the avian flu virus."

"When you said big, you meant it. What does he want us to do?"

"Get his daughter back."

They took the elevator down to the parking garage without speaking. They had gone after terrorists before, without the assistance of law enforcement or the government, but this was different.

A young woman's life was at stake if they got it wrong and millions of people could die if they failed. And they could both end up in jail for not letting the Department of Homeland Security or the FBI know that terrorists had blackmailed Berkshire into giving them a sample of the deadly virus.

Saving the life of one young woman, without letting anyone know what Drake had learned, wasn't an easy choice. But abandoning Ashley was a harder one.

It was a conundrum he would have to solve, but he wasn't going to do it by himself.

Chapter Twenty-Three

DRAKE DROVE BACK to Seattle late that night after detouring to his vineyard to pick up Lancer. If he and Benning were flying to Costa Rica, he wanted Lancer with him to search for the girl.

Lancer had excelled at scent training as a pup and won American Kennel Club Scent Work trials with his keen ability to track a scent. With Ashley's scarf that Alan Berkshire had given him, Lancer would quickly find out if she was on Paolo Pella's yacht or ever had been.

He called ahead to PSS headquarters to find out if Mike Casey was still there. He wasn't. When Drake contacted him and told him he had something important to discuss but didn't want to do it over the phone, Casey agreed to return to the office and be there when Drake arrived.

It was ten thirty in the evening when Drake knocked on Casey's open office door and walked in.

Casey saw that Lancer was with him. "Relocating Lancer to your new place on the island?"

"I'm going to need him when I fly to Costa Rica."

"Are you and Liz taking some vacation time I didn't know about?"

Drake sat down in the chair in front of Casey's desk and motioned for Lancer to lie down next to him.

"Not a vacation, but I do need your approval before I go."

"Why Costa Rica? And you don't need my approval before you take some time off."

Drake grinned. "This time I do. I've stumbled into something big and I don't know how far we want go with it."

Casey leaned back in his chair and nodded. "If it's big enough that you want to talk about it in advance, I think I need something to ease me into this discussion. Want to join me?"

"Sure."

Casey spun around and opened a door of his credenza and took out a fifteen-year old Pappy Van Winkle bourbon and two bourbon glasses.

"What have you stumbled into?" Casey asked, as he poured them each two fingers of the amber liquid and leaned across his desk to hand one over.

Drake raised his glass before answering. "The missing college student I told you about Paul Benning was hired to find, has been kidnapped. The ransom demanded was a sample specimen of the H7N9 avian flu virus and vaccine from the father's lab at the Virus and Gene Therapy Institute at OHSU. The girl's father has already delivered a specimen of the virus to the kidnappers. They killed his twin brother and slit the throat of a young woman and made him watch it on his iPhone to keep him quiet. He's agreed to let us find his daughter and allow our K and R unit to assist him with the remaining negotiation for the vaccine, but insists we don't let the FBI know anything about it.

"Is that all?" Casey said with raised eyebrows.

"There's a little more. The girl's boyfriend is Alejandro Pella, a tennis star at the University of Oregon. Alejandro's brother is Paolo Pella, of the Argentine money laundering Pellas, who are rumored to have close ties to Hezbollah in the Tri Border Area in South America."

"Holy Here We Go Again Batman! You sure you didn't leave anything out?"

Drake shook his head. "Nope, that's it."

"This trip to Costa Rica, what's that about?"

"When Ashley's boyfriend disappeared, Benning tried to find her boyfriend. Paul thought he was the last one to see her. The boyfriend is the U of O's tennis star and number one player. He's dropped out of school and Paul thought his brother in San Francisco might know where he is. Paul met with brother, who said he didn't know where his brother was. Paul didn't think he was telling the truth and followed him to a yacht club.

"He took a shot of the brother's yacht. He studied it when he got back home and saw that the younger brother was standing on the yacht partially out of view. We traced the yacht to a marina in Costa Rica. Paul intends to go to Costa Rica to find the boyfriend. I thought I would go with him."

"Do we have any idea where the specimen sample of this virus is now?"

"No idea. Alan Berkshire, Ashley's father, gave it to a guy on a motorcycle who was wearing a helmet with the visor down. The guy and the bike match the description the police have of the man who gunned down Berkshire's brother."

Casey sat his glass down and crossed his arms across his chest. After a moment, he asked, "Who do you intend to tell about what you know or think?"

"Therein lies the problem. We both know the circus this will turn into if we go to the FBI. They'll focus on the terrorist angle. Our K and R unit can handle getting Ashley better than they will. What I know and what I suspect about terrorists being involved I can't prove. It could just as well be some criminal organization that wants the specimen sample to sell on the black web. China's apparently withholding samples of the deadly virus, so a sample of the virus might be a valuable commodity."

"What about the Department of Homeland Security?"

"They would be obligated to inform the FBI about the kidnapping."

"Let's talk with Liz. She served as the Director's executive assistant at DHS. She'll have some insight about getting them involved. What are the legal ramifications if we pursue this on our own?"

"I want to look into that tomorrow morning."

"Okay then, let's meet with Liz tomorrow morning and decide what we're going to do. Would you like a refill?"

"I think both of us need one."

Chapter Twenty-Four

IT WAS ALMOST midnight when Drake rang the doorbell of Liz Strobel's condo. He'd called to ask if she would mind letting him stay over until the morning.

There was time to catch the last ferry to Bainbridge Island, but he told her he wanted to give her a heads up before their meeting with Casey the next morning. What he really wanted was to hold her and smell the fresh scent of white jasmine in her hair.

Liz was barefoot and wearing one of his white shirts with the sleeves rolled up when she opened the door. She'd just taken a shower from the look of her damp hair, and he didn't need to hold her to smell the scent of her hair that he loved.

But he did it anyway.

"You look good in that," he whispered as he wrapped his arms around her.

"Thought you might like it."

"I brought someone to see you," he said and stepped aside so she could see Lancer behind him.

Liz dropped to her knees and opened her arms. "Come here, Lancer."

Lancer looked up at Drake, who nodded, and rushed to Liz and nuzzled her cheek with his big tail drumming his welcome to her against the open door..

Liz wrapped her arms around Lancer's neck. "Has he been taking good care of you? I'll bet you're hungry. Let's see what I can find for you."

She stood, grabbed Drake's hand and walked him into the kitchen. "Have either of you eaten today?"

"We had breakfast, but you can get him something if you want."

"What about you?"

"Coffee would be great. Mike made me drink some of his bourbon when I got to headquarters."

Liz rummaged around in her refrigerator and brought out a sealed container. "It's half of a baked chicken breast and steamed vegetables from dinner. Can he eat this?"

"Sure, let me cut up the chicken and warm his meal a little in the microwave."

While Drake was cutting the chicken breast into strips, Liz popped a K-cup into her Keurig coffee maker for him.

She jumped up onto the white quartz countertop on the island. "Does our meeting tomorrow have anything to do with what Paul's working on?"

Drake put the chicken strips back in the glass food storage container with the vegetables and put it in the microwave. "Thirty seconds?" he asked.

"Try it and see."

He set the timer and turned around to face her. "Paul is trying to find Ashley Berkshire and we know she's been kidnapped. Her father gave the terrorists who kidnapped her a live specimen sample of the H7N9 avian virus for the ransom they demanded. The kidnappers haven't released the daughter and made a second demand."

Liz wrinkled her brow and said, "Do we know that they're terrorists?"

"I think they are, but I don't have anything to prove it. Berkshire's twin brother was gunned down last week by a guy on a motorcycle. Someone fitting the description met Berkshire on a similar looking motorcycle when he handed over a sample of the virus. They made Berkshire watch on his iPhone while they cut a young woman's throat as a warning to keep him in line."

"In line for what?"

"The vaccine he's working on as well."

Liz jumped down to get his cup of coffee and took it with her to the breakfast nook. "You said we might be trying to find the terrorists. What did you mean by that?" she said over her shoulder.

Drake got Lancer's food out and sat it on the floor, before following her and sitting down across the table. "Berkshire is willing to let our Kidnap and Ransom unit get involved. We need to decide if we tell the FBI or DHS about what we know. That's why we're meeting with Mike tomorrow."

"If we decide not to confide in the FBI or DHS, what will you do?"

"Try to find Ashley. If we come across terrorists in the process, then we'll have to decide if we get the government involved. If we bring them in now, there's a good chance the terrorists will find out and kill Ashley."

"Did Berkshire tell you how long it will be before he finishes his work on the vaccine?"

"He didn't say, and I didn't ask him. He did say that the problem he's having is trying to develop a vaccine for a virus that will probably be gene edited to perfect it as a bioweapon. The vaccine research currently is focused on the latest strains of the virus, not strains that have mutated to be transmissible between humans, or been gene edited. If you were still at DHS, what would you do if someone reported that a specimen sample of the H7N9 flu virus had been handed over as ransom in a kidnapping?"

Liz rubbed her forehead with her left hand before looking up and answering. "We've known for some time the U.S. is not prepared for a dangerous biological incident. If there was the smallest possibility of a bioweapon being prepared to launch against us, I would throw everything I had at investigating and mitigating that threat.

"You probably know the 1918 influenza pandemic was caused

by the H1N1 flu virus. In America, twenty-five percent of the population was afflicted, and the average life expectancy dropped by twelve years. In just a few months that pandemic killed more people than any other illness in recorded history.

"If someone is trying to bioengineer a more lethal strain of the H7N9, any responsible government would do everything in its power to prevent that from happening."

"But if we let the FBI or DHS know," Drake said, "They'll swarm all over this like honeybees when their colony is overcrowded. Ashley's safety won't be an issue."

"If the kidnappers are terrorists, in this new day of synthetic biology, that's how it has to be."

Drake shook his head. "Liz, there has to be a way to save Ashley and not endanger the lives of millions of people. There has to be."

Chapter Twenty-Five

THE CEO of Puget Sound Security had coffee, juice and bagels waiting for Liz and Drake when they entered the conference room at eight o'clock the next morning. There was also a plate of cream-filled doughnuts he'd ordered online for himself.

"I'm surprised Megan's still letting you do this," Drake said as he pointed to the plate of doughnuts.

Mike Casey laughed and said, "We reached an agreement. If I run every morning, I can eat whatever I want. She worries about cholesterol, but I never gain a pound, no matter how much I eat. Doc says my cholesterol is fine, so as long as the truce lasts, I'm good."

When they each had their selections on a plate and were sitting at the conference room table, Drake made his opening statement. "The decision we have to make is whether to inform the FBI or DHS about the possibility the kidnappers are terrorists and that the partial ransom Berkshire gave them is a sample of the H7N9 avian flu virus.

"I think we should continue to assist Paul Benning to find Berkshire's daughter and not involve the FBI in the kidnapping. If, and when, we have evidence the kidnappers are, in fact, terrorists and we can't find Ashley, we let Liz inform DHS about what we've learned.

"I think Liz is leaning toward getting DHS involved right away, but I'll let her explain."

"When I was with DHS," Liz said, "We looked at all available responses to an influenza pandemic. We found that we weren't prepared. John Hopkins did a study for the Center for Health Security and conducted a mock pandemic exercise with a bipartisan group of current and former U.S. government officials playing as presidential advisers.

"The fictional outbreak featured a virus engineered in a Swiss lab by terrorists. Because the virus in the exercise was new, no one had previous immunity to it, and it spread like wildfire. It was projected that such a scenario would kill more than one hundred million people worldwide, that health-care systems would collapse, panic would spread, the stock market would crash and government leaders, including the president and congress, would be incapacitated.

"A lot of money has been spent to develop vaccines for the existing flu virus outbreaks. But when a new strain, like the Chinese avian H7N9 virus, shows up, there are no vaccines to deal with it. The big pharmaceutical companies get huge grants to quickly develop new vaccines, but they can't do it overnight.

"That's why I think we need to get DHS, or the FBI, involved. If these kidnappers are terrorists and they bioengineer a new and deadlier strain of flu virus, they have to be stopped before we have a real-life situation like the John Hopkins mock pandemic."

No one said anything, as they thought about the possibility of a global pandemic, until Casey broke the silence.

"There are two assumptions we can reasonably make. The first is that doing anything that might tip off the kidnappers that Berkshire isn't doing what he's been told, will likely result in Ashley being killed. She's the only person who can identify them. If they think Berkshire won't be allowed to give them the vaccine they want, there would be no reason to keep her alive.

"The second assumption is that if the kidnappers are terrorists, they kidnapped Ashley to get a sample specimen of the H7N9 flu virus to use it, in some fashion, as a bioweapon. I can't think of another reason they would want the virus. Even if they want the virus to sell it on the black market to some other terrorist group, the result is the same.

"The obvious dilemma is having to choose between saving Ashley or potentially saving the lives of millions."

Drake got up to get another cup of coffee and said on the way back to the conference table, "Why can't we do both? The only lead we have is Ashley's boyfriend, who may have been involved in her kidnapping and may be in Costa Rica on his brother's yacht. We can check that out quicker than anyone else. If her boyfriend is there, there's a chance we can find Ashley if he was involved. If he was, he's our link to the terrorists and we'll have information sooner than anyone else is going to develop it."

"How do you plan to check out the boyfriend in Costa Rica?" Casey asked.

"I asked Kevin to see if he could locate the yacht. He found the marina where it's currently moored," Drake answered. "I had Alan Berkshire loan me one of Ashley's scarves. I'll take Lancer with me and see if the boyfriend is still on the yacht. If he is, I'll get him to let Lancer do some scent work. If he isn't, I still try to get Lancer onto the yacht."

"Are you going alone or is Paul Benning going with you?"

"Depends on how I'm getting there."

"Are you asking if you can use the Gulfstream?"

"Yes, if it's available."

"Liz, what do you think?"

"I'm okay with checking out the boyfriend in Costa Rica on two conditions. First, if we prove the kidnappers are terrorists, we inform DHS. Second, I've never been to Costa Rica and I want to tag along."

"I suppose you want me to stay home while you two vacation down there?" Casey asked. "I have my own condition you will have to agree to if you use the PSS jet; I get to log some flying time as Steve's copilot."

"Agreed," Drake said quickly.

"Agreed," Liz said as well.

"When do we leave?" Casey asked.

"As soon as you clear this with Megan," Drake answered, reminding his friend that his wife still blamed Drake for him winding up in a hospital in San Francisco. He'd been trying to stop an international assassin from getting into Drake's hotel room when she paralyzed him with a poisoned curare dart that was meant for Drake.

"Right," Casey nodded, "Give me a day or two and we're on our way, if I'm lucky."

Chapter Twenty-Six

THEY LANDED at the Juan Santamaria International Airport in San Jose, Costa Rica, and drove overland to the Los Sueños Resort and Marina on the Pacific coast in a rented nine-passenger van. When they arrived, the PSS team got out and stretched their legs in the marina's parking lot.

The flight from Seattle, Washington, to San Jose, Costa Rica, had taken them a little less than eight hours in the company's Gulfstream G650. The drive in the van took another hour and a quarter. It was late April, the hottest month in Costa Rica, the temperature was 92 degrees and there was a magnificent sunset to welcome their arrival.

"Any chance we could stop for a cerveza or two before we look for the yacht?" Marco Morales asked.

Drake slapped him on the back. "I thought you Army Long Range Recon Patrol guys were tough hombres."

"Even the toughest Lurps know you have to stay hydrated at all times. It has to be happy hour somewhere around here."

"Why don't all of you help Marco find a place to get a beer." Drake said. "I'll go look for Pella's yacht. It shouldn't be hard to find."

"Right," Paul Benning said, "The marina only has two hundred wet slips, it shouldn't take any time at all. The Hatteras M75 Panacera is big, but so are a lot of the other yachts out there."

"That's why I brought Lancer along. I've got Ashley's scarf in my pocket. When he has her scent, Lancer will take me to the yacht, if Ashley is or was ever on it."

"If you see Alejandro Pella on the yacht, don't scare him off." Benning said. "Call me, I want to be there when we talk with him."

"Sure, it's your case, Paul."

Drake left with Lancer on heel, while Liz, Casey, Morales and Benning took off to find a restaurant or bar.

The marina was the first government approved marina in Costa Rica and was located on the horseshoe shaped Bay of Herradura. The concrete floating dock had three fingers extending out on each side. The bigger yachts were moored in slips at the far end of the dock.

Drake strolled down the dock admiring the tournament fishing boats, yachts and a couple ocean-going catamarans. They varied in size and design, but they all had one thing in common; they looked like they cost someone a lot of money.

When he reached the end of the dock, he asked Lancer "Which way, right of left?"

Lancer stood still, looking to his left.

Drake waited for him to lead the way, but Lancer stayed where he was. "What is it Lancer, is it Ashley?"

Lancer didn't bark, as he was trained to do when he'd found his target.

"Let's check it out, Lancer."

Drake walked down the left finger of the dock with Lancer at his side. Moored halfway to the end of the finger, he recognized the sleek shape of the M75 Panacera with its open wrap around skybridge.

"Good job, Lancer. Let's have a look."

When he was twenty feet from the yacht, he heard what Lancer had heard, a low moaning and sobbing sound coming from the yacht. He walked closer and looked over the stern into the rear cockpit of the yacht.

A young man was sitting on the floor of the cockpit with a bloody white towel wrapped around his left hand.

"Do you need help with that?" Drake asked loudly enough to be heard over the sobbing sounds.

"I say, do you need help?"

The young man jerked his head up to stare blankly at Drake and nodded yes.

Drake told Lancer to stay and jumped into the cockpit of the yacht and kneeled beside him.

"How badly are you hurt?" he asked.

The young man opened the bloody towel and held up his left hand. It was missing the little finger.

"Is your missing finger here somewhere? If it is, it can be reattached."

"He threw it overboard for the crabs to eat," he cried softly.

"Who threw it overboard?" Drake asked.

"The man who cut it off."

"Is he still on the yacht?"

He shook his head no.

Drake took out his phone and called Paul Benning. "See if you can find a first aid kit and come to the far end of the dock and turn left. You'll see Lancer. It's Alejandro Pella. Someone's cut off his finger."

"Do you want me to call an ambulance?"

"Let's talk with him first. The bleeding's stopped and there isn't a finger to reattach."

Drake looked around the cockpit for a bottle or something to bring Alejandro some water. The only thing he spotted was a shot glass in the sink of the wet bar. An empty bottle of tequila was next to it.

He dumped out what was left in the small glass and filled it water. "Here," he said, "Drink this. Do you want me to call the police before we take you to the hospital? They'll want to gather evidence to allow them to identify your attacker."

Alejandro drank the water and said softly, "I can't call the police. If I do, he said they would come back and cut off my hands."

"Who said he would cut off your hands?"

"I don't know his name. He was on the boat when we left San Francisco."

Drake saw Liz and Paul Benning running toward him on the dock.

"Alejandro, why were you on the boat in San Francisco?"

From his rapid breathing and pale face, Drake knew he was going into shock.

Before he answered, Drake asked another question. "Were you involved in Ashley's kidnapping?"

Alejandro looked up and asked, "Ashley was kidnapped?"

"The night you were with her at the Inn of the Seventh Mountain in Bend."

Alejandro shook his head rapidly from side to side. "I didn't go to Bend. My brother called and said he needed me in San Francisco the next morning. I called Ashley and told her I couldn't come."

Liz was the first to reach the boat and jumped into the rear cockpit with a first aid kit in her hand. She saw that Alejandro was slumped over and was vomiting. "How long has he been doing that?"

"He just started," Drake told her.

"Ask Mike to have someone call an ambulance," Liz said. "First, help me lay him onto his back and let's get his feet elevated. And find a blanket or something to keep him warm. I'll keep his head turned to the side, so he doesn't choke on his vomit."

Chapter Twenty-Seven

WHILE THEY WAITED for the ambulance to arrive, Drake brought Lancer on board to search the yacht for Ashley's scent. There wasn't any.

While Lancer was doing his scent work, Benning had looked for anything that would explain what Alejandro Pella was doing on the yacht in Costa Rica. All he found was Alejandro's black REI duffel bag and some clothes on the floor in a stateroom. There was no evidence anyone else had been on the yacht.

Benning joined Drake in the cockpit and watched Liz comforting Alejandro.

"What did he say about Ashley?"

"He said he wasn't in Bend the night she disappeared. His brother called and said he needed him in San Francisco the next morning."

"Do you believe him?"

"He looked surprised when I told him Ashley had been kidnapped. It seemed to be a spontaneous response, but it could be what he rehearsed to say if he was asked. Given the state he's in, he could be telling the truth."

"That leaves his brother, then. Pretty suspicious, hustling

Alejandro out of the country when she disappears and telling me he didn't have any idea where his brother was. I followed him to this yacht and saw Alejandro on it. Why would he lie?"

"Did you tell Paolo Ashley was missing? Maybe he thought Alejandro might have had something to do with her disappearance and was trying to protect his brother."

"Maybe, but if Alejandro is telling the truth, why jerk him out of school and send him out of the country on his yacht? None of this makes sense. I want to talk to Alejandro when he's out of the hospital because we're missing something."

Drake heard the rumble of a rolling gurney approaching on the dock and saw Mike Casey running in front of it. "Paramedics are here, Liz," he said.

"Good, he just lost consciousness," she reported and stood up as the first EMT came aboard and bent down to examine Alejandro.

Drake and Benning stood with Liz as Alejandro was put on a stretcher and lifted out onto the gurney. As they wheeled him away, a member of La Fuerza Publica, the regular police force in Costa Rica, walked down the finger of the dock toward the yacht wearing a dark blue uniform and aviator sunglasses.

Standing at the stern, he asked Drake, "Is this your yacht, señor?"

"No, officer. I heard the boy sobbing and found him here with his finger cut off."

"Do you live here at Los Sueños?"

"No, we're here on vacation."

"Where are you staying? I may need to talk with you later."

"We'll be at the Marriott," Casey said, standing behind the police officer.

"How many are in your party?" the officer turned and asked.

"Five," Casey answered.

"Did any of you know this boy before he got his finger cut off?"

"No, we arrived today." Casey said.

The police officer took a small spiral notebook from his pocket and handed it to Casey, motioning for everyone to come off the yacht.

"Please write your full names here for me before you leave. I will come find you at the Marriott if I need to talk with you again."

Casey wrote his name on the notebook and handed it to Liz, who did the

same. When the officer had all their names, he turned and walked away.

"Looks like we might have to stay longer than we planned," Casey said.

"Paul wants to stay at least until Alejandro gets out of the hospital," Drake said.

"That might be a day or two," Benning said. "If you guys need to get back sooner, I'm willing stay in paradise a little longer."

"I'll bet you are," Drake said and waved at Marco Morales running down the

dock toward them.

"Don't turn around and look," Morales said when he stopped in front of them. "Check out the guy standing next to the marina office with the binoculars. He's been watching the yacht the whole time. There was another guy with him, who peeled off to follow the ambulance. They spoke to each other in Arabic.

"The guy with the binoculars told the other one to find out if Alejandro tells the police anything about them."

Drake casually turned ninety degrees to his right and spotted the man with the binoculars. "They must be the ones who cut off Alejandro's finger. We need to find out why."

"How are we going to do that?" Liz asked.

"Alejandro's going to tell us."

"If he lives long enough," Casey said, "If these are the guys who cut off his finger, they're likely to do more than that if they think he's talking to us or the police."

"They told him they would cut off his hands if he did," Drake said. "I don't think he'll say anything to the police. He's too frightened."

"What do you want me to do about the guy with the binoculars?" Morales asked.

Drake smiled. "Are you volunteering for something?"

"Might be nice to know where he's staying, and if there are more than two of them," Morales said with a wide grin.

"Follow him and find out," Drake said. "Meet us at the Marriott."

"Roger that, Cápitan," Morales saluted, did an about face and walked down the finger of the dock toward the marina office.

"What are you thinking? Casey asked.

"I think we're getting close to finding out who kidnapped Ashley."

Chapter Twenty-Eight

ARMIN KHOURY, the Hezbollah commander in Las Vegas, was getting a massage at the Red Rock Casino Resort and Spa when an attendant asked if he wanted his cell phone that was buzzing in the adjacent dressing room.

He lifted his head and saw the attendant standing next to the massage table.

"Bring it." He glanced at his Panerai Luminor watch on a plain leather band and saw that it was seven thirty in the evening. He had a dinner reservation at the casino's chophouse restaurant in half an hour and resented the interruption of his massage.

"Speak," he said, when he had his phone.

"I did as you ordered. The brother is at a medical clinic getting treatment for his missing finger," Hassan reported.

"Did you send Paolo a picture of what you did to his brother?"

"Yes, while the blood was still flowing and the little one was sobbing."

"Excellent. Has anyone been looking at the yacht, a new buyer perhaps?"

"There were people on the yacht today. They were the ones who found the brother and called for an ambulance. I don't know if they are interested in buying it."

"Find out who they are and if they want to buy the yacht. If Paolo hasn't found another buyer to replace his fat casino owner who had the heart attack, we'll sell it ourselves."

"As you wish, 47."

Khoury handed the phone back to the attendant and sat up smiling. Maybe the yacht would be sold after all. He jumped down off the massage table and didn't bother to wrap a towel around his waist, making the masseuse lower her eyes to keep from looking at his nakedness.

As he dressed for dinner, he reminded himself there was only one purpose for the meeting tonight; seeing if his guest showed any interest in obtaining a vaccine for the H7N9 flu virus before a pandemic started.

Paolo Pella's plan to steal a sample of the H7N9 flu virus and get the vaccine for it to sell on the black market had been genius. But he recognized a far greater opportunity for making a huge amount of money.

He'd researched and found a report that estimated the worldwide market for flu vaccines was four billion dollars a year. Each year, it was a guessing game for Big Pharma to select the strains of the virus it thought would be active in the coming year and develop a vaccine.

In 2017, the pharmaceutical companies developed a vaccine for the H3N2 flu strain, but the 2017 vaccine didn't protect anyone from that strain. As a result, the 2017 flu season resulted in a staggering number of cases reported by people who had received the vaccine.

For one of the Big Pharma companies to have a vaccine already developed for the exact strain that would be active in any given year, ahead of its competitors, would provide Big Pharma an opportunity for massive profits.

His dinner guest was a Wall Street analyst who specialized in pharmaceutical stocks. He was rumored to be someone willing to pay for news that might affect Big Pharma and happened to be attending the annual Pharma Expo in Las Vegas.

Armin Khoury was sitting at a table he'd reserved, enjoying a glass of twelve-year-old Chivas Regal, when the head waiter escorted the analyst to his table.

Khoury extended his hand and said, "Thank you for joining me for dinner, Mr. Ashton."

"Curiosity got the best of me, Mr. Nader," the analyst said. "When someone says they know how some Big Pharma company is going to make a killing, I'm always willing to listen, especially when they invite me to dinner."

"Would you like something to drink?"

"An Old Fashioned would be nice."

Khoury raised his hand and a waiter rushed over. "My guest would like an Old Fashioned."

"I don't believe I know you, Mr. Nader. Should I?"

"We travel in different circles, Mr. Ashton. There's no reason you would know me. All you really need to know is that I'm in possession of information that you will be interested in."

"Why do you think that I would I be interested in this information?"

"Each year pharmaceutical companies have to guess which strain of the flu will be active in the next flu season, yes?"

"That's correct."

"And if they guess wrong, as they did in 2017, the vaccines that are developed are not effective. What if a pharmaceutical company knew, in advance, which strain of the flu would be active in any given year? Would that information be valuable?"

Ashton's Old Fashioned arrived and he took a sip, nodded his approval and leaned back in his chair. "Who are you?"

"Someone who hears things."

"What would I do with this information you say you have?"

"Whatever you like, Mr. Ashton."

"If you're suggesting insider trading, I'm not interested. If this is entrapment and you're trying to see if I'll bite, you picked the wrong guy," Ashton said and started to get up.

"Sit down, Mr. Ashton. I'm not with the Security and Exchange Commission. I'm not suggesting you use this information for insider trading, I'm suggesting the information would be valuable to a Big Pharma company of your choosing and that each of us could benefit nicely if you offered it to them."

Ashton sat down and took another sip of his drink. "How would I know this information is reliable or that you are, for that matter?"

"If it was proven to be accurate, would you be willing to negotiate the sale of the information and share the proceeds of that transaction with me, fifty/fifty?"

"Before I answer that, tell me how in the world you think you're going to obtain accurate information that predicts the active strain of virus for a coming year?"

Khoury raised his glass of Scotch in salute and said softly, "Because I will give you a sample of the bioengineered strain of the H7N9 flu virus that will be active in the future. You can test it."

Ashton choked and reached for his glass of water on the table. After taking a drink, he stared at Khoury in disbelief. "You're a terrorist!"

"Lower you voice, Ashton. I'm not a terrorist. I happen to know someone who's developing a strain of the flu virus that will be more lethal and spread more quickly. He wants to sell it on the black market. We can't let that happen. I want you to get it to a pharmaceutical company so it can protect us all."

"And you want to be paid for doing that? You're crazy and I want no part of this."

"I'm afraid it's too late for you to make that decision. You will find that fifty thousand dollars was deposited in your savings account before you met me for dinner. I also have messages I received from your cloned iPhone that show you asked me for this meeting. If you do the smart thing, no one will be harmed, and you will have saved a lot of people from a very deadly pandemic.

"If you are not smart, and repeat anything we've discussed tonight with anyone, you will find your world is a very dangerous place."

Chapter Twenty-Nine

AFTER THEY LEARNED the resort had its own medical clinic located in the Marriott where Alejandro Pella had been taken, they drove there in their rented van. While Mike Casey was checking out what accommodations were available for the five of them, Marco Morales came out of the elevator and walked across the lobby.

"Alejandro is being treated by Dr. Juan de Francisco Mora Vargas in the clinic he operates here in the hotel. I know that because the guy I followed came straight here and met with his sidekick at the clinic. They're both upstairs in a room on the second floor. As far as I can tell, there are only two of them in the room," Morales reported.

"How is Alejandro doing?" Liz asked.

"I didn't have time to check. I'll go ask."

"Find out when he'll be released," Drake said. "We need to talk with him."

Casey joined them and handed a key card to Liz and Benning. "Let's get our things up to our rooms and go eat. I'm hungry."

"Don't I get a key card?" Drake asked.

"I didn't think you needed one."

"He doesn't," Liz said modestly.

"One of us should stay with Alejandro tonight," Benning said, "To make sure he doesn't lose another finger. He can stay with me if I have a room to myself."

"Sure," Casey said, "Morales and I can share a room. I'll see if we need a reservation for dinner."

Liz grabbed the handle of her rolling carry-on and started walking toward the elevator. "Come along, Adam. I'll show you my room."

Benning was trying hard not to laugh. "You may as well get used to it."

Drake grinned and said, "I'll try," and followed his roommate.

Casey and Morales met the three of them at the elevator.

"Marco says Alejandro will be released as soon as the anesthetic wears off. The nurse told him it will probably take another hour or two," Casey said. "I couldn't get a reservation for us until nine o'clock. What would you like to do until then?"

"I'm going to take a shower and see if Adam will buy me a drink on the terrace," Liz said.

"I think I'll grab a cup of coffee and stick around and wait for Alejandro to be released," Benning said.

"Marco?" Casey asked.

"There's a pretty señorita somewhere around here who wants to meet me," Morales said and slapped Casey on the back. "I'll see you at dinner."

"Hold on, Marco," Drake said. "The two men you said were speaking Arabic are at the front desk. Why don't you take Mike's key card and go get yourself one. While you're there, find out what they're talking about."

"Roger that," Morales said and walked away.

"I'll wait for Marco to get back," Casey said. "You two go ahead to your room."

Liz and Drake left to take the elevator up to their room. Casey watched Morales at the front desk talking with one of the receptionists. When she turned around to get him another key card, he said something to the man standing next to him.

"Was that Arabic I heard you speaking back at the marina?" Morales asked.

"What if it was?" the man said in heavily accented Spanish.

"I thought I recognized it," Morales said in Spanish and held out his hand. "My name is Morales. What's yours?"

"Why are you here in Costa Rica, Morales? Are you here for the sailfish?"

Morales turned to look back at Casey. "Actually, my boss is here to look at a boat he heard might be for sale."

The man turned to see who Morales was looking at. "Is that your boss?"

"Yes."

"Is it a boat for fishing?"

"You might be able to use if for that, I guess. It's a yacht, a Hatteras M75 Panacera. He's always wanted one."

"I hope he's successful, then," the man nodded and walked away with the other man.

When the two men were far enough away, Morales asked the young receptionist, "I didn't get his name. Can you tell me who I was talking with?"

"He's a guest here, sir. I'm not allowed to tell you his name, just as I was not able to tell him your name when he asked me."

Morales raised his eyebrows. "Why did he want to know my name?"

"He didn't say, sir."

Morales picked up the new key card, tapped it on the white marble counter and smiled. "Thank you for assisting me. Would you allow me to buy you a drink when you get off work?"

The young woman blushed. "I don't get off work until midnight."

Morales smiled broadly. "Then my night won't begin until then."

Casey watched the smiling Morales cross the lobby with a noticeable lift in his step.

"Did you just find your pretty señorita?" Casey asked.

"We'll see, boss. I hope you don't mind, but when the guy asked why we were here, I made something up."

"What did you tell him?"

"He wanted to know if you were here for the sailfish. I told him no, you heard there was a boat for sale that you'd always wanted, and you were here to look at it."

"Pella's yacht?"

"I told him that it was a Hatteras Panacera. There can't be too many of them at this marina."

"Good thinking. If he hasn't already sold it, Pella might take the bait."

"Do you want me to find out if it's for sale?"

"Ask at the marina tomorrow. Alejandro will know if it is, but we don't want those two to know we're talking with him. I'll tell Paul to keep an eye on Alejandro tonight. We can't let anything happen to him. He's the only lead we have for finding Ashley. We'll go back to the yacht tomorrow and pretend we're here to buy it."

"Do you want me to help Benning keep an eye on Alejandro?"

"That would be nice, if you think you can tear yourself away from the pretty señorita."

Chapter Thirty

DRAKE WAS SITTING at a table on the terrace admiring the view of Playa Herradura when Liz walked across the gray flagstone floor wearing a red floral print sun dress and sandals.

He pulled out a chair for her and kissed her lightly on the neck as she sat down. "You smell wonderful."

"You could smell like this, if you use the hotel's rose-scented soap when you shower."

"Thanks, but I'll stick with my Dial for Men. Besides, the natural fragrance of this place is all I need, except for your fragrance, I mean."

"Nice recovery. That's Ylang Ylang from the yellow flowers on the trees around here. It's the floral scent used in Chanel No.5."

"I thought it was familiar. My mother wore Chanel No.5."

The waitress came to their table and asked if they would like something to drink.

"What do you recommend?" Drake asked.

"For the señorita, I would recommend a Colada Fresca. For you… a chiliguaro."

"What's a chiliguaro?"

"It's our favorite drink, you will like it."

"Sure, I'll try it."

"This is a beautiful place," Liz said as the waitress walked away. "It's too bad we won't be here very long."

"If we still like it when we leave, maybe we'll come back."

"Why wouldn't we still like it?"

Drake frowned and shrugged his shoulders, "Depends on the memories we'll have, I guess. If the guys watching Alejandro aren't involved with the kidnappers and Alejandro doesn't know anything, this is a dead end. I don't like dead ends."

Liz saw the waitress returning with their drinks. "Good timing," she told her, "He needs something to brighten his day."

"This should do it," the waitress said and handed Drake his chiliguaro.

Liz raised her Colada Fresca. "Let's hope so."

Drake stared at the tall shot glass filled with tomato juice he'd been handed. "I think I should have asked what a chiliguaro is. Looks like a Bloody Mary without the stick of celery."

"She said you'd like it. Bottoms up, cowboy."

Drake took a drink and his eyes went wide. "Holy smokes! Fire water, hot sauce of some kind, tomato juice and lime. Spicy bad. I love it!"

He held it out for Liz to try.

"Not a chance."

Drake finished the chiliguaro and was signaling the waitress for another, when he saw Morales approaching.

"They released Alejandro," he said. "The two Arabic-speaking guys were hanging around outside the clinic. Paul wants to walk him back to the yacht to make sure he gets there safely."

"What about keeping him safe all night? Drake asked.

"I'll ask Paul after he talks with him. If someone needs to stay on the yacht with Alejandro, I'd be happy to do it, if Paul doesn't want to, but I might have a date."

Liz had to laugh. "Who's the lady?"

"The pretty señorita at the front desk. I was just planning ahead in case we need to find out who the two guys watching Alejandro are."

"Of course, you were, Marco," Drake said, shaking his head. "Call me and let me know what Alejandro says."

"Do you think it's safe for Alejandro to stay on the yacht by himself?" Liz asked.

"We don't know enough about what's going on here to answer that," Drake said.

"If Paul or Marco stay with him tonight on the yacht, the guys watching him will know we're more interested in him than buying a yacht."

"Good point, Liz. Let's find Mike and ask him to visit the yacht again. He didn't have a chance to ask Alejandro much about the yacht. He can ask for a meeting tomorrow. Make sure Paul and Marco leave with him. We'll watch out for Alejandro without staying on the yacht."

Drake signed for their drinks and used the hotel's courtesy phone in the lobby to call Casey.

"Mike, meet me in the lobby. There's something we need to do before dinner."

The next elevator that opened in the lobby had Casey standing in it, wearing a cream-colored pair of linen beach pants, a black long-sleeve linen shirt and sandals. His Oakley sunglasses hung from his neck on a thin black Croakies strap.

Casey smiled when he saw the look on Drake's face. "I thought I needed to look the part if I'm here to buy a Hatteras Panacera. I bought the shirt and pants in the shop here."

"Beats the cargo shorts and T-shirt I thought you'd be wearing," Drake said.

"What's the something we need to do before dinner?"

"Liz reminded me that we need to make sure we don't show more interest in Alejandro than the yacht. We don't want his watchers to know we're not who we're pretending to be. Let's walk over to the marina, so you can be heard asking Alejandro for an appointment tomorrow to discuss buying the yacht. We'll leave Alejandro alone tonight but keep an eye on him."

Casey looked at his watch. "Sure, we have time before our dinner reservation. Let's go."

The walk from the Marriott to the marina took them through the lush grounds of the resort and the warm night air made the walk all the more pleasurable.

The marina was alive with the sounds of people enjoying cocktails and dinners on their yachts and riggings slapping on the masts of the sailboats. Laughter carried across the water from fishermen telling their stories of the day's adventure and mixed with soft music from expensive sound systems. The Los Sueños Resort's marina at night was a tropical festival of cheerful bonhomie.

Except on the Hatteras M75 Panacera. The yacht was dark, and Alejandro was sobbing softly in the aft cabin.

Chapter Thirty-One

PAUL BENNING WAS STANDING in the cockpit of the yacht looking down at Alejandro when Drake asked if it was all right for him to come on board.

Benning shook his head no and told Alejandro he'd be right back. He opened the rear half-door of the cockpit and stepped out onto the dock.

"I couldn't keep him away from a new bottle of tequila," Benning explained. "He'll be drunk soon. He started crying when I asked him if he knew anything about Ashley being kidnapped. I think he was in shock when I asked him the first time, because he said he didn't know she had been.

"He said they had been having dinner in Bend when his brother called and told him he had an emergency. Paolo told him he needed him to be in San Francisco the next morning to go on his yacht to Costa Rica to deliver it to a buyer He said he explained everything to Ashley, that she understood why he had to leave, and he drove her back to the resort where she'd been staying and left her there. He said he drove all night to get to San Francisco in time and hasn't talked to her since then."

"Do you believe him?" Liz asked.

"I'm not sure," Benning said. "I asked him why he dropped out of school right before the national tennis championship in Florida and he held up the bottle of tequila. He said it wasn't his only problem, that he was afraid of being drug tested. If he was caught, he'd never be able to play professional tennis. Better to miss one championship than never achieve his dream, he said."

"Is he going to be all right staying on the yacht tonight by himself?" Drake asked.

"He seems to be at home here. It's as good a place as any to sleep off being drunk."

"Marco told one of the Arab-speaking guys watching Alejandro that Mike was interested in buying this yacht," Drake explained. "We don't want them to know we're looking for Ashley and not looking to buy a yacht."

"Alejandro will be okay. I'll tell him I'll come back to see him tomorrow."

Benning went back to talk with Alejandro, while Casey walked the length of the yacht and back as if he was inspecting a purchase he was considering.

When Benning returned, all five of Alejandro's new friends started back to the Marriott and were halfway down the main dock when Morales let them know they were being watched.

"Alejandro's two watchers are standing in the shadows of the marina office," he said softly.

"Got it," Drake said. "Mike, have you ever been on a Hatteras M75?"

Casey picked up on the lead. "A friend of mine in Seattle took me out on one, that's why I'm here. It's the ultimate party boat for Puget Sound. Think of the fun we'll have when we get it back!" he said excitedly.

"Megan and your boys will love it," Liz chimed in. "You could take them on a vacation up though the San Juan islands. It'd be one they'll never forget!"

"Any chance I can come along and crew for you?" Morales asked.

When they were past the marina office and far enough away,

Casey laughed. "Nice improv, guys. You're making me think I really do need this yacht, but you'll all need to take a cut in pay to allow me to buy it."

They waited until they were seated at their table in the Tower restaurant on the top floor of the hotel before Paul Benning asked the obvious question.

"What now? You guys agreed to help me find Ashley Berkshire, but this is turning out to be something different all together. Alejandro may or may not be telling us the truth, but I know his brother was lying to me. Paolo told me he didn't know where Alejandro was. Then I saw him standing a hundred feet away on the yacht at the marina. I appreciate your help with this, but I can't ask PSS to foot the bill for this."

"Paul, Alan Berkshire is our client once he agreed to let our Kidnap and Ransom team get involved," Casey said. "We'll figure out who pays for what later. We know there's a high probability that terrorists are involved with the ransomed avian flu virus. If they are, we need to do everything in our power to prove it and get the right people involved to stop them. Call it civic duty, but there's a reason I'm blessed to be the CEO of this company and we keep getting involved in things like this."

"Paul has a point, Mike," Drake said. "We might find out what's going on sooner, by getting answers from Paolo Pella."

"I have a hunch that's what we're about to do. Paolo owns this yacht. If he thinks I'm a serious buyer, willing to pay several million dollars for it, we can get him to come to us to close the deal. If he tries to act through an intermediary, I'll demand that he be present, on the advice of my cautious attorney, because I'm unfamiliar with Costa Rica's laws or something."

"We know Pella owns the yacht," Liz said, "But no one here knows that we know it. How do we let Pella know we want to make him an offer, if it's still for sale?"

"I'll send my attorney out tomorrow to find out who the owner is because I want to buy the man's yacht before I return home," Casey said.

Chapter Thirty-Two

ARMIN KHOURY PULLED out of the driveway of a modest residence in Summerlin, Nevada. It belonged to a young biologist who was bioengineering the H7N9 virus for him in the lab in his garage. He was satisfied that he now had a bioweapon he needed to start a pandemic that would destroy the west.

He was driving the black Mercedes G 550 SUV Paolo Pella kept in the garage of his luxury home when he got a call from Costa Rica.

"The men you asked me about are from Seattle, Washington. The rich one who owns the Gulfstream they arrived on is interested in buying the yacht. I'll send you pictures of him and the rest of his group."

"I'll let Pella know. How's his little brother?"

"Back on the yacht, drunk. The kid's a mess."

"We'll deal with him later. Stay close to this buyer. I need this sale to happen."

"Yes, 47."

Having a buyer show up in Costa Rica was good news because he'd lost faith in Pella finding one. If the sale went through and his money was returned to him washed and cleaned, he might reconsider what he was planning for the Argentine. There were others who could do what Pella did for them, but none of them had such an international organization.

Khoury used the SUV's audio control to call Pella with his synced smartphone to give him the news about a potential buyer.

"Have you sold the yacht?"

"I'm working on it."

Khoury could smell the man's fear oozing out of his pores as if he was standing in front of him.

"That's what I've been hearing since your fat casino owner died of a heart attack."

"Armin, we've had delays before. You didn't have to cut off Alejandro's finger. I always do what I say I will do."

"I warned you. You're lucky it was only his finger. Fortunately for the both of you, I have information about a possible buyer for the yacht. He's in Costa Rica staying at the Marriott next to the marina where you have the yacht. I'm sending you his picture. Don't screw this up, Paolo. Call me when you have my money."

PELLA DROPPED the phone onto the top of his modern glass and stainless-steel executive desk and growled like a guard dog about to attack a trespasser. How dare the rag head order him around like one of his lackies!

If it wasn't for El Blanco and the service he provided, the man would be living in a tent in the Tri-Border Area protecting some narcotraficante. Hijo de puta!

The biggest mistake in his life had been the agreement he made with the Hezbollah terrorist to launder his money. The second biggest mistake was hiring him to kidnap the biologist's daughter and help him steal the flu virus.

There had to be a way out this, a way to break free of his involvement with the terrorists.

His phone began buzzing and crab-walking across his desk.

When he picked up, he stared in disbelief at the picture of five people walking together on the dock of a marina.

Like a cloud suddenly blocking out the sun, a chill came over him. The man next to the woman wearing the red dress was the man who came to his condo asking about the college student who was missing, the daughter of the biologist.

Don't panic, his mind screamed! Think!

If he told Khoury one of the people in the picture was the man who came to his condo asking about Ashley Berkshire, Khoury would kill him for exposing his role in the kidnapping.

The buyer Khoury was so proud of finding wasn't a real buyer. That meant there was no opportunity to sell the yacht to get Khoury his money, which meant Khoury was going to kill him and his brother.

And there no way to get him the three and half million dollars he was expecting because he didn't have it and didn't know a soul that he could borrow it from.

There had to be a way to make Khoury think he was the one responsible for the man and his friends being in Costa Rica. Pella studied the picture Khoury had sent him more closely.

The tall man wearing the beach pants and the long sleeve shirt had the arrogant look of the rich, he was probably the buyer. The other two men looked fit and younger than the man who came to see him, but there was something about the woman that made him think he'd seen her before.

He closed his eyes to think and then it hit him. He remembered a press conference about the role the United States had played in getting governments around the world to tighten their banking laws to keep the drug cartels from laundering their drug profits so easily. He'd paid close attention because it was his family's money laundering enterprise in Argentina that had been mentioned.

The woman standing next to the Secretary of Homeland Security had been introduced as the secretary's executive assistant and former FBI agent who had worked on the FBI's money laundering task force before joining DHS. She was the same woman in the picture Khoury sent him.

Pella composed himself and called Armin Khoury.

"We have a problem."

"You mean you have a problem."

"Armin, listen to me. I thought the woman in the picture you sent me looked familiar. I thought I remembered seeing her. She was the executive assistant to the Secretary of Homeland Security. She was introduced at a press conference when the U.S. announced it was working with Argentina to tighten its banking laws. That's not a real buyer in Costa Rica. I don't know why these people are there, but they're not who you think they are."

Pella held his breath.

"It's your yacht they're snooping around. They must be there looking for you."

"Armin, they have no reason to be looking for me. Maybe they're looking for the man you put on the yacht in San Francisco. Maybe someone recognized him and called the FBI. Has he ever been arrested?"

Khoury's silence said that he had been.

"We're too close," Khoury said. "We need to get rid of them in Costa Rica, before they return to America. Contact the man who says he's an interested buyer. I'll get his number for you if you haven't got it. Tell him you'll meet him at the villa of the attorney you'll use as an intermediary for the sale. I know an attorney who has a villa there. He's handled things in Costa Rica for the cartel. I'll get you his address. I'll take care of the rest."

"When shall I call him?"

"As soon as you have his number and the address of the villa. I want this taken care of today."

"What do you want me to do with the yacht?"

"I'll send someone to get it. We'll find someone else to buy it. We need to clean up your mess first."

Chapter Thirty-Three

DRAKE AND LIZ returned from their morning run with Lancer around the resort's 18-hole championship golf course. They found Mike Casey at a poolside table drinking orange juice and trying to decide which pastry to try first from a platter of pastries set before him.

"Join me," he said. "I've got coffee coming."

"Where are Paul and Marco?" Liz asked before sitting down.

"I have no idea where Marco is. Paul's inside calling his wife. How was the run? Lancer looks like he hasn't broken a sweat, unlike the two of you."

"It's warmer than I'm used to, but that's a nice-looking golf course and the scenery was terrific," Drake said with a wink at Liz.

She stood and swiped playfully at Drake. "I'm going to see if I can borrow a couple of towels from the spa and have someone bring a bowl of water for Lancer. If you want, you can order a Bloody Mary for me."

"Roger that," Drake said and saluted.

"After we've had breakfast and you've taken a shower," Casey said, "Let's get down to the marina and ask about the yacht. We should know soon enough if Pella is interested in selling his yacht to me?"

"How far are you willing to go to convince him you're for real?"

"As far as necessary. Buying a yacht isn't something you do over a cup of coffee. You usually work with a yacht broker and there's a procedure to follow. When you make an offer, you include the timing for a survey of the yacht's mechanical, electrical and electronic equipment to understand the vessel's condition. You schedule a sea trial before closing to see how the yacht handles underway. All of that usually takes a couple of weeks."

"How do you know about buying a yacht? I've never heard you talk about buying one?"

"I've thought about it, not a boat this big, but something I might like to do someday."

A waiter brought a stainless-steel coffee carafe to the table and a tray of coffee cups. Casey poured them each a cup and picked up a chocolate-covered pastry to try.

"Have you heard anything more from the K&R unit?" Drake asked.

"Not yet, they met Berkshire for dinner. He's now wearing a microphone and they're monitoring his smartphone. He said there hasn't been any contact since they made him watch the girl getting her throat cut. He's busy working on the vaccine and trying to remain hopeful."

"I keep wondering why the vaccine is so important. They have the virus. If the kidnappers are terrorists, they have what they want. Why not release Ashley, or kill her, and disappear? Hanging around for a vaccine must mean they plan on using the bioweapon and want to be immune to the virus when it's deployed. That or they have some other reason to want a vaccine."

"Like what?"

Drake thought for a moment before saying, "If there was an avian flu pandemic, the vaccine for the virus would be worth billions. Remember the unusual shorting in the stock market just before 9/11?"

"All too well. If this is that sophisticated an operation, kidnapping Ashley is just a small part of it."

"That's what I'm starting to worry about."

Liz walked out to them carrying towels and a bowl of water for Lancer. "Mike, there's a call for you on the house phone. It's about the yacht."

"Maybe we won't need to go to the marina after all," Casey said and got up to leave. "If we're lucky, it's Pella."

Liz set the water down in front of Lancer and tossed a towel to Drake. "Where's my Bloody Mary?"

"Sorry, forgot about it," he said and waved to a waiter. "Want to order some breakfast to go along with it?"

"I would, thanks. I saw Morales coming back from the marina. He checked on Alejandro and he said he's sleeping off a hangover."

"I can almost feel sorry for the kid, but he knows more than he's telling us. There's no need for him to be here in Costa Rica to sell his brother's yacht. From what Mike tells me, you usually work with a yacht broker to sell a yacht like this."

Casey came back with a frown on his face and sat down. "I have an invitation to meet the owner's attorney this afternoon to talk about the yacht. He lives here in one of the villas. I told him that, on the advice of my attorney, I'd like to deal directly with the owner. He wouldn't reveal the owner's name, at this point, he said, "But that I was welcome to bring my attorney and anyone else that I wanted."

"Adam just told me that yacht brokers usually handle sales like this," Liz said. "If the owner isn't using one and his attorney lives here, why send Alejandro all the way to Costa Rica? This doesn't feel right."

"What time is the meeting?" Drake asked.

"Three o'clock."

"Do you have the address?"

"No, he's sending a car for us."

Drake looked to Liz and then back to Casey. "Why doesn't he come to us? That's what I would expect a local attorney to do, if he's living here on the resort. Did you get his name? Do we have any way to call him back?"

"Just his first name and no phone number."

"I'll bet Marco could ask the señorita and find out who he is and where he lives," Liz said.

"That's a horrible thing to ask Marco to do, Liz," Drake said with a grin.

Chapter Thirty-Four

MARCO FOUND Drake and Liz an hour later at the pool where they were lounging and swimming often enough to keep cool. He was wearing surfer shorts and a T-shirt and dove in on the other side of the pool and swam over.

Resting his forearms on the edge of the pool and looking up at Drake sitting on the end of his lounge chair, he passed along his report. "The lovely señorita that you forced me to see again says the attorney is a 'very bad man'. She says he is the attorney for a man who brings young girls and women from Nicaragua to be sex slaves and domestic workers. He has parties at his villa where many of these young girls have been seen. She gave me his address."

Drake got up and sat on the edge of the pool next to Morales with his feet in the water. "He sounds like the kind of man Pella would know, if he's laundering dirty money for guys like that. What do you think? Local gossip or good intel?"

"She appeared to be genuinely frightened of the man. I'd say good intel."

"Then I think we should take a closer look at the man and his villa. Liz," Drake said over his shoulder, "I'll rent a golf cart to take you and Lancer for a tour of the resort community. Are you up for that?"

"Sí, señor, let me go put a pair of shorts on first."

"Do you want me to follow along?" Morales asked.

"I think Lancer will be all the backup we need, thanks. Find Mike and Paul and let them know what we're doing. When we get back, we'll have to decide what we want to do about the attorney's invitation. You might check on Alejandro again."

"Roger that," Morales said and turned and swam back across the pool.

Drake put his sandals on and tipped the pool boy before walking to the concierge stand to rent one of the resort's golf carts. Waiting in the air-conditioned lobby for the golf cart to be driven over from the golf course, Drake was admiring the landscaped grounds outside the open-air lobby when he noticed one of the Arabic-speaking men sitting in a chair watching him.

The man made no effort to look away and Drake saw that he was staring at Lancer, who was staring at him as well.

Drake leaned down to pat Lancer on the shoulders. "At ease, boy. He's not a threat, at least not in here."

Lancer turned his head away to watch Liz walk over from the elevator and then returned to staring at the man when she was standing next to Drake.

"I see that Lancer doesn't like our Arab friend very much," she said as she slipped her arm through Drake's.

"I think the feeling might be mutual."

Drake tipped the concierge when their four-passenger resort golf cart arrived and helped her get seated. He then waved for Lancer to jump up to the backseat. "Shotgun's for Liz, Lancer. Sorry buddy."

Drake pulled slowly away from the hotel and followed the sign pointing to the Iguana Golf Course.

"The attorney's villa is on the hillside above the golf course," he told Liz. "Marco's señorita told him it's secluded and surrounded by rain forest. We'll get as close as we can and have a look."

They followed the route they'd run that morning, staying on the cart path along the course to the fourth hole, then drove downhill to the fifth tee.

Drake turned off the cart path onto an adjacent road that ran farther up the hillside. "Two hundred yards from here, there's a private drive that leads into the villa."

Liz turned around in the golf cart and looked at the vista below. She saw Playa Herradura in the distance, the Los Sueños Resort surrounded by lush rainforest and the marina filled with miniature-looking white boats. "Banana trees, orchids and all kinds of exotic plants. This guy may be a low life, but he knows how to live well."

Approaching the private drive, Drake slowed the cart down to get a good look at the secluded villa. The paved drive curved gently to the left and all he could see was dense foliage lining it on both sides.

"I thought this place was on the golf course," he said. "It must sit about fifty yards above it."

"Did you see them?" Liz asked as they drove by.

"Both sides of the drive under the trees, Ak-47's slung across their chests, I saw them."

"If this attorney needs this kind of protection, I think you should take a raincheck on his invitation to talk about the yacht."

Drake continued up the road, until he found a place to turn around, took out his phone and called Casey. "Liz thinks we should take a raincheck for this afternoon and I agree. The attorney has armed guards hiding in the bushes. Make some excuse and we'll go have a look-see tonight and find out what's going on."

"If you think this is a setup, why not tell him I've found another Hatteras and fly home?"

"Alejandro is the only lead we have to find Ashley and he's not telling us much. I'd like to learn as much as possible here before we leave. Tell the attorney you might have time tomorrow to meet with him, but you're busy today."

"Should we take Alejandro somewhere?" Casey asked. "He might be willing to open up when there's no one around to cut off another finger."

"I have a feeling these guys don't want Alejandro leaving. If they see him leaving, they're armed and we're not. We couldn't stop them from taking him. Let's check them out tonight before we decide what to do."

"All right, I'll call the attorney and I'll send Morales back to the airport. I don't like showing up at a gunfight with knives, but with the Costa Rica gun laws, all we brought with us are the CRKT M16 14SFG tactical folders we keep on the Gulfstream."

"I'm not looking for a gun fight, Mike. The M16's will be fine," Drake said and put the cart in gear to drive back to the Marriott. What he had in mind for the evening wouldn't expose them to anyone shooting at them, if they were careful.

Chapter Thirty-Five

AT SIX O'CLOCK, they were all seated at a table on the terrace of the Hacienda Kitchen restaurant for an early dinner. The sun had just slipped below the horizon to the west and they were enjoying a round of drinks before ordering their dinners.

Drake had talked Casey into drinking a chiliguaro and was laughing at his friend's reaction to the fiery local drink.

"It's got a kick, doesn't it?" Drake asked.

"Hot sauce and guaro. That will put hair on your chest."

"Thought you might need it to get ready for what I'd like to do tonight."

"Which is?" Casey asked and took another drink of the bright orange madness.

"After we have a light dinner, I want four of us to go for an evening run around the golf course. When we get near the villa, Morales and I will peel off and approach the villa from below. You and Liz will continue on back to the hotel. We'll meet you after we see what the attorney and his friends are up to."

"What about me?" Paul Benning asked.

"I'd like you to bring Alejandro here, get him something to eat and then take him up to your room. If this turns out the way I think it will, we'll be leaving. We'll need to take him with us."

"What if he doesn't want to go?" Liz asked.

"Take a bottle of whatever he's drinking up to Paul's room," Drake grinned. "When he's been drinking, he won't be able to resist taking a ride in the PSS jet with us."

"Do you think Alejandro knows where Ashley is?" Benning asked Drake. "Is that why you want to take him with us?"

"If Alejandro doesn't, his brother does. I don't think we can risk leaving him here. All of this is connected in some way; Alejandro, the yacht, Costa Rica, the invite by the attorney out of the blue, the guys with Ak-47's at the villa. Alejandro's the key."

Their waitress came back and waited patiently as they scanned their menus for the first time. When she had five orders for the evening's special, Casado with Covina, the local Sea Bass, she hurried to the kitchen when they told her they were in a hurry.

After finishing dinner and changing into their running gear, the four runners left the hotel lobby and jogged to the golf course. Liz was wearing a new white T-shirt she'd purchased in the hotel gift shop over black running shorts. Casey was wearing a lightning yellow T-shirt and cap he'd borrowed from Drake and Nike neon green running shorts. Drake and Morales jogged behind them wearing black T-shirts and black running shorts, a combination all but invisible in the dark night.

They followed the golf cart path around the golf course that Liz and Drake had run along that morning, jogging easily and talking quietly amid the rainforest night sounds of high-pitched singing mice, crickets and clicking geckos.

When they approached the course's fifth tee, Drake and Morales slipped off the cart path into the rainforest below the villa.

They each wore a black fanny pack concealing tactical folding knives and lightweight ATN PSV7-3 Night Vision Goggles.

After listening quietly for a minute while they put on their night vision goggles, Drake said softly, "The villa should be two hundred yards directly above us. I don't know the terrain around the villa, but it's probably as steep or steeper than it is here. We'll get close and see what we can see."

Morales nodded and moved forward. He was familiar with jungles and rain forests from his time as a United States Army Ranger long-range reconnaissance team member and started confidently up the steep hillside leading the way.

Drake was more familiar with the Middle East desert terrains of Iraq and Afghanistan, having served as member of the U.S. Army's 1st Special Forces Operational Detachment D, aka Delta Force, and had to work to keep up through the dense vegetation with the mountain goat ahead of him.

They stopped once, halfway to the villa to listen, before Morales moved on. When they saw light from the villa faintly beginning to filter down through the trees, they stopped again and took off their night vision goggles.

"Rules of engagement?" Morales whispered.

"Defend yourself, if necessary, but let's get in and out without letting them know we were ever here."

"Roger that."

Morales covered the last twenty yards to the edge of a clearing and pointed ahead.

The villa had an infinity pool and beyond a flagstone deck was an open-sided central pavilion with unoccupied couches and chairs. Bedrooms flanked the pavilion with glass doors that were open. In one of them, a man was sitting on the edge of a bed talking on a phone with his head bowed.

Standing outside the man's bedroom at the edge of the flagstone deck was a guard with an AK-47 slung across his chest. At the other end of the deck in front of the other bedroom was another guard similarly armed.

Drake moved up behind Morales.

"See if you can get close enough to hear what the guy on the phone is saying. You speak Spanish and I don't. If you need to get the guard out of there to be able to hear, signal me and I'll distract him and get him to move away."

"Roger that," Morales said and moved laterally to skirt the clearing and reach the concealment that the lush tropical landscaping surrounding the flagstone deck provided.

Chapter Thirty-Six

THE COSTA RICAN attorney sitting on the edge of his bed finished a quick prayer and made the call he had been afraid to make.

"What do you want me to do now?" he asked Armin Khoury, the man he only knew as "47", the Hezbollah commander.

"Do you think they suspect anything?"

"They have no reason to suspect anything. I did not tell them the name of the yacht's owner. They may know it's Pella, but not from anything I said. Your men have kept out of sight, but even if they were seen, several of the villas here have security guards."

"If the man pretending to be a buyer refuses to meet with you, let me know. I need to get him to tell us why he's there. If we can't get him to come to you, my men will have to take care of things. I don't want any of them to leave there alive. Do you understand?"

"Yes. I will try to meet with him tomorrow at my villa. Do you want me to do anything about Pella's brother?"

"He'll leave on the yacht when we've dealt with the others. He's not your concern. You've been very helpful, Alvarez. I won't forget it."

"Anything for a friend of my friends. It has been a pleasure helping you in this small way."

Oscar Alvarez dropped the phone on the bed and reached for the glass of rum setting on his antique mahogany nightstand. The small favor he'd agreed to do for his clients had just expanded his list of contacts to include the North American commander of Hezbollah. No one would dare oppose him again.

DRAKE WATCHED Morales slowly back away from his position at the edge of the flagstone deck when the guard turned suddenly and stared at the spot where he'd been standing. Morales was no longer there, but something had caught the guard's attention.

To keep the guard from investigating whatever it was that attracted his attention, Drake bent down and picked a rock he'd stepped on and threw it into the infinity pool.

The guard's head snapped around at the sound of the splash, when the attorney stepped out of his bedroom with the glass of rum in his hand.

"Probably a frog," the attorney told the guard. "They jump in the pool all the time."

The guard moved to the edge of the pool to search for the frog and saw the rock at the bottom. Instinctively, he raised the rifle slung across his chest and fired a burst of 7.62 subsonic rounds into the rainforest at the edge of clearing. Branches and leaves flew in the air near the end of the pool where the rock lay on the bottom.

Before the guard could turn and sweep his aim around the clearing, Drake dropped to the ground and began crawling backward. When he was far enough below the elevation of the clearing to be safe, he stood and ran downhill through the rainforest, dodging trees and bushes with the aid of his night vision goggles.

The sounds of the gunfire set off a cacophony of screams from howler monkeys in the trees that continued, even after the gunfire ceased and was replaced by the shouting of the villa's guards.

Drake ran through the rainforest until he reached the halfway point back to the fifth green of the golf course. When he stopped, he heard someone running parallel to him off to his left. Dropping to a knee, he flipped open the tactical folder he pulled out of his fanny pack.

When he stopped, the other runner stopped as well.

"Marco?" Drake said softly.

"Here."

"Meet me at the fifth tee," he said and took off running again downhill.

They stopped at the edge of the rainforest to see if anyone was nearby before stepping out onto the golf cart path.

"That was close," Drake said. "What happened?"

"I brushed against a tree frog and he croaked."

"Let's fast jog back to the hotel before they come looking for us."

Before they reached the green on the fifth hole, they heard the roaring sounds of the engines from several automobiles on the road that ran along the golf course.

Drake stopped and listened as the cars continued down the road past their location.

"They know it's us," he said to Morales. "They're trying to cut us off before we get back to the hotel. I need to let Mike know they're headed his way."

"If they think we're already there, they'll go straight to our rooms. Hotel security won't stop them."

Drake had his phone out and called Casey. "Mike, does Paul have Alejandro with him?"

"Yes, why?"

"Get everyone out of the hotel and meet us at Pella's yacht. Leave everything behind and hurry. Armed guards from the villa are racing toward you. We need to get everyone out of Dodge, now!"

"On the yacht?"

"On the yacht. You wanted to take it for a sea trial. We'll never make it to the airport. The yacht's our best bet."

"What happened?"

"Later."

"Okay. I hope Alejandro has the key."

"Where are we going on the yacht?" Morales asked as they started running.

"I don't have a clue, just somewhere they're not for now."

Somewhere the PSS Gulfstream could meet them later and get them out of Central America. When the odds were a little more even, he was looking forward to meeting the men who kidnapped Ashley and stole the virus from her father as ransom.

Whatever they were planning, it had to be something big. The whole thing was too elaborate to be a simple kidnapping.

Chapter Thirty-Seven

DRAKE AND MORALES crossed the road at the end of the golf course and jogged to the promenade that connected the Marriott and the marina village. There were couples walking arm-in-arm in the fragrant night air ahead of them, but there was no sign of their friends or anyone chasing them.

The Marriott was out of sight to the south of the promenade and they couldn't see if anyone from the villa was already at the marina ahead of them.

"If they find out no one's in our rooms, the yacht might be the next place they'll check," Morales said. "Do you want me run ahead and see if everyone made it to the yacht?"

"Go ahead, I'll hang back at the marina office. If they're on the yacht and they don't have company, call me. If I don't hear from you, I'll assume they do and come to help."

Morales ran ahead to the yacht and Drake followed him as far as the marina office and stepped into the shadows of the building. In the dark, he could hear his heart pounding from the run down from the villa and a sudden shot of fear that the others hadn't made it to the yacht.

Drake was about to run down the dock to the yacht when his phone vibrated in his fanny pack.

"They're all here," Morales said. "Alejandro says he doesn't have the key. We're trying to get the engine started without turning on any lights."

Drake let out a deep breath and ran out of the shadows and down the dock toward the yacht.

When he stepped into the rear cockpit of the yacht, Liz was there to greet him with a kiss.

"Marco told Alejandro what he heard the attorney at the villa say about him and suddenly he remembered where a key was hidden on the yacht," she told him and pulled him into the salon. "It's a good thing too. No one knew how to jump start the diesel engines."

Drake reached down to pet Lancer and said, "That's great, but does anyone know how to get this yacht out of the marina? It won't be long before we'll have people shooting at us if we don't get out of here."

"Mike's up on the flybridge trying to get us under way. What happened at the villa?"

"Marco tried to get close enough to hear what a guy, probably the attorney, was saying to someone on his phone when a guard got spooked. Shots were fired and we ran. I haven't had time to hear what Marco overheard. Where is Marco?"

"He's up with Mike on the flybridge."

"Where's Paul?"

"He took Alejandro below to keep him out of sight."

"Lancer stay with Liz. You two watch for men with guns running down the dock," Drake said. "I need to find out what Marco heard at the villa."

"Aye, aye, Captain," Liz said with a salute and returned to the cockpit with Lancer beside her.

Drake ran up the stairs to the flybridge and found Casey and Morales sitting in two white leather captain's chairs studying the electronic display panels for the yacht's controls and its navigation system.

"Figure it out yet?" he asked Casey.

"We'll find out soon enough."

"The sooner the better, Mike. Not sure how much time we have."

"Marco, go down and cast off the lines. I'll fire this thing up and get us going."

When Morales cleared the flybridge, Drake took his seat and asked, "Did Marco tell you what he overheard at the villa?"

"It was a setup. The attorney told someone we didn't suspect anything and that he'd try to meet with me tomorrow. That's clearly not going to happen. Walk to the back of the flybridge and tell me when Morales casts off."

Drake walked back to the flybridge lounge and saw Morales on the port side holding two thumbs up.

"You're cast off, Captain," he said to Casey. "I'll stay here and make sure you don't hit anything."

"It's not my boat but I'll try to keep from sinking us. Tell Morales to get aboard and hold on."

The rumble below confirmed that they had power. Casey slowly pushed the shifter forward to get the yacht moving and called to Drake, "Tell me when we're halfway out of the slip."

"Okay," Drake acknowledged. "You're almost there, halfway now!"

Casey slightly increased the throttle on the port engine and the yacht began swinging around to starboard.

"Tell me when we're clear of the slip," he called to Drake.

"You're clear," Drake said.

Casey gently steered to starboard and told Drake to stand beside him. "I won't put the running lights on until we're a safe distance out of the marina. You're my lookout. Tell me if I'm getting too close to a boat anchored out in the bay and we'll get out of here."

"Roger that," Drake said. "When did you learn to drive a yacht?"

Casey chuckled. "I haven't. I've been on a smaller yacht in Puget Sound with a client. I watched what he was doing, but this is my first time."

Drake held out a fist for a fist pump. "I am impressed!"

"Let's wait until we're in open water before you're too impressed," Casey cautioned.

Liz shouted suddenly from the bottom of the flybridge stairs. "You'd better gun it, Mike, guys with guns are coming. They're almost to our leg of the dock."

"Hang on!" Casey yelled and slammed the throttles forward. The Hatteras M75 Panacera yacht shot forward like a Ferrari at a stop light with the owner's son driving it.

Chapter Thirty-Eight

DRAKE WATCHED from the rear of the flybridge as a man scrambled up the ladder to the bridge deck of the tournament fishing boat closest to them on the dock and start shooting at them.

"Mike," Drake yelled, "Take evasive action! Someone's shooting at us."

Casey started zig-zagging as much as he could at full throttle, and shouted, "Distance?"

"Two hundred yards," Drake answered. "Sounds like an AK-47."

Casey continued swerving erratically from side to side for another two hundred yards before gently bringing the yacht to a straight-ahead course. "We're out of range. Where are we headed, by the way?"

Drake stood beside his friend and looked back at the lights from the resort and the hotel. "Somewhere they won't expect us to be headed, I guess. I studied the map of the area when we flew in. There's a marina north of here in the Papagayo Gulf near the Four Seasons Resort. The Daniel Oduber International Airport in Liberia is only thirty minutes away. That marina is where they'll expect us to go."

"If they check and find that we flew here in our G650, all they'll need to do is check the flight plan that's filed to know where we're going. We could file a bogus flight plan, say to an airport in Panama, and then head north to the marina you mentioned."

"How long would it take us to get to Panama?" Drake asked.

"A day or two, at least."

"If the attorney and his men are connected to the kidnapping, they'll know we're on to them. We might not have that long if we want to find Ashley before they kill her."

Casey slowed the boat and let it drift in neutral. "We should let the others know what we're thinking. Tell Marco to keep an eye on Alejandro and ask Liz and Paul to join us up here."

Drake left the flybridge and returned with Liz and Benning.

Casey spun the captain's chair around to face the others. "We have a decision to make. It's a decision we need to make carefully. It could be they're shooting at us because we took the yacht. It could be they're the kidnappers. It could be they are the kidnappers, who are also terrorists. We need to go somewhere that gives us the best chance of getting out of Central America safely.

"Adam says there's a marina up north that has an international airport thirty minutes away. Panama is south of here and we could head there. Or we could have our pilot file a bogus flight plan for Panama, take our chances and go north and hope they take the head fake. Floating around out here when the sun comes up isn't an option, with the fishing tournament sending boats out every day."

"That's a tough choice," Liz said. "Without knowing who was shooting at us."

Benning looked to Drake and then Casey. "There's someone who probably knows who was shooting at us. I don't think Alejandro has told us everything he knows."

"Do you want to take another crack at him?" Drake asked.

"I think you should, Adam. I've tried being his friend. You and Marco were at the villa. Let him know what we suspect. If he doesn't talk, ask him if he knows how to swim." Benning said and flashed a quick grin.

"Liz?" Casey asked.

"Let's find out what Alejandro knows."

"It's your show, then, Adam. See what you can find out," Casey said. "I'll stay here on the flybridge and keep a lookout."

Drake led the way and took the ladder down to the main salon. When they were gathered there, he told Benning to bring Alejandro up to the stern cockpit and ask Liz to find a bottle of tequila, a couple glasses and any raw meat she could find in the galley.

"He may not need much more persuading," Drake told her. "If he does, we'll show him how to chum for sharks."

Before Liz returned, Benning and Morales came up from the lower deck with Alejandro.

Drake motioned for Alejandro to take a seat on the white leather bench seat at the back of the cockpit.

"Alejandro, we haven't been formally introduced. My name is Adam Drake and I'm the *consigliere* for the man up on the flybridge driving this yacht. I want to thank you for remembering where the key was that let us get away from the men who cut off your finger. I think you know those men are not your friends. You should also know that we haven't decided yet if we want to be your friends. Do you know why that is?"

Alejandro looked around warily before answering. "No, I don't know why you wouldn't want to be my friends."

"It's because we don't think you've told us everything you know; about the men who cut off your finger, about why your brother pulled you out of university just before a big tennis tournament, about what you know about Ashley's disappearance. So why don't you tell us everything, we'll have a glass of tequila and be on our way."

Alejandro sat back and crossed his arms across his chest. "I told him everything," he said, jutting his chin out toward Benning.

"That's possible," Drake acknowledged, "But it's also possible that you're lying to us. Who is the man they call '47'?"

Alejandro eyes widened, then he shook his head. "I don't know anyone called '47'."

Drake stepped forward and opened the door to the swim platform to the left of where Alejandro was sitting.

"Do you know how to swim, Alejandro?"

"Sure, I know how to swim. Why?"

"Because you will stay with us, if we decide we can be friends. If we decide that's not going to happen, you're going to show how good a swimmer you are and swim back to the marina. There's no room here for you if we're not going to be friends."

"I can't swim that far! You're crazy."

"I think you can. You're young, you're an athlete. I'll even give you the extra incentive you might need to make the swim as fast and far as you possible can. Liz, did you find what I asked you to find?"

Liz stepped forward and handed him something wrapped in white butcher paper.

"What's that?" Alejandro asked.

"The incentive I mentioned." He unwrapped the butcher paper from around a large steak and held up it up. Stepping through the short door onto the swim platform, he said, "This is what you use to chum for sharks."

Drake casually tossed the steak into the dark water.

Alejandro jump up and try to push between Liz and Benning, who were blocking his way out of the cockpit.

Drake grabbed his shoulder and pulled him back onto the bench seat.

"I didn't have a choice," Alejandro pleaded. "He's my brother!"

Chapter Thirty-Nine

ALEJANDRO PELLA ROCKED BACK and forth and then rested his forearms on his knees and looked around at his captors. "I only did what I was told. I didn't kidnap Ashley."

"You knew about it, though." Drake said. "That's why you left her at the resort in Bend."

Alejandro dropped his head down and nodded. "My brother said it was an emergency, that he needed my help. I took her to dinner and back to her room at the resort. After that, he told me to get in my car and just drive straight to San Francisco that night."

"What did you think was going to happen to Ashley?"

"I didn't think anything was going to happen to her. Paolo said he was working on something that was going to save our family's business. He promised me nothing was going to happen to her."

"So, you left her that night and drove to San Francisco," Drake continued. "Then what?"

"I stayed in my brother's condo until his yacht was ready for me to go to Costa Rica on it."

Paul Benning stepped forward with his arms crossed across his chest. "You were on the yacht the day I saw you at the San Francisco Yacht Club marina. Had you been staying with your brother from the time you left Ashley in Oregon until that day?"

"Yes."

"Huh," Benning said with a quizzical look on his face. "But you did call to find out if she was okay after you left her, correct?"

Alejandro stared up at Benning, the former detective, without answering.

"Alejandro, you're about this close," Benning held up his thumb and first finger with half an inch between them, "to getting my approval for Adam throwing you off this yacht and letting you swim ashore. I suggest you start telling us everything you know unless you want that to happen."

Alejandro continued staring at Benning.

"That's it!" Drake said and grabbed Alejandro and dragged him off the bench to the swim platform and pushed him off.

Alejandro went under and came up spitting the salty water. "Help me! You can't leave me here."

Morales stepped out onto the swim platform beside Drake. "You want me to get him?"

"He's treading water, he's okay for now. There's a lifebuoy stored under the bench he was sitting on. You might get that but keep it out of sight."

"Something bumped my leg," Alejandro screamed. "Get me out of here!"

"All sorts of fish in the ocean, Alejandro," Drake said calmly. "It's probably not a shark. One more chance and then we're leaving. Where is Ashley and what is your brother planning on doing with her? If you can't tell us what we came here to find out, you're of no use to us. I'll count to ten and you'd better start talking before I finish. One..."

"Nooo...." Alejandro screamed.

"Two..."

Drake couldn't tell if Alejandro was panicking or getting tired, when his head slipped under the water and popped back up again.

"They're threatening our family!" Alejandro shouted. "They

said they would kill all of us if Paolo didn't pay them what he owed them! He's just trying to get them what they want!"

"Three..."

"They helped him kidnap Ashley so he could get the virus to sell and pay them back!"

"Where's Ashley?"

"I don't know."

"Four..."

Alejandro bobbed under water again and yelled, "I can help you find her. Please get me out of here!"

Drake motioned for Morales to join him. "Grab ahold of the buoy he's throwing you and pull yourself in."

"Do you believe him?" Morales asked after he threw out the lifebuoy.

"Not completely, but it's a start."

Drake stepped back into the stern cockpit and stopped in front of Liz and asked, "What do you think?"

"We need to get back and find Ashley as fast as possible. If the men who helped Paolo are who we think they are, they won't keep her alive if they decide it's not worth waiting any longer for the vaccine."

Drake nodded his agreement and leaned down to pet Lancer. "I'll bet you're angry with me for wasting that steak, aren't you? I'll look for something else, promise."

He waited until Alejandro was back on the yacht and talking to Benning before he took the ladder up to the flybridge to talk to Casey.

"I watched your theatrics from up here," Casey said grinning. "You're getting to be a real badass."

"I figured the kid could swim. I wasn't so sure about the sharks, though. Have you decided which way we should go, north to the marina or south to Panama?"

"We may as well go north. If they decide to chase us, they could cover the marinas and airports in both directions. We don't have any idea what their resources are. We'll get to the marina up north faster, maybe get there before they do."

"North it is," Drake said. "I'll tell the others. You want anything?"

"A good shot of whisky, if you can find it. It's going to be a long night."

"Aye, aye, Captain," Drake said and left the fly bridge.

With Godspeed and a little luck, they would reach the marina on the Papagaya Gulf by morning and make it to the airport before their adversaries found them.

Liz was standing at the bottom of the flybridge ladder when Drake climbed down.

"Morales told me he heard the attorney at the villa talking to someone he called '47'. Something's been scratching my mind about that and I just remembered who '47' is. He's the North American commander of Hezbollah. We heard rumors about him when I was at DHS."

Chapter Forty

ARMIN KHOURY WAS furious when he got the news that the people in Costa Rica had escaped with Alejandro on Paolo's yacht.

His first call was to the man he'd put on the yacht to make sure it arrived in Costa Rica.

"Get men to all the marinas where they might go. Keep their plane on the ground at the airport. They know something and can't be allowed to escape. And bring Alejandro to me. He will tell me where his brother is."

His second call was to his lieutenant in San Francisco.

"Where is he?"

"He went to the Pella's bank in Miami. He's flying back tomorrow."

"Get him a ticket to Las Vegas and bring him to me. He doesn't know that I don't have his brother. I want him here before he finds out. Our cell leaders will arrive here in three days and we're running out of time."

His third call was to the man he had watching the biologist, Alan Berkshire.

"Digame."

"No change, he's waiting for the results of the blood samples to make sure the H7N9 antibodies developed as planned. He expects the confirmation tomorrow or the day after."

"Has he met with anyone?"

"Not that I can tell. He goes to the lab, has dinner on the way home at his country club and stays in his house until he leaves for work the next morning."

"As soon as he has confirmation, get the vaccine to me. When I have it, and not before, I'll give the order to kill him, then get back here."

There were loose ends that he'd have to tie up before everything was in place. But he was getting close to carrying out the most important mission of his life. When all his sleeper cells in America's biggest cities had the virus, Iran would have the deterrent to keep the Great Satan in check when Iran began the final move against Israel.

What he needed right now was information about the people in Costa Rica. He knew the man who was asking about the yacht was the CEO of a big security company. He had the money to buy a yacht like the Hatteras M75 Panacera, but how had he found out it was for sale?

Pella had contacted the casino owner in Costa Rica because he was a link in Pella's money laundering chain. When he died of a sudden heart attack, Pella might have reached out to others he trusted, but he wouldn't have listed the yacht for sale.

He needed to source an investigation to someone in Seattle, Washington, to discover how the CEO of Puget Sound Security found out about the yacht, but that could take too long. He needed a quicker way.

Khoury called his contact in the Cartel de Jalisco Nueva Generacion, or CJNG, as the Americans called the most powerful and violent cartel in Mexico.

"I need a favor, Angel. This is 47."

"Can't one of your own men handle it?"

"I don't want to draw attention to something I'm working on right now."

"What is it you need?"

"I need you to find out where the CEO of Puget Sound Security lives in Seattle and have a talk with his wife. I need to know why he's been in Costa Rica."

"What if she doesn't know? What would you want me to do with her?"

"If she doesn't know, take her with you. I'll get her husband to tell me what I need to know when he's sees that I have her."

"If she does know and tells me?"

"Then kill her and anyone who can identify you. We'll settle up later."

"Consider it done."

Khoury knew the CJNG man didn't need to be told to eliminate witnesses, but he wanted to send a message; When you interfere in my business, you will pay a price. Men who ran big companies didn't have the cajones to take him on, if they knew what it would cost them.

The only thing he could think of to do before he called Raul to prepare his favorite nightcap, a Mezcal Negroni made with Mezcal, Campari and sweet vermouth, was to call the biologist and ask how close he was to having a vaccine for the virus.

"I know it's late, Mr. Berkshire, I just wanted to know how your work on the vaccine is coming. Your daughter says she would like to come home."

"You…"

"Don't annoy me, Berkshire! I asked you a simple question. You would be wise to answer it."

"In a day or two, three days at the most. These things take time."

"Not a day longer, if you want to see your daughter again. I will call you the day after tomorrow to arrange the exchange."

Khoury ended the call and walked to the entertainment room where he knew Raul would be watching a soccer match that he'd DVR'd from somewhere in the world that day.

When he got there, he said with satisfaction, "Raul, it's time for my Negroni. Mix one for yourself if you'd like. We're almost finished here."

NINE HUNDRED AND seventy-one miles away in Portland, Oregon, the PSS Kidnap and Rescue team member monitoring Alan Berkshire's calls slammed her fist down on the table. The call hadn't lasted long enough for it to be traced.

They were running out of time to locate the kidnappers before the ransom exchange, if Berkshire was a day or so away from having a vaccine for the H7N9 flu virus. To find Berkshire's daughter, they needed to find the kidnappers. The only chance they had now was for Berkshire to keep the kidnapper on the line when he called tomorrow for enough time to trace the call and get a rescue team in place.

Chapter Forty-One

A WEARY MIKE CASEY piloted the Hatteras M75 Panacera an hour after sunrise to within a hundred yards of the entrance of the Papagaya Marina and stopped in the calm waters of Culebra Bay.

After a night at sea, drinking too much coffee and trying to come up with a plan that would give them a fighting chance to make it to the Daniel Oduber Quirós International Airport, they had done as much as they could to stay alive and get home.

Casey had told his pilot to have the PSS Gulfstream G-650 at the airport in San Jose fueled and ready to take off at dawn with a flight plan and its destination the international airport in Panama City.

The Vista Mar Marina in San Carlos, Panama, was an hour's drive from the Panama airport. They were hoping the destination would convince the men shooting at them that they were trying to get to Panama.

When the Gulfstream was airborne, an emergency would be declared and permission requested, to divert to the airport in Liberia, Costa Rica, to pick up the gravely ill CEO of Puget Sound Security. He needed to be flown home to Seattle, Washington, as quickly as possible, according to his personal physician and team who were waiting for him.

Drake had also called ahead to the Port Captain's office to report that the captain of the Hatteras was ill and needed an ambulance to get him to the nearest hospital. To accomplish that, they would need two tenders sent to the yacht; one with a pilot and crew on it to bring the Hatteras in and moor it, and one to bring the captain and five others ashore.

The party had reservations at the Four Seasons Hotel and would be staying until the captain was well enough to fly home, the Port Captain was told.

Liz had confirmed their reservations, made as soon as they had agreed on the plan, just before entering Culebra Bay, and reserved two rental cars. Depending on who they found waiting for them at the Papagaya Marina, they would either send Casey to the hospital, where he would check himself out as soon as possible, or cancel the ambulance and use the two rental cars and make a run to the airport.

Drake swept the marina with a pair of binoculars he'd found on the flybridge.

"Looks peaceful enough," he reported. "No sign of a welcoming party."

He picked up the ship-to-shore radio to call the Port Captain's office.

"Time to find out," Casey said. "I'd better start looking sick before the tenders get here."

He took the ladder down to the main salon, where Liz and the others were waiting.

"Remember what we talked about," he told them. "Adam will take care of handing the yacht over to the Port Captain and explain things. Liz will talk with the ambulance crew and telling them about my medical history and my need to get to a hospital. The less that's said by everyone else, the better.

"Alejandro, remember we're trying to get you out of here with the rest of us. We expect you to play along to make that happen."

"I won't screw things up," Alejandro promised.

Drake came down the ladder. "Tenders are on the way."

Casey moved to the stern cockpit and stretched out on the wrap-around seat, closing his eyes and starting to breath in short, shallow breaths.

"Ahoy, permission to come aboard?" the man standing at the front of a Zodiac tender called out.

"Permission granted," Drake responded.

The first man to step onto the swim platform from the zodiac wore a dark blue short-sleeve shirt with the Papagaya Marina logo on it. Three other men wearing the same shirts remained in the first Zodiac. Another four men wearing the same marina shirts stayed in the second Zodiac. They were all watching Drake and the others intently.

"What is your emergency?" the man asked.

Drake looked down at Casey, lying on the seat behind the man, and saw that his eyes were open and that he was shaking his head from side to side, signaling that something was wrong.

Lancer was back with Liz, growling softly and confirming Casey's signal.

"We're sorry," Drake improvised and meekly apologized. "We're out of gas and couldn't make it all the way in. Did you bring some or will you tow us in?"

"That won't be necessary. We'll take you ashore and send someone out with the fuel you need. Have you reserved a slip here or are you stopping just to refuel?"

Drake looked around to his left and to his right, making eye contact briefly with Liz and Morales. He knew that Benning was standing in the back of the main salon with Alejandro to keep him from changing his mind about cooperating with them.

"Can't we take the fuel from you if you bring it out? It isn't necessary for all of you to get involved. All we need is what you can bring out. We'll take it from there."

The man standing in front of Drake started to say something when Casey jumped up and pulled a Glock from the man's holster. Spinning around, he fired two rounds into the hulls of the Zodiacs.

Drake sprang forward and shot a knuckle strike to the man's throat. "Everyone down," he shouted as the man fell to the floor.

Casey kept firing at the men in the Zodiacs, hitting the men in the first one before they could return fire. Another was hit in the sinking second Zodiac before the men in it started shooting wildly into the yacht with their handguns.

Drake dropped to a knee and yelled, "Mike, toss me the gun and get us moving."

Casey ducked down and ran to the ladder to the flybridge and handed Drake the Glock as he rushed by.

Drake moved to take his place in the stern cockpit and crouched behind the wrap-around bench seat Casey had been lying on.

"Head count?" he called out.

"All good," Morales answered. "Crawling back into the main salon."

Drake waited until the shooting from the second Zodiac paused, before raising up and firing two shots center mass to each of the three remaining men in the second Zodiac tender.

Chapter Forty-Two

CASEY STEERED AWAY from the scene of the ambush and headed straight for the entrance of the marina.

"Adam, up here," he yelled.

Drake ran up the ladder and stood behind Casey's helm chair.

"Take us slowly inside the marina. You take over as captain and explain that we were attacked by pirates dressed as marina employees and had to defend ourselves. Tell them you're former Delta Force and just reacted to protect us all and make sure I get to a hospital. I'll leave in the ambulance and take Benning and Alejandro with me. As soon as they finish with you, head to the airport. You, Liz and Morales catch the first flight back to Seattle. We'll regroup there."

"Roger that," Drake said and slipped into the helm chair as Casey got up and went below to tell the others the plan.

Drake had never driven a boat as big as the Hatteras M75. When he approached the marina's dock, he shifted into neutral too late to slow the yacht's momentum and hit the dock head on next to a massive two-hundred-foot mega yacht.

He quickly shut off the engines and looked up to see half a

dozen bikini-clad young women on the mega yacht staring down at him.

Drake waved and rushed down the ladder to see if everyone was all right.

"Sorry about that. Everyone okay?"

"Mike warned us to brace ourselves," Liz said. "We're fine."

Casey was back on the bench seat in the stern cockpit, smiling. "That's one way to make sure they know you're not the real captain."

"We have company headed our way," Liz warned as she spotted men running toward them. "Looks like marina people and one is wearing an olive-green army uniform."

"That's the uniform of the La Fuerza Publica, their regular police force," Morales explained. "Let me talk to him about the men in the tenders."

A crowd was beginning to gather to see what had happened. In the distance, police sirens were wailing and sounding closer.

"Here we go," Drake said as he left the stern cockpit to walk along the wide side deck to the bow.

Three men wearing the dark blue Papagaya Marina shirt were standing at the edge of the dock looking up at Drake when he got to the bow.

"We need to get the captain to the ambulance," he told them. "Is it here?"

"Yes, it is here," the oldest man said. "What happened out there?"

"Some men attacked us, that's what happened!" Drake said angrily. "I'll explain everything, but right now, I have a man who needs emergency medical care."

"Can he walk?" the man asked.

"Yes, with assistance. How do we get him off this boat?"

"Does your Panacera have wireless docking remote? If so, bring me the remote control. I will dock your yacht properly so we can get your man off and on a stretcher."

"Let me check. I'll be right back," Drake said and hurried back up to the flybridge. On the right side of the captain's chair, he found a small remote control with the name Dockmate on it.

"That has to be what he's talking about," Drake said to himself and headed back to the sundeck with it.

"This it?"

"Yes, hand it down. I will bring your yacht alongside and we will get your man off."

Drake did as he was told and went below to tell Casey they were going to take him to the ambulance on a stretcher.

"Not happening," Casey said. "Tell them it's my heart. Paul and Alejandro will help me to the ambulance. I'm a proud man, remind them, and won't leave on a stretcher."

The yacht's engines started and moments later the yacht backed away from the dock and began maneuvering itself to the dock using its side thrusters. When it was alongside the dock, two of the marina's men came through the starboard boarding gate to handle the dock lines.

The older marina man followed them onto the yacht.

"I am the Port Captain. Is this your port of entry into Costa Rica?"

"No, we landed at San Jose in the plane owned by the company I work for, Puget Sound Security International. Mr. Casey, the CEO of the company, is the man we need to get to the hospital."

"You are Americans and have your passports?"

"Yes," Drake said.

"Bien, take me to Mr. Casey."

Drake led the way to the stern cockpit, where Casey was reclined on the white leather bench seat.

"Señor, the ambulance is waiting. Can you make it to stretcher on the dock?"

Casey struggled to sit up and said, "With help from my friends, I can make it to the ambulance, thank you."

"What is your problem, if I may ask?"

"It's my heart, it's in afib, but I can walk."

"As you wish," the Port Captain said and walked ahead to the boarding gate.

Benning and Alejandro got on either side and Casey draped his arms across their shoulders. "Good luck," he said softly to the others.

Drake stood next to Liz and winked at Casey when he walked by. "See you in Seattle."

When the Port Captain walked ahead of Casey and his helpers on the way to the ambulance, the man in the olive-green uniform stepped onto the yacht.

"You say these men were pirates?" he asked Drake.

Morales stepped back into the main salon and retrieved the Glock the first man from the tender had been carrying. "This is what the man wearing the marina shirt was carrying when he came aboard and tried to get us to go with them. The others were armed as well."

"And where are these other men?"

"At the bottom of the bay, unless the sharks got them," Morales said without a trace of a smile.

Chapter Forty-Three

AFTER A NINE HOUR and forty-minute flight on Alaskan Airlines from the Daniel Oduber Quirós International Airport in Liberia, Costa Rica, to the Sea Tac International Airport in Seattle, the weary trio of stragglers found a PSS van and driver waiting to escort them to headquarters.

The PSS Gulstream had flown ahead of them to Seattle. CEO Casey had insisted on being discharged immediately from the hospital, so he could be treated by his doctor who was familiar with his heart condition.

Casey wanted to hear everything they'd endured after being interrogated throughout the night before about the firefight on the Hatteras M75 Panacera in Culebra Bay.

He was waiting for them in the PSS conference room with a catered dinner on the sidebar from the nearby Woodmark Hotel's kitchen.

"Airline food isn't what it used to be," he said. "I thought you might be hungry."

"Hungry and thirsty," Drake acknowledged. "You wouldn't happen to have any of that expensive bourbon left of yours, would you?"

"Liz?"

"I see a bottle of white wine over there, that's all I need," she said.

"Marco?"

Morales nodded toward a bucket of Samuel Adams on ice. "Beer's fine, thanks."

Casey left to get the bottle of Pappy Van Winkle bourbon in his office, while Liz and Morales checked out the food on the sidebar. Drake settled into a chair at the conference room table and closed his eyes.

They had some big decisions to make and he wasn't happy about any of them.

Casey came back with a bottle and two glasses and sat down next to Drake.

"Tell me everything," he said.

"They interrogated us separately until dusk. I think their divers had found the bodies of the eight men who attacked us by then, because the questions changed from 'why were we in Costa Rica to buy a yacht' to 'what involvement did we have with drug smugglers and terrorists.

"When the 'cultural attaché' from the U.S. Embassy showed up the next morning and we had a chance to talk with him, they lightened up and finally agreed to let us leave the country. We had to promise to return and testify, if they needed us."

"The cultural attaché, CIA?"

Drake took a business card out of pocket and handed it to Casey. "It's not what this says, but I'm sure that he is. He identified the guys who attacked us as Hezbollah. They provide security for the cartels' transshipment routes through Costa Rica from the TBA in South America."

"Did he say anything about Paolo Pella being involved with Hezbollah?"

"Not directly, but I'm sure he suspects it. The man who supposedly was the buyer of the yacht was the owner of the casino in nearby Jaco, Costa Rica. They suspected him of laundering cartel profits before he died."

Liz returned with a plate of Caesar Salad and a poached salmon fillet and sat across from Drake and Casey. "Did you learn anything more from Alejandro?"

"Paul got him to open up a little about his family's money laundering business in Argentina," Casey said. "He swears he doesn't know anything about his brother being involved in anything like that now. He's lying, but he's also afraid. He hasn't asked to leave Seattle. He's staying at the Woodmark with Paul until we can figure out what to do with him."

"He may or may not know about his brother's business, but does he know where we can find him?" Liz asked. "If Paolo is involved in Ashley's kidnapping, even unknowingly aided by his little brother, he's our best bet to find her."

"We haven't tried to squeeze him on that," Casey admitted. "We wanted to wait for you to get back and figure out where we go from here."

"Has the K&R team learned anything that will help us?" Drake asked.

"The kidnapper called Berkshire yesterday, wanting to know when the vaccine would be ready. Berkshire told him that it would be ready in a couple of days, three at the most. The kidnapper said he would call to arrange the transfer. The call didn't last long enough for us to trace it."

"So that means we have, what, a day or two before they call again?" Liz asked. "We're running out of time!"

Marco Morales had been standing at the sidebar sampling his dining options before he came to the table with a slab of prime rib, mashed potatoes and asparagus. "Can't we find a way to delay Berkshire from finishing his work on the vaccine?"

"How would we do that without the kidnappers thinking he's stalling?" Drake asked.

"Well," Morales said with a forkful of prime rib halfway to his mouth, "How about arranging for his lab to be inspected by some authority the lab can't refuse to let in. The Center for Disease Control or the World Health Organization or something."

Drake looked at Liz. "We don't want to get the government

involved in this. What if we had a couple of official-looking vans or trucks roll up and make it look like the CDC or WHO was there to inspect the lab?"

"That could work," Liz said, "If the kidnappers don't have someone inside. They seem to know every move he makes. What if it's someone from Homeland Security, who still has her credentials, who visits the lab on some pretext that sounds legit?"

"It's worth a try. Why not? When the kidnappers call, Berkshire might be able to take enough time explaining why his lab is tied up to allow us to trace the call. Good thinking, Marco," Drake said complimenting him.

Casey raised his glass of bourbon. "Here's to the loveliest DHS imposter I know. May her deception buy us a couple of days and keep us out of jail."

Chapter Forty-Four

CASEY WAS DRIVING HOME from the PSS headquarters when his phone signaled an alert from his home security system. The motion detection sensors in the backyard of his new home in Redmond, Washington, were detecting an intruder.

He pulled his Range Rover off onto the shoulder of the road and opened an app that allowed him to see what the surveillance cameras were recording. Two men wearing dark clothes and balaclavas were circling around the sunken firepit and approaching the steps leading up to the rear deck of the house. Casey triggered the two spotlights in the back yard.

He hit the emergency number for his wife and prayed that she had her phone close by.

"Megan," he said calmly when she answered, "Get the girls to the safe room. I'm five minutes away. We've rehearsed this, you'll be fine."

Casey checked his rearview mirror and pulled back onto the road, spraying gravel from his tires. Their new home in Westchester Estates was on a three-quarter of an acre lot surrounded by woods that provided plenty of concealment for anyone approaching from there.

It was the reason he'd installed a state-of-the-art home security system and fortified Megan's hobby room upstairs next to their master bedroom before they moved in.

Once she and the girls were inside the safe room, they would be protected from every threat he'd been able to imagine. All they needed to do was to get there in time.

Before he turned off NE Novelty Hill Road into Westchester Estates, he did two things instinctively; he took a Sig Sauer P320 X Carry out of the center console and called Adam Drake.

"Adam, need your help. Two hostiles in my backyard."

"On my way."

Casey slowed down a little as he entered Westchester Estates and raced through its quiet winding streets. Sliding sideways in a controlled drift through the turn leading onto his lane, he accelerated down it and then up the long driveway to their home.

When the Range Rover rocked to a stop, Casey jumped out and ran around to the rear tailgate. A Mossberg 590M .12gauge tactical shotgun was hidden inside a storage panel he'd modified in the rear of the SUV.

Whatever the two intruders were up to, they would be given no quarter for threatening his family and invading his home.

Casey slipped around the side of the house and chambered a round of 00 buckshot in the Mossberg. When he got to the rear deck, he saw they'd broken a glass pane in one of the French doors and were already inside.

He crossed the deck and stood beside the open French door with his back to the wall and listened. Directly inside was the family room and beyond it the kitchen. To the left of the family room was his study and then a hallway leading to the front of the house and stairs to the second floor.

The house was silent. Casey took his phone out and checked the video from the interior security cameras. From the upstairs' cameras, he saw two men wearing black balaclavas standing in the hallway. He could see that the doors to the girl's bedrooms, the door to the guest bedroom and the door to the master bedroom were open.

The only door that was still closed was the door to Megan's hobby room the men were standing in front of.

Casey moved quickly through the house and up the stairs. He stopped again to listen before he was high enough on the stairs to be seen. The men were whispering, loudly enough for Casey to hear them speaking Spanish.

He took a deep breath and took the remaining stairs three at a time. "Don't move or están muertos!"

The men spun around at the sound of his voice. Casey shot the man on the left raising a AR-15 pistol with a 30-round magazine, knocking him back onto the floor.

Casey quickly racked another round and moved forward as the hallway echoed the blast. The second man froze with his hand hovering over a Desert Eagle .50 caliber pistol in a cross-draw holster.

"You're not fast enough, amigo. Get on your knees, NOW!"

The man's eyes narrowed to slits in the eye holes of his black balaclava as he slowly lowered himself to his knees.

Casey closed to within four feet of the man with the barrel of the shotgun aimed at his face.

"Take the Eagle out slowly and put it on the floor in front of your left knee. If it moves my way a fraction of an inch, I'll blow your head off. Comprende?"

The man nodded and slowly drew the large pistol from the holster and lowered it to the floor.

"Slide it away as far as you can."

The man did as he was told.

"Why are you in my home?"

A defiant glare was the only answer.

"Take off your balaclava. I want to see the face of a man stupid enough to violate my home before I kill him."

The kneeling man didn't move.

"DO IT!" Casey yelled.

A hand reached up slowly and pulled off the balaclava.

He was young, with black shoulder-length hair and a round Latino face.

"Did you come to steal, or did you come to hurt me or my family?"

Another defiant glare was the answer.

"You haven't taken anything, so I have to assume you're here to hurt me or my family. That means I have a legal right to kill you." Casey said. "Or would you like to tell me why you're here, so I don't do that?"

The young man smiled and shook his head. "It doesn't matter what I say, I'm a dead man either way, right? So, know this. I'm not the only one who will come to find out why you were in Costa Rica. Why not just tell me, let me walk away and maybe you and your family get to live?"

Casey returned the man's smile and lunged forward, swinging the butt of the shotgun around to strike the right side of the man's head. He had enough of an answer to know who was behind the invasion. There was no reason to prolong the conversation.

He swept the Desert Eagle farther away from the crumpled body with his foot and took his phone out to call his wife.

"Megan, it's over but keep the girls there until I can take care of a few things out here."

"Are you all right?"

"I'm fine. I'm calling the police. Will you be okay in there until they get here? You haven't seen what happened out here. They won't be able to question you for very long."

"What do I tell the girls? They heard gunfire."

Casey leaned against the wall to think. He couldn't move the dead body. There was no way he could keep the girls and Megan in the safe room until the police were finished investigating the crime scene.

There was nothing he could do to prevent his innocent young girls from eventually learning something bad had happened in their home that night. The only thing he could think of was to keep them there until the carnage in the hallway was cleaned up a little.

"Tell them everything's okay and that we're all leaving on a surprise vacation tomorrow morning. Start a movie until I can sort things out and get back."

Megan asked, “Is that necessary?”

“Maybe not, but getting away might help them forget tonight a little quicker. I called Drake. I think I hear him downstairs. Call me if you think of a better way to deal with this.”

“I love you, Mike Casey. Be careful.”

“I love you too, Megan Casey,” he said and hurried downstairs.

Chapter Forty-Five

DRAKE WAS STANDING in the middle of the great room with his Kimber .45 aimed at Casey when he ran down the stairs carrying his shotgun.

He quickly lowered it when he saw who it was. "Everyone okay?"

"Megan and the girls are in the safe room. One dead tango, another unconscious."

"What can I do?"

"I'll take the live one down for a chat, you cover the other one with something. I don't want Megan or the girls to see him. Then, I'll report the break-in."

Drake followed Casey back up the stairs. "Who are they?"

"This one said he was here to find out why we were in Costa Rica. That narrows it down," he said and leaned down to grab the man's feet. "I'll drag him downstairs. Find a blanket in the guest room."

Drake walked over and looked down at the dead intruder. His chest was a bloody mess from being shot with a load of buckshot at close range. An AR-15 pistol was on the floor next to his hand and a KA-Bar combat knife was in a sheath on his belt. Whoever he was, he came prepared to do more than steal a flat-screen TV or some jewelry.

He stripped the blanket off the bed in the guest room and covered the body before joining Casey downstairs.

The surviving intruder was sitting with his head down in a chair from the breakfast nook. His wrists and ankles were duct taped to the arms and legs of the chair and the left side of his head was bloody and swollen.

Drake nodded to the man's head. "I assume that's from being knocked unconscious and not from being dragged down the stairs, in case anyone asks."

"His head unfortunately came in contact with the butt of my Mossberg when I encountered him in the hallway outside my bedroom" Casey explained. "He might remember it differently, but that's my story."

"Anything else I need to know before the police get here?"

"I don't see a need to mention Costa Rica or Ashley's kidnapping, do you?"

"No, I don't."

"I'm taking Megan and the girls somewhere safe tomorrow morning. This one said he wouldn't be the only one coming to find out why were in Costa Rica. If I told him why and let him walk away, he said they might let us live. When Megan and the kids are safe, whoever sent him is going to wish they'd never threatened my family."

Drake grabbed the man's hair and pulled his head back to see if he was conscious. He wasn't. "We need to find out who sent him, and fast. If Liz can't delay the handover of the vaccine by a couple of days, we'll run out of time.

"I'll meet with Benning tomorrow. Alejandro needs to know he's an inch away from being turned over to the police, if he doesn't help us. At the very least, he's an accessory in Ashley's kidnapping and whatever else his brother is involved in. If Paolo is working with terrorists, little Alejandro should know he's facing maximum security prison time for his involvement."

Casey took his phone out to call the police and stopped with it halfway to his ear. "I don't care what it takes to stop these guys, Adam. They made a big mistake coming after my family."

"I know, Mike. They just made this personal."

Casey called 911 and reported the home invasion and the shooting of one of the intruders. When he finished with that, he called upstairs to Megan in the safe room and told her the police were on their way. Drake reminded him that they both needed to put their weapons down before the police arrived, if they didn't want to be mistaken for the bad guys.

In five minutes, they heard the wailing sirens of the Redmond Police Department patrol cars racing toward them. Casey opened the front door and stood outside. With his left hand raised above his shoulder, he gave the tactical signal to come forward.

The first RPD patrol car stopped at the foot of the driveway with its LED roof bar flashing red and blue LED lights. Two police officers jumped out and stood behind the opened doors of their SUV with handguns covering Casey.

"All clear, officers," Casey called out. "This is my house. One intruder's been shot, the other is unconscious. We're all okay."

"Please identify yourself," driver of the SUV requested.

"Michael Ryan Casey. My wife's name is Megan. She and our two daughters are upstairs in a safe room."

The officer behind the passenger-side door was on his radio and a minute later, both officers came out from behind their opened doors and walked up the driveway.

Casey remained standing with his hands in sight until the first officer stepped forward and introduced himself.

"I'm Sergeant Hansen, this is Sergeant Alonso. You told 911 there's been a home invasion?"

"Two men dressed in black and wearing balaclavas broke in from the back yard. I was on my way home when I got the alert on my phone and came in behind them. They were upstairs outside our bedrooms when I found them. I shot the one with the AR-15 pistol when he turned on me. The other one is downstairs, unconscious and restrained."

"And your wife and daughters?"

"They made it to the safe room in time. They're still there. I didn't want them to come out until you got here. I'd like to see if we could remove the body in the hallway before they come out."

Two more patrol SUV's pulled up behind the first one, with their lights flashing but their sirens off.

"Let's have a look," Sergeant Hansen said and motioned for Casey to lead the way, as Sergeant Alonso fell in behind.

Casey stopped inside and pointed to Drake, who was standing behind the chair of the restrained and unconscious intruder at the entrance to the kitchen area. "This is my friend, Adam Drake, and that's one of the intruders. Drake serves as special counsel for my company, Puget Sound Security."

Sergeant Hansen motioned for Sergeant Alonso to go check out the restrained intruder and then motioned for Casey to take him upstairs.

By the time Sergeant Hansen came back downstairs with Casey, the house was becoming crowded as the Redmond Police Department began its investigation of the crime scene.

Chapter Forty-Six

THE SUN WAS COMING up in the east and provided a backdrop of brilliant orange and pink clouds behind Mount Rainier when Drake pulled into his parking spot at PSS headquarters. Liz Strobel's new white Cadillac CTS-V was parked in her spot next to his.

He'd called Liz to meet him that morning. He needed her advice before calling Paul Benning to tell him to bring Alejandro Pella over to PSS for a chat.

The police had quickly identified the two intruders as known members of the CJNG, the Jalisco New Generation Cartel, the most powerful and violent cartel in Mexico. Drake needed to know why they were involved in Ashley Berkshire's kidnapping. Alejandro Pella might not know, but he was sure his older brother did.

Liz was waiting for him in her office and got up behind her desk to give him a hug and a kiss. "You look like you could use a cup of coffee and something to eat. I stopped on the way, there's breakfast in the conference room."

She wrapped an arm around his waist and led him down the hall. A plate of Danish pastries, croissants and a bowl of fresh fruit were on the sidebar beside a carafe of coffee.

"The pastries are for Mike," she explained because she knew he seldom ate pastry.

"Mike's not coming. He's taking Megan and the girls to Hawaii to keep them safe. He called Riley Bishop in Hilo and asked him to find a remote location where a couple of our VIP protection guys can protect them. Riley suggested a vacation home on the northern part of the island a friend of his owns."

"Is he coming back?"

Drake went to the side bar and put a croissant and some fruit on a plate. "He wanted to see the place and get them settled in before he returns. He'll be back tomorrow."

Liz followed him back to the conference table with two cups of coffee and sat down next to him.

"What can we do before he returns?"

He took a bite of the croissant before saying, "First, that's really good. Second, we need to coordinate your surprise visit to Berkshire's lab with the K&R team. See if they can come up with a way to put a tracking transmitter in whatever he'll transport the virus vaccine in before the second ransom handover."

"That shouldn't be too difficult. Berkshire can put the vaccine in whatever he wants. What else?"

"Paul's bringing Alejandro over in an hour. Any ideas about how we get him to cooperate?"

Liz held her cup of coffee in both hands and stared at a painting of the Seattle skyline on the opposite wall for a moment.

"By the way he dropped out of school and jumped on his brother's yacht to go to Costa Rica, he's in this with his brother or will do whatever Paolo tells him to do. Either way, he knows they're both in big trouble if they're caught working with a drug cartel.

"He also knows what the cartel does with people who might break under pressure and work with law enforcement. What if we apologize for doubting him and tell him we're flying him to Costa Rica to take care of selling Paolo's yacht. We'll even tell the FBI how he was cooperative and helpful."

"You're counting on him thinking the cartel has someone inside the FBI?"

"Or at least someone in law enforcement that could let the cartel know."

"And if he doesn't cooperate?"

"We'll turn him over to the FBI for being involved in Ashley's kidnapping."

Liz got up to refill Drake's coffee cup. "When are we going to let the FBI know what we know?"

Drake crossed his arms across his chest and sat back. "We've already crossed the line when we didn't let someone in authority know about Ashley being kidnapped. Keeping the FBI out of this a little longer is the only real chance we have of getting her back alive."

Liz came back with his coffee and put her hand on his shoulder. "I want Ashley back safely as well, but I'm concerned about terrorists getting their hands on a live sample of the virus. What if we let someone in the FBI know what we know, if they agree to work with us on getting Ashley back safely?"

"You're willing to trust the FBI?"

"I'm willing to trust Special Agent Kate Perkins."

Drake turned his chair to face Liz. "How would Kate get involved in something out here from FBI headquarters? Wouldn't she have to let someone know what she was doing?"

"I don't know how she would do it, but I'm willing to ask her how she thinks we should proceed with a hypothetical situation."

"If you want to call Kate and discuss a hypothetical scenario, go for it. The worst that could happen, hypothetically, is we'll both end up in jail."

Chapter Forty-Seven

DRAKE CHECKED the messages piled up on the laptop in his office for the next hour. When Paul Benning arrived with Alejandro, he had them escorted to the conference room.

Alejandro was sitting stiffly across the conference table from with his head bowed. When Drake walked in, Alejandro's head jerked up and then started shaking from side to side.

"I have nothing more to tell you. If you won't let me go, I want an attorney."

Drake smiled and sat down across for him. "I suggest that you listen carefully, for a moment, before you decide what you want to do, Alejandro. If you want to go, we'll fly you back to Costa Rica. You can finish doing whatever it is you were doing there for your brother.

But know this before you decide.

"Last night, Mr. Casey's home was invaded by two members of the CJNG cartel. Were they the ones who cut off your finger, Alejandro? Were they the ones who tried to kill us on the yacht? Were they the ones who tried to kill my friend and his family?"

Alejandro stared at Drake and looked like he was going to cry but said nothing.

Drake slammed his fist down on the table so hard his coffee cup bounced. "Answer me, dammit!"

"I don't know who they were!" Alejandro shouted. "I don't know who tried to kill your friend and his family! I don't know why any of this is happening!"

"But you do know why Ashley was kidnapped and you do know why your brother was trying to sell the yacht. I know you know more than you're telling us, Alejandro. If you don't start talking, you'll be back in Costa Rica tonight if I have to fly you there myself."

Alejandro leaned back in his chair and looked up at the ceiling. His hands were gripping the arms of his chair so tightly his knuckles were turning white.

"Adam, before you fly him back," Paul Benning injected, "I have a couple of things I'd like to clear up, if that's okay?"

"Go ahead, he's not talking to me."

Benning pulled his chair back and turned it to face Alejandro.

"I saw you on the yacht at the San Francisco Yacht Club when I followed your brother there. Do you know who the man was that he met there?"

Alejandro shook his head no.

"Were the men on the yacht on the way to Costa Rica, were they his men?"

"Paolo told me they were. He said the man wanted to make sure the yacht got to Costa Rica," Alejandro said, turning to face Benning.

"Did you ever hear them refer to the man by his name?"

"I heard them call him '47' a couple of times, like it was his nickname or something."

"Did they ever mention where he was from?"

"Not that I heard."

"One last question, Alejandro. Do you know where we can find your brother?"

Alejandro stared at Drake. "If I tell you, will he not send me back to Costa Rica?"

Benning looked to Drake to let him answer.

Drake glared at Alejandro. "If it's helpful, we'll see."

Alejandro continued to stare at Drake for half a minute then said, "If he is still here in the U.S., there are two places where he might be. His condo in San Francisco or his villa in Las Vegas. He travels a lot, but those are the two places he owns and stays at when he's here."

"Do you know where his 'villa' in Las Vegas is located?" Benning asked.

"I've only been there once, but I remember it's not far from the Red Rock Country Club. We had lunch there and I remember he was excited about a car show he wanted to attend there sometime this year."

"Describe this 'villa'", Benning said.

"I don't remember much about it. It was big, modern looking, on a golf course in a gated community. It's the kind of place my brother always buys, expensive and…"

"What do you mean, 'the kind of place he always buys'?" Drake interrupted.

"He buys luxury homes, fixes them up just a little, and then sells them for more than he buys them for. It's one of the ways he makes his money."

Drake knew what Paolo's little brother was talking about. It was one of the ways to launder drug money for the cartels. Use dirty money to buy expensive things and then sell them to return 'clean' or laundered money back to the cartel.

"Paul," Drake said, standing up and walking to the door of the conference room, "Let's talk outside for a moment."

Benning followed Drake out into the hallway and left the conference door open. "Do you want to keep him here in the conference room?"

Drake stepped aside to let Mike Casey's personal assistant pass by. "Find someplace where he's out of sight and get someone to stand guard. I don't want him walking out of here. Did you get a photo of the man Paolo met in San Francisco at the yacht club?"

"Yes, but I don't know how good it is. I was looking for

Alejandro and took one of him on Paolo's yacht. The one with the man standing behind Paolo was before that."

"When you stash Alejandro somewhere, see if Kevin can identify Paolo's friend. And have Kevin find if there's a 'villa' near the Red Rock Country Club that Paolo owns. We're going to Las Vegas if there is. I'm going to check on Liz and find out what she's set up for her visit to Berkshire's lab."

Chapter Forty-Eight

DRAKE FOUND Liz at her desk using her laptop. She looked up and smiled when she saw him in her doorway.

"Did your bad cop good cop routine work on Alejandro?"

"A little. He says he was just helping his brother but doesn't know anything about where Ashley is now or what Paolo is up to. He did tell us that Paolo might be in Las Vegas in a 'villa' he owns there. I'm asking Kevin to see if he can find the address. He also said the men on the yacht on the way to Costa Rica referred to someone they called '47'. It might be the man Paul saw meeting Paolo at the San Francisco Yacht Club. Paolo told him the men on the yacht with Alejandro were his."

Liz's eyes widened. "Are you sure he said '47'?"

"That's what Alejandro said he heard them say. Why?"

Liz looked stunned. "We heard rumors about someone called '47' when I was with DHS. He was supposed to be the North American commander of Hezbollah. His nom de guerre was '47' because he had a custom AK-47 he used when he executed anyone who wasn't loyal to him. If he's the one who got the virus sample from Berkshire, we're dealing with Hezbollah. I need to get back to Kate Perkins."

"Whoa, slow down. Why do you need to get back with Kate?"

Liz ran her fingers through her silky auburn hair and sat back, crossing her arms across her chest. "I called her, like we talked about. I asked her hypothetically what she would do if she learned that a live virus sample of the H7N9 avian flu had been illegally obtained from a research lab. She didn't seem too concerned about it. She said there are research institutions with the samples here in the U.S. that someone could illegally get their hands on, if they wanted. She said a sample of the virus is probably available on the black market from China.

"Until she knows that the sample of the virus is in the hands of someone who wanted to weaponize it, she said the FBI most likely would let local law enforcement handle any theft of a sample of the virus as a criminal matter."

"And now we have a reason to believe that might be what Hezbollah is up to," Drake said. "Does DHS or the FBI know what '47' looks like?"

"I don't think anyone has a picture of him. As far as I know, he was just a rumor we kept hearing about."

"Paul took a picture of the man Paolo met at the yacht club. I'll see if Kevin can identify him. There must be a picture of him somewhere. Mossad or Interpol might have one if we don't."

"If Interpol has one, we would know about it and he wouldn't be just a rumor. The Mossad is a different story. Israel prefers to act alone whenever they can."

"If this '47' is the North American commander of Hezbollah, wouldn't they tell us if they knew about him?"

"They might or they might just dispatch one of their assassins to take him out. If they have a reason to want him dead, and I'm sure they probably do, operating on foreign soil doesn't seem to bother them."

"All right," Drake said. "Let's wait to see if Kevin can get something that proves our man is '47' before you call Kate. How are you coming with your visit to Berkshire's lab?"

"I'm paying the lab a surprise visit this afternoon, an hour before everyone goes home, to check on their 'security' arrangements."

"Do you need me to go with you?"

Liz forced a wide smile. "I think I can handle it myself, thanks for asking. I'll be back in time for you to take me to that Thai restaurant you and Mike keep talking about."

"Mike should be back from Hawaii by then. He might want to join us."

"That's fine, I'll have you all to myself later," she said and winked.

Drake touched his forehead in a mock salute and left chuckling, remembering his first impression of her as the 'Ice Lady'.

He took the stairs down one floor and entered the domain of the PSS IT warriors who provide internet security for clients. The head of the division, Kevin McRoberts, also did favors for him as Director of Special Projects, like identifying the man in Paul Benning's photo and finding the address of Paolo Pella's 'villa' in Las Vegas.

McRoberts was studying three PC monitors in front of him on an expansive metal and glass desk. Empty energy drink cans were stacked in little pyramids on the desk when Drake entered his corner office.

"Hi, Mr. Drake. I found the address for you in Las Vegas, but I can't find anything on the guy in the photo on Mr. Benning's phone."

Kevin McRoberts was a young twenty-something hacker Mike Casey had kept from a lengthy jail sentence after being caught hacking MicroSoft, a client PSS provided backup security for at the time. He had agreed to work for PSS as a 'white hat' hacker and was now the head of the PSS IT division.

"Hello Kevin. I like your new desk. Reminds me of the flight deck of a Navy carrier."

McRoberts laughed. "It is big, isn't it? My old desk was big enough for my monitors, but I wasted so much time carting my empty cans out of here, I talked Mr. Casey into buying me a bigger one."

“Where have you looked to try and identify our mystery man?”

“Everywhere I could, without doing something you wouldn’t want me to,” McRoberts said with a grin.

“It’s imperative that we identify this guy, anyway you can, Kevin,” Drake said. “You might want to do some of those things you think I don’t want you to do, if that’s what it takes. Just don’t get…”

“Consider it done, Mr. Drake. I won’t get us in trouble.”

Chapter Forty-Nine

ARMIN KHOURY, a.k.a. 47, was standing at the window in the master suite of Paolo Pella's 'villa' in Las Vegas, watching golfers chasing after their balls on the course that bordered the property, when his iPhone vibrated in his pocket.

He'd been expecting the encrypted message from the member of the Jihad Council of Hezbollah, the military wing of the party, that he reported to.

Our friends in the east want to know when you are ready and prepared to strike, if Israel or U.S. move against them. They have intelligence that convinces them invasion may be imminent.

He appreciated the man's caution, even though they both knew their text messages were encrypted end-to-end, using the free apps like WhatsApp available to anyone, including men like themselves to use.

What the Jihad Council wanted to be able to tell its sponsor, Iran, was that his ten sleeper cells in New York, Boston, Philadelphia, Baltimore and Washington, D.C., Miami, Dallas/Fort Worth, Denver, San Francisco and Los Angeles were in place and ready.

Each cell was to be armed with a supply of automated dispenser units filled with the weaponized H7N9 avian flu virus. The live sample obtained from the Oregon biologist had been bioengineered and developed in an aerosol form. They would target the United States' heaviest-used commuter rail systems with ridership in the hundreds of millions annually. The pandemic would start simultaneously from ten different commuter train systems and spread across every square mile of the Great Satan's homeland within a week.

His plan was to wait until he had the vaccine to equip each of the cell members with it to survive the pandemic and be able to exploit the collapse of the nation. His men were prepared to attack and destroy as much of its infrastructure as possible while America's defenses were down.

The 1918 Spanish Flu pandemic that killed millions of people in the world had started in the military at a fort in Kansas. Soldiers had been infected and then deployed to Europe in World War 1. It had mutated and spread from the soldiers to the civilian population and then around the world.

They calculated that American law enforcement and military would be neutralized, along with the rest of the country, leaving vital components of the infrastructure unprotected.

To be able to strike while the iron was hot, as the Americans liked to say, required his men surviving the pandemic. To do that, they needed the vaccine to be immune to the flu virus.

The problem was a nervous Iran didn't care if his men survived. Hezbollah's fighters, as members of an Iranian proxy army, were expendable. They were expected to die as martyrs in the jihad against the West, if necessary. Iran wouldn't care if he didn't have the vaccine. It was up to him to make sure the biologist completed his task as quickly as possible.

Cell leaders are meeting with me in two days. They will leave and return to their posts by the first of next week. They will be ready to strike when ordered to do so.

. . .

I WILL RELAY MESSAGE, **commander. Alláhu Akbar.**

Khoury slipped his phone in his pocket and shouted, "Raul!"

His orderly burst through the door and stood at attention in front of him. "Sí, jefe."

"Has Pella arrived?"

"No, jefe."

"Tell him I want him here tonight! No excuses. I want to know where his brother is and how much he knows about what we're doing."

"Sí, jefe."

"That's all for now, Raul."

The orderly nodded, did an about face and left the room.

Khoury took out his phone again and returned to the window to call the biologist's watcher.

"Where is he now?"

"In his lab. He didn't leave for lunch as he usually does. Someone from the Department of Homeland Security showed up to do an unscheduled security inspection of the facility. From what I can hear, she's saying she's inspecting all the labs, just now his. She's been in there for two hours."

"Call me when she leaves his lab. I need to remind Berkshire I need his vaccine now, not next week. If we're forced to proceed without it, you will see to it that Berkshire suffers the consequences along with his daughter."

"Understood."

He had promised the biologist that no harm would come to his daughter, if he cooperated. He had, so far, but the man was taking more time delivering the vaccine than he'd said he needed.

Symptoms of the H7N9 avian flu, he knew, usually appeared within ten days after exposure to the virus. Berkshire's field trials had been going on for two weeks. Some of the delay, of course, could be explained by the stress of his daughter's kidnapping.

It was time to make sure the biologist knew he was deadly serious about the consequences to his daughter if he failed to get the vaccine to him before his cell leaders left Las Vegas.

There were things a father never wanted to see happen to a daughter, besides having her throat cut. Tonight, he would show Alan Berkshire one of those things with the help of a few of his men.

Chapter Fifty

MIKE CASEY HAD ARRIVED at Puget Sound Security headquarters late Thursday afternoon, angry and tired.

His family was safely enjoying an unplanned vacation in Hawaii without him, guarded by his hand-picked VIP protection team in the Kohala Lodge Vacation home on the north end of the Big Island of Hawaii. Riley Bishop, the owner of Royal Hawaiian Helicopter Tours, had located the hideaway and flown them all there.

When Casey was satisfied with the remote location and the timber-framed reproduction of a Hawaiian Cowboy ranch house he was renting, Bishop had flown him back to Hilo to catch his flight on the PSS Gulfstream back to Seattle.

Now he was driving Liz and Drake in his Range Rover across the Evergreen Point Floating Bridge, the longest floating bridge in the world, to have dinner in a Thai restaurant because Liz had begged him to join them.

Going to check on the repairs to his home that were underway after the two cartel members had attacked it was foremost on his mind, but he had to admit he was hungry. The in-flight meal had been okay, but it wasn't enough to keep his stomach from growling while he was driving.

"Has Kevin been able to learn anything about this '47'?" he asked, gripping the steering wheel hard with both hands. "I have a score I'd like to settle with him!"

"We don't know for sure that he's the one who sent the two killers to your house, Mike," Drake reminded him, sitting in the seat behind Liz.

"I know it's him. He's the only one that knew I wasn't really in Costa Rica to buy Pella's yacht. They tried to get us on the yacht when we left the resort in Costa Rica. Why wouldn't he try again when he knows we were there and left with Alejandro?"

"It could also be Paolo Pella, trying to find his brother," Liz offered.

"Paolo doesn't strike me as the type, the way Paul Benning described him when he met him at his condo. Paul said Paolo seemed to be taking orders from the man he met at the yacht club, the one who put his men on the yacht with Alejandro. That's the guy I think I'm looking for, the one giving the orders."

"We need to find Paolo," Drake said. "He's our ticket to finding the guy."

"And you think he's in Las Vegas?" Casey asked.

"Alejandro thinks he might be there if he's not at his condo in San Francisco. Alejandro said Paolo was excited about a car show at the Red Rock Country Club that's not far from Paolo's home in Las Vegas. I checked and the Concours d´ Elegance of Las Vegas is being held at the Red Rock Country Club this weekend. I think Paolo's going to be there and if he is, he might lead us to '47' so you can talk with him."

"I want to do more than talk to him," Casey promised. "Let's go to Vegas, then, and find Paolo."

"Who do you want to go with us?" Drake asked.

"Just the two of you. You can get Paolo to talk, if anyone can. We have his little brother. He'll talk."

"Are you sure you want to go?" Drake asked Liz. "I may have to persuade Paolo to talk to me in ways you might not be comfortable with."

"I've interrogated felons before."

"I'm not saying I'll torture the guy. I just want him to think I might. Your sweetness might give him the impression I wouldn't do what I'm saying I'll do."

Liz turned around and pointed a finger at Drake sitting behind her. "You're forgetting what I did to that guy who escorted me to the bathroom in Volkov's villa. My 'sweetness' didn't get in the way of me hurting the guy."

Drake broke out laughing. "I also remember the pair of cut-off jeans and a tank top you used to throw him off his game."

"It worked, didn't it?"

Casey joined Drake laughing. "Indeed, it did. Let's hope this time you have enough clothes on you to hide your Glock."

"That's enough, boys. Get your wallets ready, because I'm going to make you pay for your misogynistic banter when I order dinner tonight."

"I'm sure glad you talked Mike into joining us," Drake said. "This is a company business planning dinner, isn't it, one we can expense?"

Casey looked over his shoulder at Drake sitting behind Liz. "Yes, it is. A planning dinner that's going to be hosted by the Director of PSS Special Projects and come out of his budget, not mine."

"Fair enough," Drake said. "As long as I get to order drinks. They're supposed to have a tequila cocktail they call 'Cheap Sunglasses' that we'll have to try."

The evening did begin with 'Cheap Sunglasses'. After finishing all the dishes that Liz wanted to try, Drake paid for the night with his company credit card and drove Mike Casey back to PSS headquarters to sleep in his office. Until it was safe for his family to return and the man called '47' was dealt with, Casey wanted to be in full-warrior mode marshalling the resources of his company.

Chapter Fifty-One

THE PSS GULFSTREAM G650 landed at Henderson Executive Airport located twelve miles south of Las Vegas strip at eleven o'clock Friday morning. Drake walked with Liz through the beautiful terminal building to a white Jaguar F-type convertible parked outside. He'd reserved it to surprise her from the Enterprise Exotic Car Collection.

"I thought we needed to look the part when we drove through the gated community to find Paolo's villa at the Ridges in Summerlin. Besides, I've wanted to drive an F-type Jaguar like this since I lusted for an E-type Jag when I was in college."

Liz slipped into the passenger seat of the low-slung sports car and ran her hand lovingly over the premium leather of her hip-hugging sport seat. "I'll ride shotgun this time, but I want some time behind the wheel."

Drake loaded their two travel duffels in the boot of the car and got in beside her. He pushed the button on the center console and smiled at the raspy burble of a three hundred horsepower V-6 supercharged engine when it fired up.

"That's what I'm talking about!" Drake shouted above the

revving sounds of the exhaust as he blipped the throttle. "That's what a car should sound like!"

"Drive on, Mario," Liz ordered. "You have twenty-three miles from here to Paolo's place to enjoy this before it's my turn."

Drake pulled away from the terminal building and followed the GPS navigation route to County Road 215 West. They were on their way to Summerlin, Nevada, where Paolo Pella's three and half million-dollar custom-built villa was located in a gated community northwest of the city.

"Have you spent much time in Las Vegas?" Drake asked.

"This is my first visit," Liz said.

"Darn, I wish I'd known that. I made reservations for us at the Red Rock Casino and Spa. It's away from downtown but closer to Pella's and the country club where their holding the Concours d ´Elegance tomorrow. Let's have dinner on the strip tonight so you can see the place in all its night-time splendor."

"I'd like that."

Drake took the exit onto I-15 N as they skirted the western edge of Las Vegas heading north. In a short time, too short for Drake, they exited onto West Sahara Avenue and drove a short distance to Red Rock Ranch Road. Once there, they followed directions to the gated community on the private mountain course of the Red Rock Country Club.

"How are getting into this gated community?" Liz asked.

"Kevin took care of that. He printed out a guest pass that will get us past the gate."

"Do I want to know how he did that?"

"I guess he found it on the internet somewhere," Drake grinned.

"Right."

They stopped at the gated community's guard house and waited for the security guard to step out.

He approached their convertible and said, "Good morning, folks. May I help you?"

"We're visiting a friend, Mr. Pella," Drake said and handed him the guest pass.

"Does Mr. Pella know you're coming?"

"He does. We called ahead. He said he'd meet us at his home."

The security guard studied the guest pass and handed it back to Drake.

"Mr. Pella isn't home, but some of his friends are there so I guess it's okay," the guard said, looking down at his iPad. "Follow…"

"Thanks, we've got the map to his house on the GPS screen," Drake said and pulled forward when the guard rolled the gate back.

When they were past the gate, Liz asked, "Who do you think Pella's friends are?"

"I guess we'll find out."

Pella's 'villa', as his brother called it, was an imposing architect-designed two-story custom home on a large one-acre lot. It was clearly designed for maximum privacy with narrow, high windows facing the street.

"That's some house," Drake said and slowed as they got closer.

"Drive on by," Liz said softly.

"I see them. Guards in front on each end of the house. Probably more in back. It's on a golf course."

"Pella has something or someone in there to merit that much security, if he's not home."

"I'm guessing it's a someone."

Drake drove on and turned around when they were out of sight and drove back by Pella's home.

"We need to get a closer look," he said as they passed it.

"How?" she said. "Those guards won't let that happen."

"We'll see. How's your golf game?"

"Why?"

"When I was checking out the location and terrain around Paolo's place, I saw there are two golf courses next to each other, one private and one public. We could rent a cart and clubs on the public course, get lost and wind up on the private course. If we can locate the hole his house is on, we can lose a ball in his back yard and get a closer look."

"I hope you're not suggesting I distract the guards with another 'short shorts and tank top' display?"

'I wasn't going to but now that you mention it…"

Liz stared straight ahead and shook her head before saying, “If you take me to lunch, get us checked in at the casino so I can change my clothes, I might consider it. But you’ll owe me.”

“A debt I’ll gladly pay.”

Chapter Fifty-Two

AFTER A QUICK LUNCH in the Red Rock Casino and Spa's Yard House Restaurant, Drake talked the front desk into an early check in. He was in their room studying the confusing layouts of the Red Rock Country Club's private Mountain Course and the Arroyo Golf Club's public course, while Liz was in a shop downstairs buying golfing attire.

The two courses were built side-by-side and from what he could see, it was possible to cross over from the twelfth hole on the Arroyo course to the tenth hole on the Mountain course. From there, they could follow the cart path to the ninth hole where Paolo Pella's villa was located. He'd been able to identify the house on Google Earth.

He changed into a pair of cargo shorts and a white polo for their golf outing. When Liz came back from her shopping spree, he was surprised to see that her new outfit included a very short black skirt and a sleeveless lightning yellow top that was unbuttoned halfway down the front.

"You're staring," she said. "Don't worry, the skirt has a liner."

"What's this going to cost me?" he smiled and asked.

"For starters, with the golf shoes in my new accessory bag, about four hundred dollars. I haven't finished adding up what you're personally going to owe me."

Drake picked up the golf course brochures and walked over and kissed her. "Let's go see if we can find Paolo."

Liz held out her hand for the keys to the Jaguar and led him out of their room.

They had to wait for almost an hour for a tee time to play just the back nine. By the time they teed off at the twelfth hole, the weather was in the low nineties, ten degrees warmer than the average for April, and Liz was three strokes up on Drake.

"I remember why I never liked this game," Drake said to himself while he searched for his ball after hooking a decent drive into the rough.

"They're waiting to tee off behind us," Liz called out from their golf cart. "Come get in and we'll cross over to the Mountain course."

Drake complied and gladly joined her. "I thought I finally hit a good drive until the ball veered left. There must have been a gust of wind or something."

Liz turned and saw that he was smiling. "That is one of the hazards when you hit a ball as high as you did."

"Very funny, just drive."

Liz pulled over onto the cart path and drove on to the twelfth green. When they were out of sight from the foursome behind them, she veered across an open area and onto the cart path that ran along the tenth hole of the Mountain course.

When they came around a curve driving back toward the green of the ninth hole, they both saw the trouble ahead at the same time. The course Marshal was driving toward them, waving for them to pull off the cart path.

He pulled alongside and stopped. "Something wrong?" he asked.

"I left my pitching wedge somewhere and we're backtracking trying to find it," Liz explained.

"I just drove the front nine and I didn't see one on any of the holes," he said, looking back at their two bags of rented clubs. "If it's a rental, don't worry about it. Someone will turn it in."

"I know, but I'd like to finish this round with it. We're here from Seattle and I've always wanted to play this course. We won't get in anyone's way, I promise."

"All right," the Marshal said, trying hard to keep from looking at her legs. "Go ahead. I'll wait ahead and work you in when you get back."

"Thank you so much," Liz gushed. "We'll be right back.

She drove back onto the cart path and sped away before he changed his mind. Not only were their clubs rented, the 'Arroyo Golf Club' was stenciled in black across the dash of the golf cart.

"Quick thinking," Drake complimented her. "Of course, that short skirt helped as well."

"Let's hope it works again. Paolo's place is just ahead."

Liz checked to see if anyone was teeing off back on the ninth hole and then drove out onto the fairway to detour around Paolo's villa. When she was fifty yards past the back yard, she got out to grab a club. Drake got out to stand beside the golf cart and took a ball out of his pocket.

"Ready?" he asked.

"As ever."

Drake threw the golf ball as hard as he could over a tree on the side of the course, landing it in the rough ten yards from the security fence at the rear of Paolo's landscaped backyard.

Liz marched toward the area where the ball landed and began looking for it, while Drake got in and followed slowly in the cart behind her.

As she approached the area where the ball landed, she started sweeping her club back and forth to expose her ball hiding somewhere in the deep grass.

The rear security fence consisted of a three-foot-tall cement wall and a nine-foot wrought iron fence with spikes on top to keep golfers or unwanted visitors from climbing it. Two stern-faced security guards were walking toward the fence, motioning for her to leave the area.

Liz waved at them and said, "I'm looking for my ball."

"Leave, you can't be here," one of them said.

"I certainly can!" she straightened up and said. "This is part of the golf course. I have every right to be here."

Drake stayed seated in the golf cart, using his iPhone to capture the scene, first using the telephoto camera before switching to the wide camera, and then finishing with the video setting. At the back of the villa, he saw that one of the guards was holding a radio to his ear.

"Honey," he said loudly, "Just drop a ball and let's go. I want to finish this round sometime today!"

Liz turned to glare at him and then stomped through the grass to the fairway, where she dropped a ball, took her time getting ready and then hit it cleanly out of sight.

Drake drove up beside her and slowed to let her jump in. "Two at the fence, two more with AK-47 folders back against the house and one on a radio talking to someone. I don't think they like having their pictures taken."

"Hand me your phone," Liz said. "I'll send the photos to Kevin in case they try to stop us and take your phone."

"I'd like them to try. They have no idea what you're capable of."

Chapter Fifty-Three

ARMIN KHOURY, A.K.A. "47" watched the couple in the golf cart drive back onto the fairway. He was standing at the window of the master bedroom in Paolo Pella's villa with a hand-held two-way radio held to his ear.

"Find out who they are," he ordered. "That golf cart was rented from the public course. It doesn't belong here on the private course."

The Hezbollah commander stormed downstairs to confront Paolo Pella, who had just arrived from San Francisco. He found him in the entertainment center putting ice into a whisky tumbler.

"You were followed! You've been here for twenty minutes and we have people snooping around outside. I'd shoot you right now, but you owe me money. Who are they?"

"How should I know? No one followed me. You and your men have been here a week, maybe you're the ones who were followed."

"Enough! I'm tired of your excuses. You didn't sell the yacht and my men, who were there to assist you, were killed. We should have never trusted you with our money."

Pella spun around, throwing ice out of the tumbler in his hand. "We are the ones who should have never gotten involved with you and your money. And I should never have told you about my idea to kidnap the biologist's daughter."

Khoury smiled broadly. "Yes, that was a mistake. One that you will regret."

"What's that supposed to mean?"

Khoury nodded to Raul, who walked up behind Paolo and put a pistol to the back of his head.

"It means that when I am finished here, you will die along with the girl you kidnapped."

"You won't kill me, Khoury."

Khoury stepped into Paolo's personal space and took a deep breath. "Enjoy each breath, Paolo, while you still can."

Khoury turned to leave the room and said over his shoulder to Raul. "Take him to the basement. Have someone keep an eye on him. I don't want him going anywhere."

He went to the villa's study and took a cigar from his humidor. He needed to think, and a good cigar always helped him do that.

When the cigar was lit and burning evenly, he sat down behind the inlaid mahogany executive desk and swiveled slowly from side to side in the chair.

The final meeting with the leaders from his ten sleeper cells was two days away. Their instructions about how to place the dispensers on the commuter trains weren't complicated. The demonstration of how to handle the vaccines and inject each member of their cells was more complicated, but it was beginning to look like they might not get the vaccines before the cell leaders had to leave Las Vegas.

If that happened, he would have to discuss martyrdom and how to get their men prepared for that, but martyrdom wasn't in the plan. The collapse of civil order in the U.S. offered too many opportunities to cripple the country's infrastructure in a way that would make it difficult, if not impossible, for their enemy to ever recover.

He had to get the vaccines before Monday. With Berkshire dragging his feet and the delay caused by the unexpected security inspection by the DHS woman, he couldn't count on Berkshire delivering the vaccines in time. Even with what he was arranging for Ashley's father to see tonight, he would have to get more directly involved with the man than he'd planned.

Khoury took his iPhone and sent an encrypted message to his man watching Berkshire.

Berkshire will be instructed tonight to go to his lab and give you the vaccines. When you have them, get them here as arranged.

Khoury sat back and blew smoke rings in the air until his phone signaled his message had been received.

Understood.

That was all he could do right now to speed up delivery of the vaccines. The next item on his mental list of concerns was the couple in the golf cart.

"Raul," he yelled.

When he jogged in, Khoury asked, "What have you learned about the two in the golf cart?"

"The golf cart was rented from the public course in the name of Jameson Bond, on an American Express card issued to Puget Sound Security in Seattle, Washington."

"Jameson Bond! How clever. It's that company that was poking around in Costa Rica, with the wife of the CEO we went after. They must have Pella's brother. We'll relocate to the warehouse tomorrow until we're finished here."

"What about the girl and Pella? Are they going with us?"

Khoury tipped his head back and blew another smoke ring. "Pella isn't but we might need the girl. Make it look like he had too good a time and overdosed."

Whoever this guy was calling himself Jameson Bond, it would be a pleasure to kill him. The West idolized its fictional heroes. But this wasn't Hollywood. Jihad was real and it had real heroes, men like themselves who weren't afraid to die.

They would soon find out if their enemy was willing to risk dying by the millions, because that's what would happen if it refused to leave Iran alone in the Middle East.

Chapter Fifty-Four

WHEN THEY WERE BACK in their room at the Red Rock Casino and Spa, Drake called Mike Casey in Seattle.

"We found Pella's place but I'm not sure where we go from here. It's heavily guarded."

"Guarded to keep us from talking to Pella or guarded because they have Ashley there?"

"There's no way to tell without getting past the guards."

"Are the guards standing post outside the house?"

"They are, why?"

Drake heard Casey walk to the door of his office and close it before he said, "We know how to immobilize guys who are guarding a place. If that's all it would take to get to Pella, we could use the same thing we used in Colorado."

To get past armed guards on a ranch in Colorado, Casey had borrowed a non-lethal strobe light weapon from a defense industry client. They had mounted it on an unmanned drone and immobilized armed men within its pulsing beam for long enough to restrain them without a shot being fired.

"Do we still have the weapon?"

"I talked them into loaning it to us for additional testing in nonmilitary urban situations, like hostage rescues made by our HRT team."

"How soon could you get it here?" Drake asked.

"How soon do you need it?"

"Tomorrow."

"Would you like me to send the HRT team? They've been training with it."

"Does Norris have the team he put together ready?"

"I'll find out and call you."

"Thanks Mike."

"You know I'll be coming too."

"I figured you would."

Drake knew there was no way his friend would pass up the chance to be there when they questioned Paolo Pella, if it got him closer to finding the man responsible for sending killers to his home.

Liz came out of the bathroom wearing a pastel green coverup over a black bikini swimsuit. "I thought I'd go for a swim. Want to join me?"

"Mike's going to call me back. He's checking with Dan Norris to see if the new HRT team is ready if we need them. I will come along to keep an eye on you. Dressed like that, I don't want anyone thinking you're here alone and available."

Liz laughed and batted her eyes coquettishly. "Why Mr. Drake, aren't you the jealous one?"

"It's not jealousy if I want to protect you from lecherous men in this city, Ms. Strobel. It's my duty," Drake said and offered her his arm.

When they walked out of the elevator down in the hotel lobby on their way to the Sandbar Pool, Drake noticed two men who looked out of place. It wasn't the way they were dressed or their nationality, which was most likely Central or South American, it was the way they searched the lobby, moving their eyes sector by sector as they moved. They were hunters, looking for their prey.

Drake put his hand in the small of Liz's back and said softly, "There are two men at ten o'clock who look a lot like the guards at Pella's place. They must have checked the rental card for the golf cart that showed we were staying at the casino. We'll see if they follow us out to the pool."

Liz turned her head toward him and looked over his shoulder. "The one on the right is looking at me. Now he's looking down at his phone. They must have taken my picture when I was searching for my ball."

Drake took his phone out and stopped walking. "Let them get closer and then we're going to turn around and walk back the way we came. I'll take their pictures when we pass by and we'll see if Kevin can identify them."

"If they let us pass by."

"They will. They're not going to try anything in here."

"They're ten feet away."

Drake took Liz's arm and turned her around. She was on his right side when he saw how close the men were and he lowered his shoulder before he collided with the man closest to him.

As the man took a step back to regain his balance, Drake feigned surprise and said, "I'm sorry, I didn't see you there."

The man stared at Drake but didn't say anything.

Drake narrowed his eyes as he studied the man's face. "You look familiar, have we met before?"

The man's partner looked around to see if anyone was watching them, before smiling and saying, "We know who you are. Why were you taking pictures at the villa?"

Drake returned the smile. "I heard Mr. Pella might be selling the place. Do you work for him or do you work for '47'?"

When there was no response, Drake continued, "You must work for '47', then."

The surprise that registered on the man's face answered the question.

"You work for someone you call '47' because he uses an AK-47 when he executes people. That must make you nervous when you screw up and let yourselves be spotted looking for us. I'll make you a deal. I won't tell him about this if you leave right now and let us enjoy the rest of our stay here. What do you say? Do we have a deal?"

The talkative one stepped closer to Drake. "You're going to regret this," he said and walked away.

"I probably will,' he said softly. "That was easier than I thought it would be."

"Do you think we should let Kate Perkins know that '47' is involved?"

"We don't know that he is. This guy could have been surprised that I knew the name and that he's one of Pella's guys. Kate will want more than a surprised look on a guy's face."

"Do you think they'll be back?"

"Not if he keeps our deal and lets us enjoy the rest of our stay."

"I wouldn't count on that."

"I'm not."

Chapter Fifty-Five

THE HEZBOLLAH COMMANDER was sitting at the island in the kitchen of Pella's villa eating lamb stew, called *'aleb khodra* one of his men had prepared for him, when Raul came to him.

"The men you sent to the casino have returned."

"Did they find the couple?"

"Yes, in the lobby of the hotel. They were asked if they worked for Paolo Pella or '47'."

Khoury slowly finished chewing the chunk of lamb in his mouth and wiped his mouth with the back of his hand. If they knew who he was, it was possible his identity was compromised but perhaps not his mission. As far as he knew, no security service knew what he looked like or had fingerprints or DNA that could identify him. So how had someone known he was involved with the girl's kidnapping and the ransom demand?

Whoever the couple was, they were threatening everything he had worked all year to put in place.

"After I call the biologist tonight, I'll move to the warehouse with the girl and one shift of guards. If these two know about me, they'll return here. When they do, have the men kill them and then take care of Pella as we talked about."

"Sí, jefe."

"For tonight, select four men, the youngest ones, and have them wait outside her bedroom when I call her father. I'll tell them what I want them to do when I'm ready to make the call."

"Sí, jefe."

"Go."

When he was alone in the kitchen, Khoury searched through the bowl of stew with his spoon, looking for the choicest piece of lamb. He remembered sitting at a table with his three brothers watching his father eat a stew much like before him and wondering when it would be his turn to sit at the head of the table.

His father and his brothers had been killed fighting the Jews. Now he was sitting at the table, alone, fighting the same war against Israel and its American sponsor they had fought, eating lamb stew. The war was the same war, but the fighting was different now and that would make the difference. This time the military might of the enemy wouldn't matter.

Khoury finished the stew and poured himself another glass of red wine before heading up the stairs to the girl's bedroom. She had been in her room for a week now, left alone and not frightened in any way, so her father would believe that she would be unharmed when she was released. But with the delays and the people looking for her here in Las Vegas, that was going to change.

Four of his men were standing in the hall outside her bedroom when he got there.

"Take off your shirts and stay out here until I call for you. When you come into the room, walk around behind the girl in the chair and stand in a line. She will be wearing only a bra and her panties. I want you to look like you can't wait to undress her and have sex with her. Her father will be watching. He must believe she will be returned to him unharmed if he does what I tell him to do. So, you will not touch her. Do you understand what I'm telling you?"

All four men said that they did.

Khoury entered Ashley's bedroom and saw that she was standing in the middle of the room facing him.

"What's going on?" she asked. "I heard voices outside."

"I have been very patient with your father, Ashley, but he's not keeping his end of the bargain. I also have men here that I promised could go to town to find girls when we got here and they're saying I have not kept my end of that bargain.

"I haven't been able to do that because your father has taken so long to do what he agreed to do. So, I've had to make a deal with them. If your father agrees tonight to do what I tell him to do, they will not be allowed to do with you tonight what they've waited to do with girls in town. If your father does not agree, then I will have to keep my promise to them because he has not kept his promise to me. Do you understand what I'm telling you, Ashley?"

The "deer in the headlights look" on her face said that she did.

"Don't be afraid, Ashley. I won't let them do anything if your father cooperates. But I need for him to know that I'm serious. So that he understands, I want you to strip down to your bra and panties and sit in that chair that you sat in the last time while I call him. Will you do that for me?"

Ashley began shaking and then started crying. "Please don't make me do that," she sobbed.

"Do what I told you or I will have them come in and do it for you," Khoury said softly. "You don't want them to do that, Ashley."

He crossed the room to the straight-backed chair, brought it to the center of the room and backed away. "No one will touch you or do anything to you, if you do what I'm asking you to do, I promise."

Ashley moved slowly to the bed and sat down. She looked straight ahead, pulled her shirt over her head and then stood up to unbutton her jeans. When she pulled them off, she walked to the chair in the center of the room and sat down. Without making a sound, she stared at a place on the wall with the far away look of someone transported in a memory to another place and time.

Chapter Fifty-Six

AFTER A LIGHT DINNER of Linguine and Clams and Veal Ravioli on the patio in the Terra Rossa restaurant, Drake and Liz returned to their room to wait for Mike Casey to call. To pass time, they looked for something to watch on TV.

None of the movies available to rent appealed to them and April wasn't a good month for any of the sports Drake enjoyed watching, except for watching Formula One racing. Round Four of the championship in Azerbaijan was a week away. They settled on a rousing game of Double Solitaire and Liz was winning when Casey called.

"You're on speaker Mike," Drake said. "What's the news?"

"The kidnappers called Berkshire tonight and he's rattled. They had his daughter sitting in a chair in her bra and panties with four bare-chested men standing behind her, looking like they couldn't wait to gang rape her. At least that was the implied threat, if he didn't do as he was told. They told him to go to his lab tonight and hand over the vaccine he's been working on."

"Is he able to do it?" Liz asked. "When I was there on my fake security inspection, he gave me a note that said it wasn't ready."

"He's been coordinating that with our K&R team. He's going to hand over a vaccine that works on one strain of the avian flu, but not the H7N9 strain. He hasn't developed one that's effective yet. He says even if he had, it wouldn't make any difference, if the sample of the flu virus he gave them has been substantially altered when it was weaponized."

"Will we be able to follow the sample when it's handed over?" Drake asked.

"There's a tracker K&R concealed in the transfer case the vaccine will be in. They won't be able to discover it without ruining the vaccine."

"How are you going to protect Berkshire? When they have the vaccine, there's no reason to keep him or Ashley alive."

"Berkshire came up with the answer. There's a label on the outside of the shipping container that will tell the kidnappers he has to see that Ashley's been released and that she's safe before he'll tell them how to get the vaccine out of the shipping container without ruining it. The shipping container has a heat and cold monitor that usually has instructions on how to read the monitor to know the temperature the vaccine has been transferred at and must be stored at to keep it viable. He removed the instructions."

"That might take care of things on his end," Liz pointed out, "But what are we going to do at this end to get Ashley back?"

"Here's the good news, Liz. The K&R team was able to trace the call the kidnapper made tonight. He stayed on the call too long when he forced Berkshire to watch his daughter sitting in the chair. The call came from the address you have for Pella's place."

"Then we should be over there getting her out, tonight!"

"Not by yourselves," Casey said. "We'll be in the air within the hour. Dan Norris and his HTR team are coming with me. Marco Morales is coming along with the Black Hornet nano drone if we need it. Wait for us to get there."

"We should keep an eye on the place until you get here," Drake said. "I don't want them moving Ashley to a new location before we hit them."

"Can you do that without tipping them off they're being watched?"

"We'll find a way."

"Can we do this without getting the police involved? Kate wanted us to let the local law enforcement handle the kidnapping," Liz reminded them.

"I don't know anyone in Las Vegas that I trust to work with us on short notice?" Casey asked. "The Las Vegas Police Department isn't going to take your word for it tonight that Ashley's being held at Pella's place. We'll be there before you could get them to take your word for it and do something."

"Mike's right," Drake said. "We have a better chance getting Ashley out safely when he gets here, without getting the LVPD involved tonight. The FBI has jurisdiction here because Ashley was kidnapped and transported over state lines. By the time we explain things to the LVPD, and they bring in the FBI, nothing will happen anytime soon. We'd be asking them to jump into something on a weekend without any concrete evidence to back up our story."

"Are you two equipped to stake out Paolo Pella's residence?" Casey asked.

"Yes, we're carrying our PSS armed security guard permits," Liz answered.

"And they're armed with AK-47 folding stock automatic assault weapons. I wish you could wait for the cavalry to arrive."

"We'll be okay, Mike," Drake promised. "Call us when you're a mile or two out and we'll guide you in."

"See you then."

"Roger that."

"It's a good thing we're in Las Vegas," Liz said. "I didn't bring clothes for a nighttime stakeout, but it's only supposed to get down to the mid-fifties tonight."

"I thought we might keep each other warm if it gets too cold."

"Sitting in the Jaguar you rented with its bucket seats? That could be a little awkward."

"We'd find a way if we wanted to."

"I'm glad you said 'we', cowboy, because I'm a little to old for that kind of thing."

"You're right about the Jaguar, though. It's not the right car for a stakeout. We could have a rental car brought over, something that wouldn't stand out."

"Like what?"

"I was thinking of something like a big black Suburban like the FBI always use in the movies."

"And you don't think that wouldn't stand out?"

"It might, but it would give us the room we would need if we had to find a way to keep warm."

Liz called down to concierge service and rented a Ford Taurus with bucket seats.

Chapter Fifty-Seven

BY ELEVEN O'CLOCK Friday evening they were parked in their rented tan Taurus three houses down the street from Pella's villa. Drake handed Liz the pair of Vortex Optics Crossfire binoculars he'd checked out from the PSS Quartermaster, retired Master Sergeant Pat Mallory, before leaving for Las Vegas.

"Two armed guards at the front corners of the villa, a step back so they're out of sight," he said. "With the two we saw earlier in the back, there could be at least eight of them, if they're rotating every four hours or so."

Liz focused the binoculars on the closest guard. "Ak-47, forty-five and a radio on his belt, the same as this afternoon."

She shifted her focus to the high windows on the front of the house. "They designed this place to have maximum privacy. I hope Marco can find a way to get the nano drone inside."

"If they leave a window or door open a couple inches, he'll get it inside and have a look around, as small as it is."

"That'll make our job easier."

"Speaking of our job, did you think you'd be doing something like this when you took Mike up on his offer to work for PSS?"

Liz lowered the binoculars and handed them back to Drake. "I hoped that I'd being doing exactly what I'm doing right now. I didn't leave Washington to sit behind a desk and let you have all the fun. I liked being an FBI special agent and I like this. Besides, I get to spend more time with you this way."

Drake's phone vibrated in his cup holder.

"We're turning onto Pella's street, where are you?" Casey asked.

"Tan Taurus down the street."

Drake saw a white van coming toward them in the rearview mirror.

When it slowed and parked behind them, Casey got out and joined them in the Taurus.

"Morales, Dan Norris and four men from his HRT team are in the van. What's the situation?"

"Third house ahead on the left," Drake said and handed the binoculars to Casey in the back seat. "Four armed guards outside and probably more inside. We don't know how many."

Casey leaned forward between the front bucket seats and trained the binoculars on the villa. "The UAV and the strobing searchlight can take care of the guards outside. I'll have Morales have a peek inside with the Black Hornet and see what we're up against."

Casey handed the binoculars back to Drake and returned to the van.

"When we get inside, go find Ashley," Drake told Liz. "She'll be scared until she knows who we are."

"I can't imagine what she's feeling, knowing her boyfriend was involved in this."

"She probably wants to rip his face off."

"That might help her get through this better than dwelling on his betrayal."

Casey knocked on the window and got in the back seat. "Come back to the van. We'll decide how we're going in."

Drake and Liz got out of the Taurus and followed him back to the white Chevrolet Express Passenger van. With seating for twelve, there was plenty of room for them and the six men Casey brought with him.

Casey got in the van with them and introduced them to the four members of the new PSS Hostage Rescue Team.

"Liz, Adam, meet Peter Collins, Mark Gunderson, Tim Taylor and Rico Gutierrez."

After reaching back and shaking hands with the men in the rear seats, Drake asked Dan Norris how he wanted to handle the rescue.

"On my signal, Taylor will activate the strobing searchlight hovering over the villa on the UAV and immobilize the four guards outside. Peter, Mark, Rico and I will restrain and silence the guards and look for anyone else immobilized we didn't count on being outside. Taylor will hand off the UAV to Morales and join us.

"With the code Pella's brother gave us for the electronic keypads, we'll enter from the front and back when I signal Kevin back at headquarters to kill the lights. Kevin got the builder's plans for the villa from the county building department, so we know where the rest of them are likely to be.

"We'll avoid shooting anyone, if possible, using NVG, flash bangs and stun guns to secure the house. When the lights go back on, we pull the van and your car in the driveway and you come in through the front door. When we have Ashley, we'll leave the kidnappers, or whatever they are, flex-cuffed and duct-taped for the police or FBI to deal with."

"If these guys are who we think they are," Liz said, "I'd like to call Kate in Washington and let her decide how to handle this before we leave."

Casey looked to Drake, who nodded in agreement and said, "I'm okay with that. The FBI has jurisdiction for kidnapping and dealing with terrorists. I trust Kate more than the locals."

Dan Norris, as the leader of the new hostage rescue team, looked at each of them to see if everyone agreed with the plan before saying, "That's it then. We'll go as soon as Morales has a look inside with the Black Hornet. When he gets it back, we'll get the UAV up and in position. There's body armor in back for everyone but we only brought tactical helmets and radios for HRT."

Morales got out to get the Black Hornet ready to fly. When he had its field case hanging from his neck and turned the handheld controller on, he held the sparrow-size black drone in his right hand and gently tossed it in the air.

Chapter Fifty-Eight

THEY SAT SILENTLY in the van while Morales flew the Black Hornet above and then around the villa, locating the guards and hovering outside windows looking for Ashley.

"Guards at the four corners and one in the kitchen near a window, no sign of anyone else. No windows or doors were left open," Morales reported.

"All right, time to take out the guards. Tim, get the UAV in the air. When it's in position, activate the searchlight on my count. Deactivate after one minute before we head across the street," Norris ordered.

While the UAV was being set up, the other three members of HRT got out and stood behind their leader on the sidewalk.

Casey was sitting in the front passenger seat with the window down. Norris saw that Casey was tapping the barrel of his Sig Sauer M17 up and down on his leg. "I know you have a score to settle, Mike, but let us do our job."

Casey realized he'd been holding his breath and exhaled before saying, "Understood, this is your show."

Drake sat in the second row of seats with Liz and behind Casey, remembering his friend's anger when they tried to abduct his wife from their home. He leaned forward and put a hand on Casey's shoulder. "Dan's right, Mike."

"I know."

Tim Taylor walked up beside Norris. "UAV's in position."

"Activate," Norris ordered.

The Xenon based searchlight attached below the UAV began pulsing with its unique modulating effect that immobilized anyone within its beam. A minute later, Taylor deactivated the searchlight, handed the controls to Morales and sprinted after Norris and the other members of HRT crossing the street.

Morales stowed the UAV in the rear of the van and ran around to get in the driver's seat just as the lights in the house went out.

Drake jumped out and ran to the Ford Taurus to get ready to pull it into the driveway with the van when the lights came back on.

Both drivers waited a seemingly interminable length of time before the house lights flashed back on and they drove up the street and pulled their vehicles into the villa's driveway.

Dan Norris opened the front door when Casey knocked twice and then a third time.

"The first floor is clear," Norris said. "Four hostiles in the entertainment room. They were watching TV and didn't put up a fight. The guy in the kitchen did and I had to shoot him. We haven't searched the rest of the house. There are four bedrooms upstairs and a basement. Why don't you four take the bedrooms, the stairs are around there, and I'll clear the basement."

Drake led the way around the corner Norris pointed to and started up the stairs, one step at a time with his Kimber .45 drawn. Liz was right behind him. Casey was on the other side of the staircase with Morales behind him. When they reached the second floor, Drake and Liz started down the hall on the right and Casey and Morales started down the left side.

The bedrooms were all empty, but the last one on the right looked like it had been occupied recently when they searched it.

Liz entered the walk-in closet and come out shaking her head. "Nothing there. If Ashley was here, they took her clothes with her."

"I didn't find anything in the bathroom," Drake said and walked to the bed and pulled back the covers. "The sheets and the pillowcase aren't fresh."

He started to walk away and went back to take a closer look at the pillow. "Ashley's a blond and there are a couple of blond hairs here on the pillow."

Liz came over and leaned down to see. "I'll tell Kate. She can see if they match something from her sorority."

"This has to be her room," Casey said from the doorway, pointing to the straight-backed chair at a small writing desk against the far wall. "Her father had to watch while she sat in a chair like that in her bra and panties last night."

"Down here," Norris called from the bottom of the stairs. "I found Paolo Pella."

He led them to the basement where Pella was slumped over in the sauna with a bullet hole in his right temple. A baby Glock 26 was laying on the bench next to his right hand.

"This wasn't a suicide," Norris said. "Look at the discoloration on his wrists."

"If he doesn't have Ashley, then who does?" Morales asked. "It was his idea to kidnap her, according to his little brother. This is his place. So, who has her?"

"Whoever he was working with," Drake said. "Dan, is anyone talking upstairs?"

"We haven't had time to question any of them."

"No time like the present."

Morales stayed behind to search the basement and the others followed Norris up to the entertainment room.

Eight men were lying side by side with their wrists and ankles flex-cuffed and duct tape across their mouths. One man was shouting muffled threats at them from the angry look on his face when they entered the room.

"He looks like he wants to say something," Norris said. "Let's take him to the kitchen where his dead buddy is and find out."

Collins and Gunderson grabbed his feet and dragged him out of the room and down the hall to the kitchen. They picked him up and forced him to sit in a chair they turned around so he could look into the dead eyes of the man lying on the floor beside him.

Norris stood in front of the man and studied him for half a minute. In his late twenties, the man had a beard and long black curly hair, wore jeans, a T-shirt and had tattoos that ran up his neck and down both arms. He was trying to look as tough as his squinted black eyes could make him.

"I'm going to take the duct tape off so you can tell me where the girl is," Norris said. "Your friend wouldn't tell me, so I shot him. I'm going to ask each one of you the same question until I have the answer I'm looking for, even if it means I shoot each one of you. Just so we understand each other, I am not the police. You do not have a right to a lawyer, and I have all night. This is the one and only chance I'm going to give you tell me where she is, *comprende*?"

Norris reached down and ripped off the duct tape from the man's mouth.

"Where is the girl?"

The man grinned and spit at Norris.

Norris grinned back and then turned around and said, with a wink the man couldn't see, "Why don't you guys go in the other room, you don't need to see this."

They filed out of the room without a word and walked a short way down the hall before they heard the man start talking.

A couple of minutes later, Norris walked out of the kitchen and told Collins and Gunderson to take the man back with the others.

"I have to ask," Morales said, "How did you get him to talk?"

"I put the duct tape over his eyes and started praying for his soul," Norris said straight faced. "I'm Catholic and I figured he was too."

"What did he tell you?"

"He said the man called '47' took her away just before we showed up."

Chapter Fifty-Nine

WHEN THEY FINISHED SEARCHING Pella's villa, they met in the foyer to decide their next move. Ashley wasn't there, none of the men had cell phones that might lead them to her new location and the talkative one in the kitchen had proudly identified himself as a member of Hezbollah.

"We need to call Kate Perkins and find out what she wants us to do," Liz said. "We don't have any idea where they've taken Ashley. Local law enforcement will eventually turn these guys over to the FBI anyway. I'd rather have her running things for the FBI than someone we don't know."

"I think we should get out of here as soon as possible," Dan Norris said. "A neighbor is going to wonder what's going on and call the police before long. If we make sure these guys aren't going anywhere, Kate can take credit for arresting a bunch of terrorists."

Drake looked at Casey. "The Gulfstream's at the airport. Why not send everyone back to Seattle except Liz and the two of us? We can explain what brought us here without them."

"You don't have first-hand knowledge of the takedown," Norris pointed out. "That may or may not be a blessing. I shot the guy in the kitchen. I should be the one to explain why I had to."

"Liz, what do you think?" Casey asked.

"I think Kate will listen to us, if we can get her here. If she's tied up in Washington, the fewer of us there are to detain and question, the better. I agree that sending HRT back to Seattle, minus Dan, is the way to go."

"All right," Casey said, "I'll call ahead to get the plane ready to go. Get rooms for Dan and me at the casino. We'll meet you there as soon as we get back from the airport. Let's make one more sweep to make sure we're not leaving anything behind and clear out of here."

Five minutes later, Casey and Norris were headed to the airport in the van and Drake and Liz were driving back to the Red Rock Casino and Spa.

Drake glanced at the dashboard. "It's three o'clock in the morning, D.C. time. Do you think you should wait awhile before calling her?"

"I don't think we can wait. The FBI need to be the first one on the scene, so she has control of this. If we wait and someone calls the police, it will take her longer to be able to help us. The sooner we find Ashley the better. '47', or whomever is in charge, won't keep her alive much longer when he learns his men might be talking to the police."

"Okay, go ahead and call her. Let's hope she's had a good night's sleep before we ask her to jump on a plane and fly to Las Vegas."

Liz found Kate's number in her contact list and called her.

"The one night I'm home and in bed before the sun comes up, you call. I hope you've forgotten that it's four o'clock here."

"When I was in the FBI, I was already at work by four o'clock."

"That's BS and we both know it. What's on your mind, Liz?"

"I'm sorry about waking you, but we need your help Kate."

"I can guess who the 'we' is. Where are you?"

"Las Vegas."

"What kind of help?"

"There are nine Hezbollah terrorists we came across in our search for a kidnapped girl. Eight of them are duct taped and flex cuffed on the floor in a villa here. One of them tried to shoot Dan

Norris and didn't survive the encounter. We'd like you to come here, arrest the terrorists and we'll tell you everything we know. You should also know we have reason to believe the terrorist known as '47' is in possession of a stolen sample of the H7N9 flu virus. He may be trying to bioengineer a bioweapon with it."

Liz had her phone on speaker and Drake silently counted to thirty before Kate said something.

"If this was anyone else calling me, I would think this was a bad dream and go back to sleep. This is a bad dream, but I can't go back to sleep because now I'm involved, whether I want to be or not. You counted on that, didn't you, Strobel?"

"We didn't know who else to call, Kate. I know this involves you, but it also involves a terrorist we only knew about from the rumors we heard. He's here and you could be the one who brings him down."

"He's a ghost, Liz. No one even knows what he looks like."

"He's real, Kate. One of the terrorists identified the man he called '47' as the one who has the kidnapped girl. We also have a picture of the man we believe to be '47'."

Drake only counted to ten before Kate Perkins, senior special agent in the FBI's Washington field office, said something.

"Are you at this villa now?"

"No, we're on our way back to the Red Rock Casino and Spa in Summerlin, Nevada. Adam Drake is with me. Mike Casey and Dan Norris will meet us later at the casino's hotel."

"Give me the address of the villa. I'll send someone I know from the Las Vegas office to check out an anonymous tip I just received. I'll catch the next flight to Las Vegas as soon as I can and meet you at the hotel. If there's anything else I need to know before I get there, send me a text with the information. I hope this isn't going to be a career ender."

"It won't be, Kate, I promise. It might be for us but not for you."

Chapter Sixty

THE PSS foursome of Drake and Liz, Casey and Norris met for breakfast at eight o'clock Saturday morning in the Grand Café at the casino.

Drake and Liz got there first and ordered two carafes of coffee to make sure there was an ample supply of caffeine to get their motors running after the late night.

Casey and Norris hadn't returned until sometime after three o'clock that morning from the Henderson Executive Airport with unsettling news. The Kidnap and Rescue team in Portland had called Casey to tell him Alan Berkshire had handed over the flu vaccine to the kidnappers as instructed. The courier on the motorcycle with the vaccine had been followed to a room at a hotel near the Portland International Airport. The courier was believed to be the same man who gunned down Berkshire's brother.

Berkshire was safe, but the tracer in the vaccine shipment container had gone silent. When the hotel room was surreptitiously searched, the original shipping container was found torn apart and the tracer smashed on the floor.

Someone had slipped out of the hotel room with the vaccine in a different shipping container and K&R had no idea where it was now. Without the tracer, there was no way of knowing where it was going or where the kidnappers were holding Ashley.

The morning sun was warming the patio where they had asked to be seated, but the mood at their table was as dark as the thunderclouds forecast for the afternoon.

"'47' is a pro," Dan Norris reported. "There were no cell phones at the villa that could be used to locate him. Not one of the eight men I questioned knew where he had taken Ashley. Everything was compartmentalized. The one I unfortunately shot was '47's' second in command. He probably knew where they'd gone, but there was nothing at the villa that told us anything."

"He knows by now that we're here and looking for him," Liz said. "Ashley could be anywhere by now."

"They have the virus and the vaccine, she could also be dead by now," Casey pointed out the obvious.

"She might also be alive because he needs a hostage," Drake offered. "We need to keep looking. We can't allow this sample of the virus to be weaponized by terrorists. The Spanish Flu pandemic started here in Kansas. If that's what this guy is planning and we don't stop him, we'll be blamed for everyone who die because we didn't get the FBI or DHS involved."

"I think we could all use a strong Bloody Mary about now," Casey said and waved for a waiter. "Do we know when Kate is going to get here?"

"If she caught a red eye from Washington, she could be here this morning," Liz said. "She said she'd meet us here at the casino."

Casey opened his menu and started scanning it when his phone buzzed softly in his pocket. He saw it was the head of his VIP Protection division and walked to the far end of the coffee shop's outdoor patio.

"Are Megan and the girls okay?" he asked, fearing that something had happened to his family in Hawaii.

"They're fine, Mike. I didn't mean to alarm you. This is about Alan Berkshire, the man K&R asked us to protect. The man they followed to the airport with the vaccine came to Berkshire's home early this morning and tried to break in. Shots were fired and he's dead. We have his phone. He's had calls from Area Code 702, that's Las Vegas. I thought you'd want to know."

"Take the phone to Kevin McRoberts and have him see if he can get anything else from the phone. This might be the break we need to find Berkshire's daughter. Have Kevin call me as soon as he has anything."

"I'm on it."

"Thanks, Bill," Casey said and walked briskly back to their table.

"Everything okay?" Drake asked.

"Better than okay," Casey said and picked up his Bloody Mary as if he was going to propose a toast. "We might have a way to find Ashley."

"How?" Drake and Liz said at the same time.

Casey sat down, took a big drink of his Bloody Mary and smacked his lips. "That's a great Bloody Mary!"

"How?" Drake and Liz said together, louder this time.

"The guy who picked up the vaccine from Berkshire tried to break into his house this morning. K&R had a protection team guarding him and they shot the guy. We have his phone and he's had calls from someone here in Las Vegas. Kevin's going to see if he can find the location of the caller."

"'47' kept his men in Las Vegas from giving away his location, but he had to be in communication with his man in Oregon," Norris said. "He never considered the possibility we'd get our hands on the guy's phone in Oregon."

"If Kevin gets a location for us, what then?" Norris asked. "We sent our HRT guys back to Seattle."

"We find out where Ashley might be and wait for Kate to get here," Liz said. "We need her to take over. This is getting to big for the four of us and we can't wait to recall HRT from Seattle."

"Liz is right," Drake admitted. "As much as we want to rescue Ashley before the FBI storm in and get her killed, '47' knows we know who he is. He has the virus and vaccine and no reason to keep Ashley alive any longer. Hezbollah isn't going to slink away just because we discovered his hidey hole at Pella's villa. He needs to be stopped, before he kills Ashley and slips away out of Las Vegas. The FBI has the resources to help us do that, better than we can do it by ourselves."

"Did I really hear someone say there's something the FBI can do better than you can do it alone?" Special Agent Kate Perkins of the FBI said as she came around the corner and walked out onto the patio of the Grand Café.

Chapter Sixty-One

KATE PERKINS WAS WEARING a blue blazer, tan slacks and a blue button-down shirt and looked very much like an FBI special agent on a mission, grumpy after a sleepless night despite the forced smile on her face.

She pulled a chair over from the closest table and sat down straddling the chair with her forearms resting across the top. "Who gets to tell me what the hell is going on? I have one hour before I'm expected at the Las Vegas field office.

"They want me to explain why they found nine terrorists, one of them with a bullet between his dead eyes, and the dead owner in the basement of the home in Summerlin, on an anonymous tip I gave them. Anyone?"

"Would you like some coffee?" Drake asked.

"I'd like a Bloody Mary but what I want is to understand what's going on!"

"It's a long story…" Drake began.

"Then I suggest you give me the Cliff Notes version."

"The daughter of a research biologist in Oregon was kidnapped. Her father asked us to get her back. The ramson demand was a live sample of the H7N9 Avian flu virus, which he gave the kidnappers. Then they demanded that he develop a vaccine for the virus before they released his daughter. We followed the trail here to Las Vegas and the villa owned by Paolo Pella, the known money launderer."

"I know who Paolo Pella is, was," Perkins said. "Go on."

"Pella was involved with or working with a Hezbollah terrorist known as '47'. Those were his men they found in Pella's villa. We went there to rescue Ashley Berkshire, the biologist's daughter, and found Ashley was gone. In the process, one terrorist was killed. The others were left unharmed. We don't know where Ashley or the other terrorists are, but we think they're still here in Las Vegas. That's why Liz called you, to help us find her."

"We don't know this '47' even exists. Why do you think these were his men or that he's here in Las Vegas?"

"Because one of them told me '47' took the girl," Norris said.

"We also have a picture of the man with Paolo Pella," Casey added. "We haven't been able to confirm it, because we couldn't find anything in any law enforcement data base that identified him."

"Why was Pella working with a Hezbollah terrorist?" Perkins asked, "And why a sample of the virus as ransom?"

"Pella's younger brother told us Pella planned to sell the live sample of the virus on the black market," Drake explained. "You can imagine how terrorists would like a sample of it when they find out it's there for the taking."

"Liz said Pella's brother was involved. I need to talk with him."

"He's at our headquarters in Seattle," Casey said. "I can have him flown here if you want."

Perkins looked around the table and shook her head. "Why in the world didn't you tell me this earlier?"

"Remember the hypothetical I ran by you?" Liz asked. "You said the FBI wouldn't get involved unless there was evidence that terrorists were the kidnappers, who were demanding the virus as ransom. Otherwise, the theft of a sample of the virus was something local law enforcement would handle. We didn't have evidence Hezbollah was involved."

"Would someone order me a Bloody Mary? I need something to

calm my nerves before I face the most perfect storm of my career. You're asking me to go in and say that I have evidence that the rumored North American Commander of Hezbollah is real and here in Las Vegas, that he's in possession of a live sample of the H7N9 flu virus, that he might be trying to weaponize and that he's kidnapped the daughter of the biologist that gave him the virus.

"And the worst part of it all is that I'll have to explain why I didn't involve my chain of command before I agreed to help you and flew here."

"Just remind them the last time you agreed to help us, the FBI was credited for exposing two traitors, one CIA agent and a senior FBI agent," Drake suggested. "We didn't ask to be recognized then and we don't want to be this time either. There are some good 'atta boys' to be spread around, if they back you on this and the FBI takes down '47'."

Perkins's Bloody Mary was brought to her and she stirred it slowly with the stick of celery before asking, "Do we have any idea where '47' might be right now?"

Drake didn't want to explain why they were in possession of the phone of the man who tried to break in and kill Alan Berkshire. The story was complicated enough as it was, but he knew she would have to be told sooner or later.

"When Alan Berkshire gave the kidnappers a fake vaccine for the virus last night, we had the courier who took it followed. He returned early this morning and tried to break into Berkshire's home. We had a team protecting Berkshire and they shot the guy. We have the man's phone and there are calls he received from and made to Las Vegas. We're trying to trace those calls. If we succeed, we might know where '47' is."

"That phone is in Seattle?" Perkins asked.

"Yes," Casey said. "I can have it brought here when we fly Pella's brother to Las Vegas."

"Do that," Perkins said and stood. "As much as I would like to finish my Bloody Mary, because it might be the last Bloody Mary I have for a while, I need to go. If you do trace the calls on that phone and I can't get you the help you need, do what you need to do get the girl back."

Chapter Sixty-Two

ARMIN KHOURY CHECKED his Seiko military-style field watch for the fourth time in the last thirty minutes. Something was wrong. Raul wasn't checking in from Pella's villa and he hadn't received confirmation that the biologist was dead.

The flu virus had been weaponized and the vaccine was on its way from Oregon. It was time to accelerate the plan.

Khoury marched across the concrete floor of the vast warehouse and pointed to his bomb maker to meet him upstairs. When the door was closed behind them, he stood at the small window of the manager's inner office. The biologist's daughter was tied to a chair and her head was slumped forward on her chest.

He couldn't tell if she was sleeping or had passed out, but it didn't matter. She was always going to die. The terror she would experience, if she was conscious when the suicide vest was strapped on her, wouldn't change the outcome. It would only make her more aware that no one could protect her or any American from their inevitable fate as an enemy of Allah.

"Prepare a martyr's vest for her," he ordered. "I want to be able to detonate it from a cell phone."

When his bomb maker left, Khoury followed him down the

stairs and went to the shipping department of the industrial supplies distribution warehouse he'd purchased the year before.

The industrial deodorant dispensers the company sold had been modified and filled with aerosol particles of the H7N9 avian flu virus. It had a much higher mortality rate than the strain that killed people in China. If Israel and the United States invaded Iran, it would be released in commuter trains where the dispensers would be placed.

"Are the shipments ready?" he asked his shipping clerk.

"Yes, sir. The dispensers are in boxes, but without the vaccines you wanted to be included, I haven't closed the boxes."

"Close them up and call UPS. I want them out of here today."

The vaccines would have to be shipped to his cell leaders after they were back in their assigned locations. He'd been given a deadline that had to be met.

For that to happen, his ten cell leaders had to make it out of Las Vegas before anyone discovered who they were and why they were here. In hindsight, he'd been foolish to fly them to Las Vegas. He'd planned it as a reward for the years they'd lived in the U.S., posing as loyal immigrants who loved the culture, ate fast food and laughed at all the stupid offerings on television.

He wanted to meet each of them and salute their fidelity to jihad. Now he could only tell them to leave as soon as possible and wait for his signal to carry out their mission.

Khoury took out his phone and sent an encrypted text message to Groupo Aves, the name he'd given his cell leaders for the roles they played in an operation that made use of the bird flu, or *gripe aves* in Spanish, as its bioweapon.

Check out of your rooms and fly home immediately. Packages will be UPS'd to you. Await further instructions.

He started walking to the far end of the warehouse to give him time to think about his next move. Once his cell leaders were repositioned and their supply of dispensers was delivered, he would be able to report that the last phase of his mission was completed.

When he was given the signal to deliver on the threat Iran had made, a blow more devastating than 9/11 would be unleased. At that point, his orders were to retreat from the populated areas of the country to the mountains of southern Idaho and a hideout he'd established there.

With the aid of an Iranian communication satellite, he was to direct attacks on the U.S. infrastructure using two hundred Hezbollah warriors in-country in his command. With the vaccine the biologist had developed, his men would be immune to the pandemic sweeping the country.

What he was struggling with now was the timing of his retreat to Idaho. The men he'd brought to Las Vegas would not be going with him to Idaho. For operational security, none of them knew his hideout was a small ranch in a valley below Diamond Peak in Idaho. From there, he would command the mission alone.

There were two vehicles waiting for him to use in the adjacent and smaller warehouse across the compound. One of the vehicles was the black Mercedes sedan he'd been driving while in Las Vegas.

The other vehicle was the Bugatti Chiron Paolo Pella had intended to sell at the Red Rock Country Club's Concourse d´ Elegance. Pella bought the car with money he was laundering for them and there was no way he was going to leave it behind in Pella's garage.

He also wasn't going to leave it behind in Las Vegas. That meant he had to find a buyer before he left or drive the car to Idaho. In rural Idaho, the Bugatti would be noticed, but if he couldn't find a buyer it would be a risk he'd have to take.

When he turned around to walk the length of the warehouse back to where he'd started, his mind was made up. He would spend the afternoon trying to find a buyer for the Bugatti and leave for Idaho when it got dark.

Chapter Sixty-Three

AFTER BREAKFAST, Drake and Liz left the casino to return the Jaguar F-Type they'd rented, while Casey and Norris left for the airport to meet the PSS Gulfstream arriving from Seattle.

Paul Benning and Marco Morales were bringing Alejandro Pella for his meeting with the FBI, along with the cell phone of the man who tried to kill Alan Berkshire.

"Did you notice the way Dan and Kate avoided looking at each other at breakfast?" Liz asked Drake.

"That and the way they didn't speak to each other. I thought they might get back together, after they spent time together in Washington last year. It doesn't look like that's happening?"

"I'll see if Kate will open up to me when this is over. And thinking about when this is over, there's something I want to do here in Las Vegas before we return to Seattle?"

"What would that be?"

"You always wanted to drive the Jag F-Type. I want to drive the new mid-engine Corvette. If they have one available, I'd like to rent it."

Drake didn't hesitate to say yes. "If they have one, rent it!"

He wanted to drive one as well. Zero to sixty miles per hour in

2.9 seconds, a top speed of one hundred ninety-four miles per hour and there was even a convertible model with a retractable hardtop. The only production sports cars he could think of that were faster were super-exotic and super-expensive limited-edition sports cars like the Bugatti Paul Benning had seen Paolo Pella driving in San Francisco.

Liz was looking on her phone to see if the rental agency had a C8 Corvette available when Drake got a call on his phone.

"Kevin called me," Casey said. "He was able to trace the calls on the guy's phone who tried to kill Berkshire. The location of the last couple of them is a warehouse in northeast Las Vegas, out near Nellis Air Force Base."

"Were any of the other calls made from Pella's villa?"

"Half a dozen of them were."

"It has to be '47' at the warehouse. Have you heard from Kate Perkins?"

"No."

"I haven't either. Text me the location of the warehouse. As soon as we return the Jag, we'll head to the warehouse."

"I'll ask Benning to stay with Alejandro on the Gulfstream and come join you. I don't want Alejandro with us, in case '47' knows what he looks like."

"Let's hold off letting Kate know we've traced calls to the warehouse until we have a better idea of who's there. If it looks like Ashley might be there and there's a chance to get her out safely, I'd like to try it without the FBI."

"We're not going to have a nonlethal way to do that, like we did at Pella's villa. Not sure the FBI is going to overlook more terrorists joining their virgins without getting upset at us."

"Let's see who's at the warehouse before we decide if we're going in alone," Drake said. "In case we have to, bring whatever you have on the Gulfstream with you."

"Roger that. You'll have the address of the warehouse as soon as we end this call."

They were a block away from the exotic car rental agency when Drake put away his phone.

"Kevin located the warehouse where they might be holding Ashley. Mike's sending me the address for the warehouse. He'll meet us there as soon as he picks up Morales and the phone Kevin traced the calls on at the airport."

"Do you want me to call Kate?" Liz asked.

"She said to do what we had to do to get Ashley back. She hasn't called and we have the address of the warehouse. We can't wait for the FBI, if it looks like we have a shot at getting her out safely."

"That's the question, isn't it? How are we going to get her out of a warehouse guarded by who knows how many Hezbollah terrorists?"

"Let's see if we can find away, okay? While I'm turning in the Jag, come in with me and see if they have a Corvette. Then let's go scope out this warehouse and see if we need to call in the cavalry."

Twenty-five minutes later, they were driving on Hwy. 604, the Las Vegas Boulevard North, in an arctic white Corvette following the GPs navigation directions to a warehouse northeast of Nellis Air Force Base.

The closer they got, the more certain they were that they were not going to be able to approach the warehouse without being noticed. The area was undeveloped for the most part, except for a scattering of industrial buildings and warehouses built on sprawling parcels of land with chain link fencing protecting most of the buildings.

When they passed Nellis AFB and turned left onto North Hollywood Boulevard to approach the warehouse located on East Howdy Wells Avenue, they saw the warehouse they were interested in had chain link fencing, as well as concertina razor coils on the top.

There was one gate and one paved road leading into the main warehouse. A smaller warehouse that looked like it had been built some time before the main structure sat close to the perimeter fencing on the south side near the gate. The only area of the five-acre parcel that was paved was surrounding the main warehouse for fifty yards on each side.

Liz slowed down as she drove past the main gate and then drove on west on East Howdy Wells Avenue. "If that's where they have Ashley, there's no way to get in without being noticed."

"It looks like a distribution warehouse of some sort," Drake said, craning his neck around as they drove past. "There's a loading dock on the west side at the end of the road leading in. The gate has to open for trucks going in and out."

"That's great if there's a truck going in or out. If there isn't one?"

"Then we'll find another way in. Let's drive on until we're out of sight and wait for Mike."

Chapter Sixty-Four

LIZ TURNED the Corvette around a quarter of a mile past the warehouse compound and drove back. When they were within a hundred yards and had a clear view, she pulled off onto the shoulder of the road.

"Binoculars would have been handy," Drake admitted. "Looks like the telephoto lens on my phone will have to do."

He focused on the main warehouse and zoomed in as much as the lens would let him. "No sign of anyone outside. There's one door under the company's sign, NEVADA INDUSTRIAL SUPPLIES AND SOLVENTS, and one door to the left of the loading docks. There are security cameras above each door and one facing the main gate."

"The warehouse could be empty," Liz said. "Did Mike say when the last call was made that Kevin traced?"

"He didn't say."

"I'll call him."

"Are you at the warehouse?" Casey asked.

"Parked a hundred yards down the road. It's a fenced compound, one way in and out, and no sign of anyone. When was the last call Kevin traced on the phone from the guy in Oregon?"

"Last night."

"Any word from Kate? Is the FBI going to get involved?"

Casey laughed. "You could say that but not in the way we wanted them to. They want all of us to come in to give our statements before the sun goes down so they can verify what's she's telling them. The Las Vegas SAC isn't willing to trust Kate that we're the good guys."

"Mike says the last call Kevin traced was last night and that we're on our own," Liz told Drake.

"How far out is he?"

"How far away are you?" she asked Casey.

"Best guess, ten minutes."

"When you pass Nellis Air Force Base, turn left onto North Hollywood and left again on East Howdy Wells. We're parked a hundred yards past the warehouse compound."

"Roger that."

Drake sat beside Liz, enlarging and studying each of the pictures he'd taken of the warehouse compound. "Unless the gate's open, the only way we're getting in is by cutting through the fence somewhere and going in on foot."

"If they're in there waiting for us, we'll be completely exposed."

"Unless we wait for it to get dark."

"Do we want to wait that long?"

Drake's silence was her answer as they waited for Casey and the others to arrive.

The white Ford van Casey had rented to take Norris and the HRT guys to Pella's villa turned onto East Howdy Wells, drove past the Corvette and did a U-turn to pull up behind them.

"Nice job hiding in plain sight," Casey said when he called Drake. "Who would notice a white Corvette convertible in a place like this?"

"Better than a black Suburban the FBI use or a white twelve passenger van with men inside."

"What now?" Casey asked, scoping out the warehouse compound with his binoculars from the front passenger seat in the van.

"Unless we follow someone in through the gate, we cut through the fence or wait until it gets dark," Drake said. "We can't wait until it gets dark."

"That's a lot of open ground to cross completely exposed if we go in now."

"Not if no one's in there."

"That's a big if."

"Open to suggestions."

"Going in with a helicopter would work, if we rent one somewhere."

"How long would that take?"

"No way to know."

"Then we cut though the fence and go in from two sides. Are there wire cutters in the van, by any chance?" Drake asked.

"Marco's getting out to check."

After a long minute, Casey said they were out of luck; the van didn't come equipped with wire cutters.

Liz touched Drake's arm and pointed down the road. A UPS truck was slowing down and signaling for a left turn as it approached the gate of the compound.

"Mike," Drake shouted, "Take the lead and follow that UPS truck in. We caught a break! Keep your phone open."

The van shot around spewing gravel in the air, as Liz fired up the Corvette with a roar and fish tailed onto the road to follow it.

The UPS truck waited in front of the gate for it to roll all the way back and started forward.

The van with Dan Norris behind the wheel was twenty yards away from the open gate when the UPS truck drove through. Accelerating to follow it, Norris turned sharply and slid the van sideways to a stop in the middle of the opening.

When the gate closed and hit the side of the van, it rolled back again and allowed Norris to drive through with the Corvette now behind him.

The van and the Corvette stayed close behind the UPS truck, until it started to swing around to back up to the loading dock.

"Mike, take the main door. We'll veer right and enter through the loading dock door," Drake said quickly.

Liz swung out to drive around the UPS truck to get to the loading dock door.

Before she got there, they heard gunfire erupt on the left by the main door.

Drake jumped out and sprinted to the door on the side of the loading dock with his Kimber .45 in hand. Liz ran to his left with her Clock extended in front of her at eye level, ready to acquire a target and cover him.

When they reached the top steps, Drake stepped to the right side of the door and Liz to the left side.

Drake whispered "Ready?"

Liz grabbed the door handle and signaled with a nod that she was ready.

Drake said "Go" and Liz pulled the door open.

Chapter Sixty-Five

THE CEMENT FLOOR to the right of the door was stacked high with boxes, but no one was in the shipping area.

To their left, booming gunfire continued to echo down the length of the vast open warehouse.

"Four maybe five AK-47's," Drake shouted and took off running toward the unforgettable sounds firing on full auto. Liz chased after him, making sure there were no surprises coming out from between the rows of pallet racks or coming up behind them.

Drake also recognized the three-round suppressed pops of .300 caliber Blackout rounds from the SIG MCX Rattlers Casey kept aboard the PSS Gulfstream. They were coming from outside the warehouse, where the terrorists were keeping them at bay.

When they reached the last row of pallet racks, Drake ducked behind the tall pallet rack on the end of the row to his right. Ahead of them, the warehouse opened onto a reception area with a long counter and secretarial desk behind it. There was a closed solid door at the rear of the reception and along the far wall, stairs led up to an office with windows looking down on the reception area.

Two terrorists were crouched behind the counter, popping up randomly to shoot outside through an open door. Two other terrorists flanked the open door, leaning out to fire when the two behind the counter crouched down and stopped firing.

Drake pulled Liz close and whispered into her ear. "Go down this row and come up behind the two at the counter. I'll take out the two at the door, if the guys behind the counter don't shoot them in the back first. Go on three."

Liz sprinted down the row and stopped at the end. When she turned to look at him, he held up one finger, two fingers and then a third.

Drake took two quick side steps to his left and shot the terrorist standing with his back to the wall on the left side of the open door. The terrorist on the other side of the door turned at the sound of the gunshot from inside the warehouse and fell with a head shot from Drake's Kimber .45.

In his peripheral vision, he saw the terrorist on the far end of the reception counter spin toward him. Liz dropped him to the floor and swung her Glock to the left to shoot the second terrorist behind the counter. Before she got off a shot, his head jerked back, spraying a red mist of blood back on the door behind him.

"Clear!" Drake yelled.

Casey was the first man through the door, followed by Dan Norris and Marco Morales. "Any more of them?" he asked.

"We didn't see any when we came from the other end of the warehouse. Not sure about whatever's behind that door or the office upstairs," motioning with his pistol.

"I'll check out the rest of the warehouse," Morales said and headed down the aisle between the rows of pallet stacks

Casey made sure the terrorist he shot was dead and started toward the door at the back of the reception area. Norris stopped to check the two terrorists at the front door and then came around the counter to see about the man Liz shot.

"Nice shot," Liz told Casey.

"You got him turned to look your way, easy shot," Casey said as he passed her.

"I'll check the office," Norris said, after making sure the terrorist Liz shot was dead, and started up the stairs to the office.

Casey returned and reported that there was no one in the room behind the reception area. "Nothing but a copier and office supplies."

"She's here," Norris shouted from the office, "But we have a problem. Stay there, I'm coming down."

He ran out and put both hands on the stair's railing, sliding then down as far as he could and swung forward to land on the middle step. He repeated the maneuver to clear the stairs in two steps.

"They put a martyr's suicide vest on her," Norris said, "It's got cell phone trigger. Get outside and call Kate. Tell her to bring a bomb squad and a KingFish device to block any signal that can detonate the thing. I'll see if I can get the vest off her."

Drake grabbed Liz's arm when she started toward the stairs. "You have Kate's number. Go outside and call her. I'll see if I can help Dan."

"Ashley has to be terrified. She needs…" Liz began.

"She needs you to go call Kate," Drake said and started up the stairs.

Norris was kneeling behind a rolling office chair that Ashley was sitting in. She was crying softly as Norris quietly told her what they were going to do.

She had gray duct tape around her forearms and ankles and a couple of wraps around her upper body that kept her in the chair. A black bag was laying on the floor at her feet.

Drake leaned down and whispered to Norris, "What do you need?"

Norris stood and backed away from the office chair. "I'll need the bomb squad to get it off her."

"He's kept her alive to bargain with in case we caught him."

"He knew we were coming. He would have had more of his men here if he was sticking around."

"He could be anywhere by now."

Norris shook his head. "He's got to stay within range of a cell tower, if he wants to trade her for his safety."

"Have you asked her about who was here?" Drake asked. "Was it 47?"

"She was crying too hard when I told her who I was. She's calmer now, I can ask her."

Norris walked back to Ashley and knelt beside her. "Ashley, you'll be out of here soon, I promise. The FBI is on the way. Until they get here, would you be able to help us? Do you know the men who kidnapped you? Do you know who their leader is?"

Ashley turned with tears still streaming from her red teary eyes and nodded. "I don't know all of them, but they called the leader '47'. He was in this office just before the shooting started."

Chapter Sixty-Six

AFTER THEY MADE sure there were no other terrorists hiding in the warehouse, Liz waited outside for Kate Perkins and the FBI to arrive.

Casey and Morales stood beside her while Drake and Norris stayed with Ashley Berkshire to keep her calm until her martyr's suicide vest could be removed.

Liz looked across the black-topped area in front of the warehouse to where the UPS truck was still parked. "Has anyone talked with the UPS driver? Is he still in his truck?"

"I'll go find out," Morales said and jogged toward the truck.

He stopped beside the passenger-side door and knocked on the window. After a moment, a man opened the door. He was wearing a set of black wireless headphones over his ears.

Morales motioned for the driver to get out of the truck, stepping back with his SIG MCX raised in case the man was armed. He wasn't and they talked for several minutes before Morales jogged back after the driver got back inside his truck.

"He didn't hear a thing," Morales laughed. "He said he was told to wait until the loading door opened before backing up to load the truck. He was listening to his music the whole time."

"Does he know anything about the men in the warehouse?" Casey asked.

"This is his second visit. He said he's only seen one man at the loading dock when he's been here. He did get a glimpse of a man a little while ago leaving from the smaller warehouse over there. He said he didn't think he worked here because of the car he was driving."

"What car was he driving?" Casey asked.

"A black and gold sports car. Said he's never seen one like it before."

"Damn!" Casey exclaimed. "That had to be '47' driving Pella's black and gold Bugatti. I'll tell Drake."

Before Casey made it to the warehouse, a caravan of black GMC Suburbans pulled up to the closed front gate.

"Go find the gate opener in the office," Liz said to Morales. "I'll get Kate to rush the bomb squad to the office."

Liz ran to the front gate and saw FBI special agent Kate Perkins getting out of the lead SUV.

"Thanks for getting here so quickly," Liz told Perkins. "We'll have the gate open in a minute."

"Everyone okay?"

"We're fine. Four terrorists aren't. They started shooting before we reached the office."

The gate started to roll back and Perkins stepped though the opening. "Show me where she is."

They ran side-by-side to the warehouse office.

When they entered the reception area, Casey and Drake were standing at the bottom of the stairs.

"Dan's upstairs with Ashley, Kate. Are you blocking cell signals?"

"We started as soon as we got close enough," Perkins said. "We couldn't shut things down any sooner."

"Dan says it's a sophisticated vest. Are your bomb squad guys good?"

"They tell me they are. I guess we'll find out. Tell me everything that happened before the rest of them get here."

"We parked up the road, watching the warehouse and looking for a way in," Drake said. "When the UPS truck drove up, we followed it in. They made a mistake and started shooting at us as soon as we got close to the warehouse."

Perkins looked around at the four bodies lying on the floor. "Is this all of them?"

"They were the ones shooting at us," Casey said. "We just learned another one, possible '47', slipped out during the shooting. He's driving a Bugatti like the one Pella owns."

"A car like that shouldn't be hard to find. We have a drone overhead. I'll have the operator start searching for it," Perkins said and started up the stairs.

Dan Norris was kneeling beside Ashley's chair in the office and raised a hand to keep Perkins from approaching. "Signals blocked?"

Perkins nodded yes.

"Is the bomb squad here?"

"Right behind me."

"Ashley says she heard them talking about shipping industrial air dispensers out today. She thinks they have something to do with the virus sample they got from her dad."

"There's a UPS truck outside. I'll see if that's what he's here for."

"Agent Perkins?" an FBI agent called out from the bottom of the stairs.

Kate Perkins looked down and saw a bomb squad agent dressed in his protective suit. "Up here," she said.

She stepped aside to let him enter the office and waved for Norris to follow her.

He shook his head no. "I told Ashley I would stay until we get this thing off."

Perkins looked at him for a long moment before nodding that she understood and left to join the others in the reception area.

Drake and Liz were standing aside while two FBI agents searched the bodies of the dead terrorists.

"Dan says Ashley heard them talking about shipping air dispensers somewhere. She thought it had something to do with the virus sample they got from her dad," Perkins told them. "Let's go check out the loading dock. If we're lucky, that's why the UPS driver is here."

Drake led the way to the other end of the warehouse where boxes were sitting on the floor just inside the first overhead door of the loading dock. The boxes were all the same size, a foot long, a foot wide and ten inches high.

He picked up a box from the top row and looked at the shipping level. "Going to a travel agency in Atlanta. Let's see what's inside," and took out his CRKT M-16 tactical folding knife.

Cutting down the middle of the packing tape, he lifted the two halves of the top of the box and saw four smaller identical boxes inside.

The plain white label on the outside of the first box he took out read "Dispenser-Wall Mount, Evergreen scent". The other boxes had the same label on them.

"These remind me of the dispensers we found loaded with nerve agent the terrorists tried to use on the light rail system a couple of years ago in Seattle. Simple but effective."

Drake checked the shipping label on the next four boxes and saw they were all going to the same travel agency in Atlanta, Georgia.

"Twenty deodorant dispensers, all going to one travel agency," he said. He walked around and counted fifty boxes. "If they each contain the same number, that's two hundred deodorant dispensers. If these are the dispensers Ashley heard them talking about and they're filled with a weaponized flu virus, they planned on a lot of us coming down with a bad case of the flu."

Chapter Sixty-Seven

IT TOOK a long and tedious hour for the bomb squad team to get the martyr's suicide vest off Ashley Berkshire. She looked fragile and withdrawn as Dan Norris walked past with her on the way to an EMT van the FBI called to take her to the hospital.

"I sent the Gulfstream to Portland to fly her dad here," Mike Casey said, standing with Drake, Liz and Special Agent Perkins. "She's going to have a tough time putting this behind her."

"Our Victim Services Division will have a counselor with her when she gets to the hospital," Kate Perkins said. "Having her dad there will help. She's tough, she's going to be okay."

"I hope so. I don't think you'll be able to say that about her former boyfriend, if they ever cross paths," Drake said.

"Hopefully, they won't," Casey said. "Paul Benning told me the FBI have him in custody. They're trying to figure out how much he knew about what his brother was doing. He'll get some credit for the help he provided, but he'll still get some jail time."

Drake looked over Kate Perkins' shoulder and saw Marco Morales headed their way. He'd been talking with the agent flying the FBI drone that was searching for the Bugatti that left the warehouse.

Morales shook his head as he approached them. "There's no sign of the Bugatti. They're flying a two-mile grid, but he could be anywhere by now."

"Won't the Bugatti have a GPS Tracker," Liz said. "I'll bet there's a tracker on the Corvette we rented."

"There must be," Drake said. "Exotic cars have a hard time finding an insurance company. The ones that do insure them will require a GPS Tracker on it so they can find the car if it's stolen. Pella would have insured the Bugatti. Find the company and we'll find the car."

"When you recovered Pella's body at his villa, did he have a wallet?" she asked Perkins. "There should be an insurance card in it."

"I'll ask Spawn," Perkins said.

"Who's Spawn?" Drake asked.

"I'm sorry, I should have introduced you. 'Spawn' is Janell Raymond's nickname. She's the SAC here in Las Vegas."

Drake watched Perkins with raised eyebrows as she left to find the Special Agent In Charge of the Las Vegas field office. "Spawn?"

"Kate must know her well," Liz said with a smile. "She hates that name. There's an old saying that left-handed people are the 'spawn of Satan'. They gave her that nickname at Quantico because she's left-handed and her dad was a pastor. Not many agents are willing to pay the price for calling her that name."

Drake saw that Casey had turned around and was watching boxes of air freshener dispensers being loaded into an FBI Hazardous Materials Response Unit van at the loading dock.

"They've been planning this for years," Casey said. "Buying this warehouse, developing a capability to weaponize a virus, finding a way to get their hands on a live sample of a virus that's top of the list of the WHO for starting a world-wide pandemic. Why put a plan like this in place when you're as likely to die as your enemy?"

"They weren't planning on dying with the rest of us, Mike. The vaccine Berkshire was developing would make them immune to the strain of flu he was working on. Without a live sample of a strain of the flu they were weaponizing, no one would have time to develop a vaccine to prevent a pandemic. It's as evil as it is brilliant."

"Right, as a deterrent," Casey said. "If an enemy wants to make sure we never attack them, why not have a pandemic-causing bioweapon hidden around to threaten us if we didn't back off?"

"It's possible," Drake acknowledged, "But the U.S. isn't threatening to attack anyone?"

Casey shook his head. "Iran doesn't know that. We've considered attacking Iran if they get close to having a nuclear bomb. "47's" supposed to be the North American commander of Hezbollah. Maybe this is Iran's deterrent, having a killer virus they can release if they think we were about to attack them. You mentioned those boxes over there were being shipped to cities here in the states."

Drake knew his friend might be right. "Then we need to find "47". If this is Iran's play, he knows what they were planning. We need to let Kate Perkins know what we're thinking."

They looked around for her and saw her standing beside the lead black Suburban and waving at them.

When they ran over to her, she said, "We identified the insurance company, but we have a problem. They won't use their GPS Tracker to locate the Bugatti in real time without a warrant or a court order."

Drake and Casey exchanged looks and Casey took Perkins' arm to lead her a couple of steps away from the Suburban and the FBI agents standing there.

"If you tell us the name of the insurance company, I might be able to locate the Bugatti," Casey offered.

Perkins started to ask how, looked at Casey and then Drake and turned away with her back to the other agents. She held her mobile phone in the shadow of her body so Casey could read the message on the screen.

Hagerty Insurance

"I can't tell you the name of the insurance company, Mr. Casey, she said loudly enough for the agents behind her to hear. "Information you obtain could jeopardize our court case. I'm sorry."

"Understood, I certainly wouldn't want to jeopardize your case, if it ever makes it to court."

"It won't unless someone finds the guy driving the Bugatti."

Chapter Sixty-Eight

CASEY WALKED AWAY from FBI Special Agent Perkins and called Kevin McRoberts, his IT guru and white hat hacker.

Kevin had hacked the Pentagon without getting caught. He was even better now and could hack Hagerty Insurance without leaving a trace to taint any evidence they obtained searching for '47'.

"Hi Boss, everyone okay?"

"We rescued Ashley from the warehouse but '47' got away. I need you to find the GPS tracker on Pella's Bugatti we think he's driving. He insured the car with Hagerty Insurance."

"Right away. Anything else?"

"Be careful."

"Always."

"Also, see if you can find anything on traffic cams around the warehouse that show which way '47' went when he left the warehouse. We might have to explain how we found him."

"Roger that."

Casey jogged back to Drake and Liz. "Kevin's going to access Pella's insurance company IT system and use its GPS Tracker system's 'stolen vehicle recovery' mode to locate the Bugatti. When he does, we need to be ready to go."

"If we share the information with Kate, she's not going to let us ride along," Liz said. "We told her to come to Las Vegas so she could lead the FBI and take down '47'."

Casey stepped in front of Liz and leaned down to say, "I have to be there when we catch him. It's personal for me, Liz. We're not going to tell her if we locate the Bugatti, because I'm going to be there to see the look on his sorry face when we catch him."

"Liz, Kate won't want to locate '47' with information she gets from us. That doesn't mean the FBI won't get the credit for stopping his plan, if we're the ones who track him down," Drake pointed out."

Casey nodded. "Kate told me she didn't want to use any information we came up with that wasn't obtained without a warrant. If we find '47' and then call in the FBI, she wouldn't have to worry about it."

"She's still not going to like it. Trust me, the FBI is not going to pat us on the back for getting ahead of them on this. I wouldn't have when I was FBI."

Casey's phone buzzed in his pocket and he stepped away to answer it.

"We don't have a choice," Casey said when he returned. "Kevin says the Bugatti is headed north on Highway 93. He's two hours ahead of us in a car that'll do two hundred fifty miles an hour."

Drake's eyes widened. He knew that Nevada Highway 93 connected with State Route 318 and the ninety-mile open-road course of the famous Silver State Challenge, the fastest automobile race in the world.

Nevada closed a stretch of the highway for the race each year and the current record was an average speed of two hundred nineteen miles per hour over the ninety miles of the course. It was a race he'd always wanted to drive his Porsche 993 in.

"Highway 93's called the Great Basin Highway. It runs north through the desert to the course of the Silver State Challenge I told you about, Mike. If '47's' driving the Bugatti, he might be tempted to drive two hundred and fifty miles an hour, but he won't. We could catch him in the Corvette. It'll do almost two hundred miles an hour."

Liz saw the look Drake exchanged with Casey. "By 'we' do you mean you and Mike?"

"No, it was a collective 'we'. I didn't mean to exclude you."

"I was the one who rented the Corvette," she reminded him.

Casey hesitated before saying, "Technically, I rented it. You used the company's American Express card. I need to ride shotgun on this one, Liz."

"I understand, Mike," she finally said. "I'll follow you guys in the van with Norris and Morales. Should I tell Kate we're leaving?"

"She'll be better off if you don't," Drake said. "Let's just slip out. She'll know what we're doing."

Liz left with Casey to tell Norris and Morales what they were doing, as Drake strolled nonchalantly across the compound to the Corvette to drive it over to the van.

They needed to beef up their firepower, but loading more armament into the convertible Corvette without being noticed by the FBI agents standing around, wasn't going to be easy.

Drake circled around to the far side of the van and pulled the Corvette as close as possible while still being able to open his door.

"Dan, Marco," he waved them over and said, "Have you sat in one of these new Corvettes? Come take a look. I'll show you how the Corvette's first retractable hardtop works."

He got out and walked around to the back of the car while the retractable hardtop raised up and lowered into place, blocking the view of the closest FBI agents while Casey beefed up their firepower; the two SIG MCX Rattlers and extra magazines he was loading into the rear trunk.

"Throw a pair of binoculars and a radio to coordinate with the van while you're at it, Mike," Drake told Casey.

"Dan," he continued, "Liz is going to ride with you and Marco. When we leave in the Corvette, give us a couple of minutes before you follow. Kevin will give you directions to the Great Basin Highway to join us".

"I'll be driving as fast as possible without getting stopped until we're clear of the city. Then we'll open it up and see if we can catch up to the Bugatti. If we get the Bugatti in sight, we'll back off a little and come up with a plan."

"What's there to plan?" Norris asked.

"We need him alive," Drake said, "He's a well-trained terrorist. He's not going down without a fight. Let's just make sure this fight ends on our terms."

Chapter Sixty-Nine

WHEN NORRIS and Morales had taken turns sitting behind the wheel of the C8 Corvette, Drake got in and started the engine and let them listen to the music coming from its exhaust pipes.

Liz walked over and leaned in to kiss him. "Be careful."

"You do the same. We'll finish this and take some time off. There are some things we need to talk about."

Drake winked at her and pulled away.

Casey sat next to him with a quizzical look on his face.

"What?" Drake asked.

"Something you need to tell me?"

Drake looked in the rearview mirror and saw Liz watching him drive away.

"Check with Kevin and find out how far ahead of us he is."

"I'm reading that as a yes."

"Okay, maybe. Can we just focus on getting this bastard?"

Casey reached behind his seat for the two-way radio. "Maybe's good enough for now."

When Drake pulled onto the Las Vegas Boulevard heading east, it was two thirty in the afternoon.

"Kevin said take the Las Vegas Boulevard, then get on the Las

Vegas Freeway, I-15, until we get to the Great Basin Highway," Casey said. "'47' must have stopped somewhere. He's only fifty miles ahead of us."

"How fast is he going?"

"Kevin didn't say, but he'll stay close to the speed limit to keep from getting stopped. The speed limit on 93 is seventy miles an hour."

Drake did a quick calculation in his head. "If he drives ten miles over the speed limit, say eighty like most people do, and we average a speed of one hundred and fifty, we should catch up to him in about two and a half hours."

"If you average a hundred and fifty, we'll be the ones who get stopped," Casey said. "Why not have Liz get someone to set up a roadblock for him?"

"She'd have to explain to Kate how we know '47's' on 93 and then explain to the FBI how we knew the Bugatti was insured by Hagerty Insurance. We can't do that to Kate. We'll get him, Mike, don't worry."

Drake kept his speed at eighty-five on the Las Vegas Boulevard and the Las Vegas Freeway until he slowed for the exit onto Highway 93. When he passed Love's Travel Stop and headed north on Highway 93, he increased his speed to ninety miles an hour to get past the two cars ahead of them in the slow lane and put his foot down.

"I'm not worried about anyone behind us," he told Casey, "but you might want to use the binoculars and see if we have a trooper up ahead. This doesn't come equipped with a radar detector."

"I'm surprised, it looks like it has everything else," Casey said and looked over at the speedometer. "You need to get a move on if we're going to average one fifty."

"Happy to. You have Google Maps on your phone?"

"I do. Are you needing directions?"

"I need to keep my eyes on the road at this speed. 93 runs fairly straight to the north, but it would be nice to know if we're approaching a town that might have a speed trap waiting for us."

Casey put down the binoculars and pulled up Google Maps on

his phone. "Two small towns in the first hundred miles or so. First one's just past the fifty-mile post."

Drake had the speedometer pegged at one fifty when Casey's phone buzzed. Liz was calling them.

"We just turned onto Highway 93. How far ahead are you?"

"We're approaching Coyote Springs," Casey told her.

"Kevin tracked the route of the Bugatti and thinks it spent some time off the road just before the I-15 and Highway 93 junction. We didn't see anything except a cluster of two mobile homes and a shop of some sort when we drove by. Do you want us to go back and check it out?"

"If he picked something up, it's in the Bugatti with him. He's too well-trained to leave anything behind that would tell us where he's going. Stay on 93."

Drake and Casey settled in for a fast trip through the desert of central Nevada. The ride in the Corvette was surprisingly quiet at high speed as the center stripes on the road became a solid white line.

They drove past the master-planned community of Coyote Springs that was never built, because there was not enough water to support the development, Casey explained, acting as their navigator and tour guide.

Alamo, Nevada was just a wide spot in the road and no commentary was required for the next two towns. Ash Springs and Crystal Springs had a combined population of one hundred and twenty people, who lived on the surrounding farms and ranches. Crystal Springs was a ghost town, a real ghost town, and was on the map as a historical footnote.

Their average speed as they approached Hiko, Nevada, was one hundred and sixty miles an hour since leaving Las Vegas. In that distance, they'd only passed two cars.

"Are we going to need gas before we reach the next town?" Casey asked, leaning over to look at the gas gauge.

"Why?"

"Because gas is another one hundred and twenty-eight miles beyond Hiko."

"Maybe there's a gas station in Hiko?"

"Not if it's like the last four 'towns' we passed."

Casey's suspicion was right on the money. Hiko was a ghost town. The only things they saw as they sped past were and old abandoned red brick building and some tomb stones beyond it in the town's cemetery.

"Maybe we'll get lucky and catch up with him before we run out of gas," Drake said.

"And if we don't?"

"We'll wait for the van and borrow some gas. It'll have a bigger gas tank than this thing. Until then, let's see how fast this thing will go with the gas we have left. He can't be that far ahead of us."

Chapter Seventy

WITH NOTHING but a straight flat road ahead to concentrate on while driving the Corvette just short of red-lined on its tachometer, Drake started worrying about how they were going to stop the Bugatti when they caught up with it.

"Any thoughts about how we stop '47' when we catch up to him?" he asked Casey.

"None that will keep him from dying in the process."

"I remember something I saw on TV. State troopers used a GPS tracker to slow a stolen car down so they could catch up to it. The car had OnStar installed at the factory with functions for recovering it if it was stolen. If Hagerty Insurance has a GPS tracker system on the Bugatti with stolen car features, could Kevin activate it remotely?"

"We can ask him, if there's cell coverage out here."

"We would have to be there when it happened. If he takes off running, we might never find him out in the desert."

"That's all right by me. The buzzards around here are probably hungry."

Casey used his iPhone to call Kevin McRoberts and found that he had a weak but steady cell phone signal. "Kevin, is it possible to access Hagerty's GPS tracking system and use its stolen vehicle modes to slow down or turn off the ignition in the Bugatti?"

"Give me a couple of minutes and I'll find out."

"Mike, look at your Google Maps and see if you can locate a stretch of highway that links four sweeping corners north of Hiko. There's a canyon they call the 'Narrows' on the course of the Silver State Challenge.

"I watched a YouTube video of a car racing through there. There are rock cliffs close in on both sides of the highway and the posted speed limit drops to forty-five miles an hour. If we could stop him there, he'd be boxed in with no place to run."

Casey opened the Google app again and traced the path of Highway 93 north of Hiko. "I've got it. We're getting close to the canyon, another thirty or forty miles."

"Call Kevin and see if he's in Hagerty's IT system yet."

"Why?"

"Because we have traffic ahead. If it turns out to be the Bugatti, we won't have much time before it reaches the Narrow's canyon."

Drake was closing fast on the cars ahead and saw that it was two black Suburban traveling together. He pulled out to pass the slower vehicles and was surprised to see that there was another car in between the two SUVs…a black and gold Bugatti!

"Look," Drake said as they swept passed the convoy of three vehicles. "It's him!"

Casey looked up from his phone and stared at the face of the driver as they passed the Bugatti. "Kevin, are you in the Hagerty system?"

"I'm there. What do you want me to do?"

"Be able to slow or stop the Bugatti on our command."

"On it."

"I didn't expect that," Drake said as he pulled back into his lane. "Did you get a look at how many men he has with him in the SUVs?"

"Two in front, probably two more in back in each SUV."

"Nine of them and two of us. We need an advantage to even the odds."

"I think the odds are pretty even."

"Not if these guys are trained Hezbollah fighters," Drake cautioned. "If we keep them from abandoning the Bugatti and getting away in their SUVs, we can bottle them up in the canyon and wait for the cavalry to arrive."

"We're getting close to the start of the canyon. Two quick questions. How do we keep them from getting away in their SUVs and what cavalry? Liz and our guys in the van? They won't be here for a while."

"We have to try, Mike. This might be our only chance. I'll drop you off at the mouth of the canyon. Call Kevin when they pass you and have him slow the Bugatti to a stop. Find a perch above them and disable the SUVs. I'll drive on and block the road and come back to you. We'll keep them pinned down in the canyon."

"That's our plan?" Casey asked.

"You think of anything else?"

"Only calling the FBI in and that would mean I might not be there when he's taken down. We got this."

Drake maintained their speed entering the canyon until he was around the first bend in the road to keep the lead SUV from seeing his taillights as he stomped hard on the brakes. The Corvette stopped like it's tailhook had snagged the wire on a navy carrier.

Casey jumped out and got one of the Rattlers out of the trunk. "Leave '47' for me," he said over his shoulder as he sprinted to the base of the cliff.

"Roger that!" Drake shouted and raced away.

Two hundred yards ahead of Casey's position around the bend, he slid the Corvette sideways blocking the highway and jumped out.

If Kevin disabled the ignition on the Bugatti on Casey's command and it slowed to a stop in time, the Hezbollah's North American commander would have nowhere to run.

Chapter Seventy-One

CASEY WAS LYING prone on a ledge fifteen feet above the floor of the canyon watching the headlights of the three-vehicle convoy approaching the entrance to the Narrows White River canyon.

Through the scope on his MCX Rattler he saw there were four men in the lead SUV. They were all smoking and the one in the passenger's seat was looking down at something he was holding in his hands. Casey imagined he was playing a game on his phone.

When the first black Suburban was a hundred yards from his position, he leaned down toward his phone on the ledge and told Kevin to be ready to activate the GPS tracker on the Bugatti to kill the ignition.

"On my count....three, two, one, now!"

The first Suburban swept past and the gap between it and the Bugatti slowly widened, as the black and gold luxury supercar slowed and fell back. The sudden deceleration surprised the driver in the second Suburban and he had to hit the brakes to keep from running over the smaller car.

The lead Suburban drove on, unaware that the Bugatti was falling back. When it came around the bend and saw the white

Corvette blocking the road, it slammed on its brakes and slid to a stop.

The ten seconds of confusion before the driver realized his leader in the Bugatti wasn't behind him gave Drake time to fire a round into each tire and put three rounds through the grill from his position leaning against the cliff wall of the canyon.

The doors flew open and terrorists jumped out to hide behind them, shouting at each other as they decided what to do.

At the sound of gunfire behind them, as Casey fired rounds into the rear tires of the second Suburban, the two men behind the back doors of the lead Suburban took off running back to the stalled Bugatti.

The men behind the front doors of the lead Suburban fired blindly at the Corvette, with no idea where the rounds fired at their vehicle had come from.

From his position, Drake had a clear shot at the legs of the closest man standing behind the open passenger side door and fired a three-round burst, dropping the man to the road. Drake shot again as the man tried to drag himself to safety at the rear of the SUV, killing him.

Hearing the screams go silent from the other terrorist, the driver in the lead SUV turned and ran after the two men who had been with him in the lead Suburban.

Drake didn't have a shot at the man from his side of the highway and ran after him, staying close to the wall of the canyon.

It was easy to distinguish the 300 Blackout rounds from Casey's Sig Sauer Rattler from the distinct sound of AK-47 7.62 x 39mm rounds and Drake knew his friend was taking fire from the men protecting '47'.

He ran back toward the Bugatti and saw two terrorists were shooting at him from behind it. The other terrorists were shooting at Casey from behind the safety of the second Suburban.

Drake darted across the highway and dove into the shallow depression between the highway and the wall of the canyon. From his prone position, he had a clear shot at the men standing on the side of the second Suburban firing up at Casey. He also had a shot at the men crouching behind the Bugatti seventy-five yards away as they raised up to shoot at him.

Sighting through the reflex sight on his Rattler, he put the red dot on the head of the closest man behind the Bugatti and fired. He moved the red dot ten degrees to the left and saw the second man's head behind the Bugatti jerk back when he fired.

Swinging his Rattler to the right, he dropped the first man standing at the side of the second Suburban. When the man fell forward, Drake saw there were two remaining terrorists standing on either side of '47'. Two other terrorists were on the ground at the rear of the Suburban.

Realizing the crossfire they were in, the man standing to '47's' left side took a chance and ran across the highway toward the base of the cliff.

Casey shot him from his perch on the ledge before he made it across the highway.

Drake shot '47's last guard, leaving the Hezbollah commander standing alone beside the second Suburban with nowhere to run.

"It's over, Khoury," Drake shouted. "Drop the rifle and raise your hands over your head."

The Hezbollah commander's head snapped around at the sound of Drake's voice. Defying Drake's order, he remained standing with his AK-47 in his left hand. When he slowly turned to face Drake, he had a grenade in his right hand.

"Unlike you, I am not afraid to die," he said and started walking toward the Bugatti.

Drake fired and the glass in the Suburban's left headlight exploded near Khoury's head.

Khoury hesitated and moved forward. "You want me alive, we both know that."

"Look to your right, Khoury," Drake said and stood up. "The man standing there would rather see you dead. You sent your men to his home to kill his wife and daughters."

"Ah, Mr. Casey," Khoury said and started to take another step forward.

Drake centered the red dot in his reflex sight on Khoury's left hand and fired.

A 300 Blackout round from Drake's MCX Rattler tore through Khoury's left hand. It knocked the AK-47 to the pavement, leaving bloody bone and severed tendons hanging below his wrist.

Khoury stood still without looking down at what remained of his hand. "You can kill me, but you will not win this war," he said through clenched teeth, and started forward again toward the Bugatti ten feet away.

Casey ran along the side of the highway to get ahead of Khoury and bent down to look in the Bugatti and shouted, "There's a brief-case in the passenger seat. He's going to destroy it with the grenade."

Khoury lurched toward the Bugatti and Casey cut him down with three rounds from his Rattler.

The grenade dropped from Khoury's hand and Drake and Casey ran for cover.

Most grenades have a delay of three or four seconds. but they had no way of knowing if Khoury had pulled the pin before he started toward the Bugatti.

Khoury had. The grenade exploded, rocking the Bugatti that shielded Casey and sending shrapnel flying over Drake lying in the depression on the other side of the highway.

Chapter Seventy-Two

WITH THE HIGHWAY blocked and dead bodies lying around, Drake searched the lead SUV and found emergency road flares to warn approaching traffic of the roadblock ahead.

When the flares were set out to the north and south, Casey and Drake decided that it was time to call the FBI and let Special Agent In Charge Kate Perkins decide how to handle the situation,

Drake called Liz in the van that was still an hour away and asked to talk to Dan Norris after telling her what had happened.

"Dan, it's only a matter of time before local law enforcement gets here and we have to explain this. It would be better if the FBI got here as quickly as possible and took charge of things."

"I'll call Kate. What do you want me to tell her?"

"Tell her we found the man she was looking for and we need her help. We'll let her take all the credit for this. She can decide what the government wants everyone to know, if anything at all. The public doesn't need to know how easy it was for Hezbollah to get a bioweapon developed under our noses to use against us."

"Where are you?"

"On Highway 318 at the White River Narrows. The highway is

blocked. We have emergency road flares set out. If she comes in a chopper, she'll see us."

"I'll get her ETA and call you."

Drake put his phone away and stood quietly next to Casey in the middle of the highway as they looked around at the enemies they'd killed. Today's war was being fought in small skirmishes like this all around the world.

Casey just shook his head. "It's never going to end, is it?"

"Not in our lifetime."

"Let's police our brass. We're the good guys here but I'm not willing to trust that everyone will see it that way."

"Including some of our friends in the FBI," Drake agreed and retraced his steps to pick up his spent shell casings.

Dan Norris called back to say that Kate Perkins was on her way in a UH-60 Blackhawk helicopter that was in Las Vegas. One of the FBI Hostage Rescue Teams was here for a training exercise simulating a terrorist takeover of the Hoover Dam. Members of the team would be with her.

Norris had suggested when she mentioned the HRT being in Las Vegas that she might consider having them take the credit for the takedown of Armin Khoury, the FBI's Number One Most Wanted Terrorist. Norris said she seemed to like the idea.

With nothing to do until the van with Liz, Norris and Morales arrived, Drake and Casey stood guard near the emergency road flares they'd set out to keep vehicles from trying to drive through the scene. In the forty-five minutes it took the HRT Blackhawk to arrive, only three vehicles had arrived at the scene.

Casey heard the HRT UH-60 Blackhawk before he saw it begin its descent to land on the highway fifty yards south of the flare at the mouth of the Narrows canyon. Eight members of an assault team jumped out and ran forward in two four-man lines on each side of the highway. Casey waved them forward and saw Kate Perkins jogging behind them.

When she reached him, she said, "Get Drake. We need to talk."

Casey turned and followed the HRT men as they confirmed for themselves that no remaining threat from the terrorists existed and secured the scene. When he rounded the bend on the highway and could see Drake, he waved him back as one of the HRT men ran out to take his place.

They met Special Agent Perkins next to the remains of Armin Khoury, a.k.a. '47'.

"I could ask how the two of you managed to take out nine terrorists, but I'm not sure I'd believe you if you told me," she said.

Drake laughed before saying solemnly, "It looks to me like this is the work of a team of elite FBI agents who managed to track down a terrorist and his bodyguards. I'd imagine they somehow got ahead of him and blocked the canyon so he couldn't escape.

"When he refused to surrender, the agents were forced to defend themselves. With their superior training, they prevailed. Also, '47' tried to get to the Bugatti he'd been driving with a grenade. He wanted to destroy the briefcase you'll find in it. The grenade unfortunately exploded before he got there and killed him."

"Will I find evidence of any other cause of his death?" she asked.

"Not if the grenade did what I expect it did," Drake offered.

Perkins furrowed her brow as she considered his explanation. "Who else knows about this?"

"Liz, Dan and Marco in the van that should be here anytime," Casey said. "We haven't let anyone else in here."

"Let's keep it that way," Perkins said. "I'll tell the team leader how we're going to handle this. He should be pleased."

When she walked away, Drake said, "Good thing we policed our brass. If the HRT guys can keep a lid on it, we might get to keep our names out of this."

"It's in their best interest to do so. Kate's too. She might get another promotion out of this."

"She deserves it. She took a big risk trusting us," Drake said and saw Liz running toward them.

When she reached them, she gave Drake a hug and then stepped back and punched him in the chest. "I told you to be careful!"

"I was! Mike did all of this."

Casey smiled and raised his hands before stepping aside. "I'm sorry Liz, I can't lie. I did because he's not as good as he once was."

"But I am good once as I ever was," Drake chimed in with the words from a Toby Keith song with a wide grin on his face.

"I can't believe you two," Liz said and walked away to the sound of their laughing.

Chapter Seventy-Three

IN THE DAYS following the FBI's announcement that it had discovered a sleeper cell of Hezbollah terrorists and staged an assault on them in the Nevada desert that resulted in the death of Hezbollah's North American commander, two things happened in quick succession.

Special Agent Kate Perkins was credited with the takedown of the Hezbollah leader and an unspecified number of his terrorists with assistance from the FBI's HRT. She was promoted and was taking the place of Assistant Director Thomas R. Danforth, III, as the head of the FBI's Counterterrorism Division.

Danforth had been hospitalized and had been in a coma, after being ambushed by members of MS 13 in a park in Washington, D.C. He never regained consciousness. He was survived by his wife, who made the difficult decision to remove his life support after being advised by specialists brought in by the FBI that there was no hope that he would ever recover.

There were rumors that he'd been a friend of Victor Volkov, the Russian oligarch who was being tried for treason, due to his dual citizenship as an American. The relationship was never investigated by the FBI, the *Washington Post* or the main-stream media.

After being allowed to leave while the FBI was conducting its investigation of the scene where the terrorists' convoy had been stopped, the Puget Sound Security (PSS) Gulfstream G650 returned to Seattle, Washington, with eight of its employees on board.

Mike Casey, the CEO of PSS, flew to the Big Island of Hawaii in the G650, after it was refueled in Seattle, to bring his wife, two daughters and the PSS security team protecting them home to Seattle. The Casey's home had been repainted and repaired and there was no sign of the damage resulting from the failed terrorist attempt to abduct and torture Megan Casey.

Drake and Liz caught the first ferry the next morning in Seattle to Bainbridge Island to rescue Drake's German Shepherd Lancer from the kennel and spend a quiet day or two to discuss their future together before returning to work.

The day they returned to PSS Headquarters, Drake received a call from his father-in-law, Senator Hazelton.

"I understand you were blocking traffic out on some road in the Nevada desert," Senator Hazelton said.

"Who did you hear that from?"

"One of the men you met at our cabin in Oregon last summer."

"Are you calling to confirm what he told you?"

"I'm calling to invite you and Liz and Mike Casey to join us for dinner tomorrow night."

"In Washington?"

"At our home in Georgetown."

"That's not much notice," Drake said. "Why in D.C.? Won't you and Mom be back in Oregon next month? We could drive down to Portland easier than flying to Washington."

"There are some men here who would like to hear more about your recent activities."

"Do I know them?"

"You met them last summer at the cabin."

Drake did know the men who were at the senator's cabin in central Oregon the previous summer. They were members of a small group that called itself "the committee with a small c". They all had experience at the highest levels of government dealing with foreign intelligence and terrorism.

Like his father-in-law, they were concerned the entrenched bureaucracy in Washington had its own agenda that didn't always serve the country well. More dangerous than that, in the experience they shared, the bureaucrats paid little or no attention to the will of the people and their duly elected leaders in Congress or the White House.

"I'll check with Liz and Casey and see if we can come."

"Let me know what time you're arriving. I'll send a car for you," Senator Hazelton said and ended the call.

As the senior senator from Oregon and the chairman of the Senate Select Committee on Intelligence, Senator Robert Hazelton was used to getting his way. Even so, the sudden invitation to come to dinner in Georgetown was out of character for him and more so for his wife, Meredith, whose coveted invitations to attend one of her dinner parties were sent months in advance.

When the PSS Gulfstream took off from Seattle, Mike Casey stayed home with his family and sent his regrets. The trauma experienced by his wife and daughters was still too fresh for them to be left alone while they settled back into their home.

The senator's car and driver were waiting for them, as promised, when they landed to drive them through the warm spring evening in the capitol. It was too late in the month to see the cherry blossoms in peak bloom, but there were still cherry blossoms on the trees as they drove from the airport to the Hazeltons' stately white row house on N Street NW in Georgetown.

The men the senator said wanted to hear from him were standing around an assortment of chafing dishes full of appetizers on the kitchen island and drinks in their hands when Drake and Liz were ushered in by the senator's bodyguard, a retired Oregon State Trooper.

Senator Montez, the ranking Democrat on the Senate Select Committee on Intelligence with Senator Hazelton, was the first to notice them as they walked in.

"Liz, great to see you again," he said. "You too Drake. We're hearing you two had something to do with Kate Perkins' promotion at the FBI."

Senator Hazelton held up his hand. "Let's wait until later to hear the full story, Monte. Let them have a chance to get one of those Dungeness Crab Puffs before they're gone. I'll get them a drink. Bourbon for you, Drake, and red wine for you, Liz? Oregon pinot noir okay?"

"Yes, please," Liz said. "Where's Meredith?"

Senator Hazelton look at his watch. "She'll be along in a minute. Now, let me get your drinks."

Drake got a plate and loaded it with two of the crab puffs and a couple of the stuffed button mushrooms and returned to stand beside Liz. She was talking with Michael Montgomery, the former Director of National Intelligence, about how she liked living on the west coast.

There was a commotion at the front door, and everyone turned to see Meredith Hazelton walking across the foyer with the President of the United States at her side.

Chapter Seventy-Four

PRESIDENT BENJAMIN RONALD BALLARD was the newly elected president and had been in office for less than three months. Drake had voted for the man because he liked the promises he made during the election. Some politician made promises they never intended to keep. He hoped this president wasn't one of them.

President Ballard had been a two-term senator from Nebraska and an Army Ranger with combat experience in both Iraq and Afghanistan. He was also the second-youngest president ever elected and was shaking things up in the capitol by nominating younger people to fill cabinet positions than were usually nominated.

The president shook hands with Senator Hazelton and said, "Thanks for setting this up so quickly, Bob."

He looked to each of the other members of the "committee" and said, "Gentlemen, I hope to meet with each of you when things settle down. Senator Hazelton has hinted that you share my concerns about our ship of state that isn't always sailing in the direction its elected leaders are trying to steer it. He suggested that it would be worth my time to hear your thoughts about how we get things back on course, if you're willing to share them with me."

A chorus of "Certainly" and "Be glad to, Mr. President" was their answer.

President Ballard walked over to Liz Strobel and extended his hand. "Ms. Strobel, nice to see you again. I know Senator Hazelton was sad when you left his staff but took some comfort in knowing you'd be working with his son-in-law in Seattle. I hope you won't mind if I borrow Mr. Drake for a few minutes. I asked you both to come to Washington tonight so I could hear what really happened in Nevada."

"He's all yours, Mr. President."

"Bob. If I could get some of that twenty-year old Oregon whisky you keep talking about, I'd like to take Mr. Drake somewhere we can talk privately."

"You're welcome to use my study upstairs, Mr. President. Adam will show you the way. He knows where I keep a bottle of Pendleton Director's Reserve for special occasions."

Drake led the way upstairs to the senator's study and motioned the president toward his pick of the two dark brown leather armchairs at the far end of the room.

The president walked along the floor-to-ceiling bookcase on his side of the study, admiring the titles of the books in the senator's American history collection.

"He's read them all," Drake said over his shoulder as he poured two fingers of the senator's favorite whisky into two crystal tumblers.

"I know, we're friends. I served on several of the committees he chaired. I know how he loves our country and its history. I expect that's why he's so concerned about its future."

Drake waited until the president was seated, handed him a tumbler and sat down in the other leather armchair.

"Tell me about what really happened in Nevada. Your father-in-law didn't say much at the briefing we attended at the White House. When the FBI was finished and we were alone, he said if I wanted to hear how it really went down, I should ask you about it," the president said. "We're analyzing the bioengineered virus. I'm told it had the potential to kill millions of people and cripple the economy.

If Armin Khoury was acting on behalf of Iran, I have to decide how we're going to respond."

Over the next hour, Drake told the president everything that had happened since they'd begun the search for Ashley Berkshire, the biologist's daughter.

"You, Mike Casey and Liz did all that using the resources of Puget Sound Security? There was no government involvement?"

"Special Agent Kate Perkins flew to Las Vegas when we discovered Khoury was there. But we hit the warehouse ourselves. Mike and I took down Khoury in the desert before Kate and HRT got there."

"That's an amazing story, Adam. May I call you Adam?"

"Of course, Mr. President."

"Then you'll have to call me Ben."

The president stared into the whisky he was swirling around in his tumbler for a moment before he continued.

"You and the men downstairs are valuables resources I'd like to know I can call on from time to time. You have a quite a record for dealing with situations without the government being involved. I might need your help if there's something that I determine needs to be handled privately. Would you be willing to help me with something like that, if I call you? No one will need to know that we're talking, unless we decide there are others who need to be included or involved."

"Would that include Liz and Mike not knowing about it? I'm not interested if it does."

"You would decide who needs to be included, and that includes your father-in-law and the men downstairs. Before I leave tonight, there's an encrypted app my aide can put on your phone that will keep our messaging secret and confidential."

Drake didn't hesitate before saying, "I'd be honored to assist you in any way I can, Mr. President."

The president stood and held out his hand. "That's Ben, Adam. Pour me a little more of your father-in-law's whisky and we'll join the others downstairs before I have to get back to the White House."

THE END

Next book in the Adam Drake series

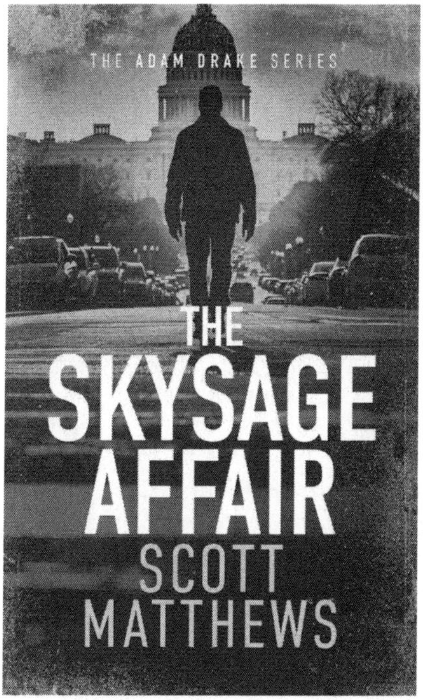

America is developing a new space weapon that will change the way future wars are fought.

But China has a covert espionage operation in place to steal it.

When Adam Drake accidentally uncovers the plot, he becomes the target of an enemy desperate to protect its spies and their mission. To defeat the CCP, Drake must first survive.

Printed in Great Britain
by Amazon

50134475R00163